D1572381

CONFLICTING VENTURES

BELLES OF BROAD STREET BOOK 1

AK LANDOW

Conflicting Ventures: Belles of Broad Street Book 1

Published by Author AK Landow, LLC

ISBN: 979-8-9882335-1-0

Edited and Proofread By: Chrisandra's Corrections

Cover Design By: K.B. Designs

Photo By: Jane Ashley Converse

Cover Models: Maddie Hansen & Dane Peterson

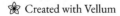 Created with Vellum

To my youngest daughter:
Just because your star shines differently, doesn't mean it shines
any less bright.

"A girl should be two things: who and what she wants."
Coco Chanel

Knight & Lawrence
FAMILY TREE

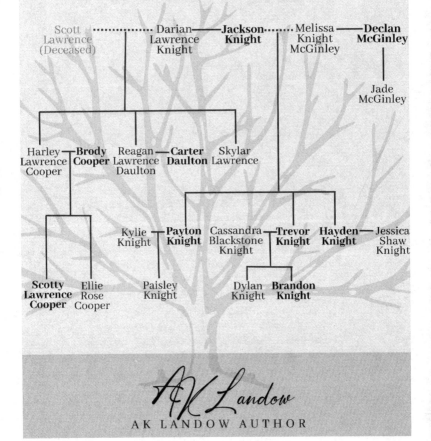

Scott Lawrence (Deceased) ·········· Darian Lawrence Knight — **Jackson Knight** ········· Melissa Knight McGinley — **Declan McGinley**

Jade McGinley

Harley Lawrence Cooper — **Brody Cooper**   Reagan Lawrence Daulton — **Carter Daulton**   Skylar Lawrence

Kylie Knight — **Payton Knight**   Cassandra Blackstone Knight — **Trevor Knight**   **Hayden Knight** — Jessica Shaw Knight

Scotty Lawrence Cooper   Ellie Rose Cooper   Paisley Knight   Dylan Knight   **Brandon Knight**

AK Landow

AK LANDOW AUTHOR

PROLOGUE ONE

ONE YEAR AGO

SKYLAR

My naked body is on top of Jason's as I move my hips over his at a rapid pace. He grabs onto my breasts and dusts his thumbs over my nipples. "Sky, you're so fucking beautiful. Keep going, baby. You feel amazing."

I look down at my handsome boyfriend. His shaggy brown hair is messier than normal. His lust-filled hazel eyes locked with my green ones.

I ride him as hard as I can for as long as I can. I know we don't have much more time together. He's leaving town for a job, and he doesn't want to try a long-distance relationship. I'm devastated. I'm in love with him. I thought he was the one for me.

We've been dating for four years. Two while in college, and two while we attended business school together.

He's leaving and wants a clean break and a fresh start. He

thinks it's best for the both of us. I tried to explain to him how we could visit each other on the weekends, but he thinks it's a mistake. We both need to focus on our jobs, not be constantly running to the airport.

There's nothing I can do about it. His mind is made up.

He lifts his upper body flush with mine and pulls my lips to his while he thrusts up into me. He whispers into them, "I can't hold off anymore, baby. Come with me."

I don't want it to end. We only have one more week together before he leaves. I want to be close to him and enjoy every moment that I can.

He licks up my neck and breathes into it, "I love you, baby." That sets me off and I feel my body spasm around his. I yell out as he shouts my name into his own release.

I slow my movements until we're still. Our arms are wrapped tight around each other, both knowing how much we'll miss the other. Our chests are moving rapidly in unison. Our heartbeats in sync.

As we each catch our breath, he looks up at me. I see tears welling in his eyes. "That was out of this world. I'm going to miss how it is with you."

I play with his hair, as I often do. "It's always out of this world. It doesn't have to end, Jason. We can make the long-distance thing work. I'm willing to try. Please, let's try. I'm not ready to let you go. We're the only ones for each other. I know it. I can't imagine ever being with anyone but you."

I feel his entire body stiffen in my arms. I look down and his face looks pained.

I run my fingers over his sexy square chin. "What is it? What's wrong?"

He gives me one more soft kiss before he shatters my world. "I have to admit something to you."

"Okay. What is it?"

He chews on his lip, which I know to be a nervous habit

of his. "Sky, I was with someone else recently. I cheated on you. I'm so sorry, baby. I feel horrible about it. I wasn't sure if I should tell you since I'm leaving, but it's getting hard to keep lying to you. I can't do it."

My body goes numb. Despite my overheated body temperature and being wrapped in his warm arms, I now feel cold. Of all the things that could have come out of his mouth, that's just about the last thing I expected.

I struggle for words for a moment. My head is spinning, but I eventually muster, "Who? When? Why?"

He swallows. "Who it was doesn't matter. It was a few weeks ago. I was drinking at a bar and upset about the end of our relationship. A woman approached me, and I forced myself to do it because I knew it was what we needed to help us make a clean break. It's time for us both to move on. I wasn't into it, but I did it for us."

That may be the most fucked up thing I've ever heard in my life.

My mouth is open in shock, struggling to form words. I look down. He's still inside me. He told me he cheated on me while his dick is literally still inside me. I'm filled with him. His come is starting to leak out of me.

The reality of it hits me and I practically catapult myself off him. I grab the closest T-shirt and quickly cover myself. Even though he's seen me naked a million times, I've never felt more uncomfortably exposed. I don't want him seeing my body.

"Did...did you use protection? Am I at risk right now?"

He nods. "Of course I used protection. I would never put you at risk like that."

"You'd fuck somebody else and break my heart, but not risking disease is your hard moral line?"

He runs his fingers through his thick hair that I've wasted four years lovingly running my own fingers through. "Sky..."

I hold up my hand, tears streaming down my cheeks. "No, don't. You don't get to talk to me."

He pops out of bed and starts toward me. "If you'd just let me…"

"Stop." Tears are now coming out like a waterfall, but I gather every ounce of strength I have and manage to say, "Don't come near me. Don't touch me. You never get to touch me again. You broke something so pure and beautiful. That was my love for you. Pure and beautiful." I point toward the door. "Get out. I don't ever want to see you again."

He pauses for a moment, tears also streaming down his cheeks, but he eventually nods, gathers his clothes, and walks out the door.

As soon as he does, I fall to the floor and sob. I sob in a way I haven't since my father suddenly passed away six years ago.

I have no clue how long I lay there. At some point, my tears dry up and my head is throbbing. Why did this happen? What have I done to deserve this? I loved him. I thought he loved me. How could I have been such a fool? I'm suddenly so ashamed. Ashamed that I didn't see it coming. Ashamed that a man would cheat on me. Am I not enough?

I would give anything in the world to have my dad at this moment. He was my best friend. I love my older sisters, Reagan and Harley, and of course I love my mom, but my dad and I were so close. His death left a gaping hole in my life, and for four years Jason helped to fill it. Now he's gone too. I've never felt more alone.

I look up and whisper, "Help me, Dad. I need you. Give me a sign that everything is going to be okay. That I'm going to be okay."

My eyes automatically find my most precious possession. A special book my father gave me as a little girl. I stand, walk to it, and carefully remove it from its designated spot. I need to be careful because he left me many notes over the years that are stuffed inside the pages of the book.

I close my eyes and reach my hand into a random page. I let fate dictate which. I pull out the note on that page and read it. It's an old quote I've read hundreds of times.

I will welcome happiness for it enlarges my heart; Yet I will endure sadness for it opens my soul. I will acknowledge rewards for they are my due; yet I will welcome obstacles for they are my challenge.

I look up and let a small smile creep out from my quivering lips. I whisper, "Thanks, Dad. You never let me down."

I place the note back in the book and return it to its special spot. I take a deep breath of fortitude and turn back toward the bed. I remove the sheets and run them through the washing machine. I get in the shower and scrub my skin until it's red and irritated. I need every trace of Jason expunged from my body.

When I get out and dress, I move around my apartment to purge it of all reminders of Jason and begin my new life without him.

PROLOGUE TWO

ONE YEAR LATER ~ PRESENT

REAGAN'S TWENTY-EIGHTH BIRTHDAY PARTY

LANCE

"Aunt Melissa, are you sure I'm invited to the party? I don't know Reagan. I've heard of her a bunch of times from my cousins, but I've never met her or her husband. I feel like a party crasher."

Aunt Melissa nods. "Yes, sweetie. I asked Reagan, and she was more than happy to have you. You'll know a bunch of people. Of course, you have us." I look around the Uber at her, her new husband, Declan, and Declan's teenage daughter, Jade.

"My boys and Jackson will be there too." Jackson is her ex-husband, and now my boss. I also work with two of my cousins, Trevor and Payton. Aunt Melissa's third

1

son, Hayden, is a pediatric resident at a local hospital here in Philadelphia.

Reagan is Jackson's stepdaughter. She's the CEO of one of the biggest companies in the world. Her husband, Carter, is the president of the company. They must be quite the duo.

"Will it be a stuffy corporate event, or do you think it will be fun?"

The three of them look at each other and laugh. Jade turns to me and smiles. "Reagan's the exact opposite of stuffy. She's one of the funniest people you'll ever meet in your life. She has no boundaries and no filter."

I guess I just assumed she was stuffy because of her job.

Jade continues, "And her husband, Carter, is funny, smart, and the hottest man in existence." Jade gives a dreamy smile.

Declan growls. "Enough with that, Jade. He's more than twice your age. *And* he's married to your cousin. *And* he's your boss."

Jade shakes her head. "I turned eighteen last week, Dad. He's no longer more than twice my age, and he never will be again." She sighs. "I know he's *very* happily married to Reagan. They can't keep their hands off each other at the office. He's just so damn dreamy. I want one just like him."

I can't help my smile. I see Aunt Melissa trying to hide hers as well. Declan looks like he might punch a hole straight through the glass. I learned quickly that Declan has a temper. That, and he's very possessive of my aunt. He doesn't like any man coming near her or even looking in her direction.

I turn to him. "Remind me how you're related to

them?" This family is fucking confusing. I need a visual chart to understand it all.

"Jackson's wife, Darian, used to be married to my brother until he passed. Reagan and her two sisters are Jade's first cousins, which is why Jade needs to cut her crap and stop drooling all over Carter."

I better redirect this conversation. "How old is Reagan?"

Aunt Melissa answers, "Twenty-eight."

My eyes pop open. "She's only twenty-eight? I thought she'd be much older. Wow, I feel like such a failure. She's only two years older than me and look at all she's accomplished. I've done nothing."

Aunt Melissa touches my shoulder. "Lance, you're at one of the best business schools in the world. Jackson told me that you've been incredibly impressive at the office. You're well on your way to making a name for yourself."

I roll my eyes. "I've only been there a few weeks. All I've done is their training program. I haven't done any real work yet. And I only have the job because you asked Jackson to give it to me."

"Well, Jackson said you've genuinely impressed the trainers. He mentioned that he's going to give you a lot of responsibility right away. Everyone there thinks you can handle it."

I can't help but smile with pride. I'm happy they're pleased with my performance so far. I busted my ass during the training. I worked twice as hard as everyone else. I know I only got this incredible opportunity because of Aunt Melissa. Every business school classmate of mine would kill for the job I have. I want to prove my worth a thousand times over.

We arrive at a big, fancy hotel. I've never been

anywhere like it, being from a small, rural town in the western part of the state.

I've only been in Philadelphia for a few months. I arrived early, in part to secure a job because my father cut me off and I'm paying my own way through graduate school, but also because it was only prolonging the hurt for my longtime girlfriend, Roseanne, to see me leave.

Moving to a big city is just something I've always wanted to do. After battling with my father over it for years, including a few deals with him that kept me in town much longer than I would have preferred, I'm finally living my dream. Unfortunately, small town life is what Roseanne wanted, so we parted ways. It broke my heart to see her suffering. So I left a little earlier than planned to spare her the long goodbye.

It was nice to get settled before school started anyway. I was also able to reconnect with my Aunt Melissa. She and my father, her brother, haven't spoken in years, so I hadn't seen her since I was a boy.

She welcomed me with open arms. I was waiting tables to help pay my tuition, but she insisted on getting me a job with her ex-husband. He owns one of the biggest development companies in Philadelphia. It was an opportunity I couldn't pass up. It's also going to be fun to work with my cousins. I haven't seen them much because I've been in training, but now that the training is over, I imagine that will change.

We walk through the front doors into the lobby of the hotel. It may be the nicest room I've ever been in. I can't help but look around in awe. Every inch is decorated. It looks like a beautiful, old church that you'd only see in movies. The biggest chandelier I've ever seen hangs in the middle.

Aunt Melissa stops us for a moment. She turns to me

and fixes my tie, smiling up at me. "You look very handsome."

I smile back. "Thank you, and thank you for this nice suit. Thank you for all ten nice suits you bought me."

Aunt Melissa offered to pay my tuition for business school. I declined. I plan to pay for it myself. She insisted on buying me suits for my new job though. I indulged her in that one thing because I really did need them and can't afford them. I plan to find a way to pay her back one day.

Declan clears his throat. "What about me? Do I look handsome too?"

She winks at me and then turns to him. "Baby, you're always so handsome."

She takes a step toward him and fixes his tie as well. She finishes it off with a soft kiss to his lips.

He runs his hands up and down her sides, and unashamedly says, "You look edible."

Maybe not *edible*, but she does look great. She always does. She's a beautiful woman. She's got our family's height, blonde hair, and dark blue eyes.

Jade walks between them. "Ugh. Cut it out. The honeymoon phase is over. I can't handle you two playing kissy-face all night. It's bad enough I now live with it half the time. You know, Mom and Rick aren't like this, and they just got married too."

Aunt Melissa and Declan are definitely in love. It's kind of cute. I wouldn't mind a relationship like theirs one day. They're always touching each other. Roseanne wasn't the touchy-feely type though, with the right woman, I think I might be.

Declan is way more possessive than I would ever be though. He's a lot to handle at times, often acting like a bull in a China shop, but he loves her and I'm happy for that.

I hated having to miss Aunt Melissa and Declan's wedding, but my grandmother on my mom's side passed, and the funeral was the same day. I had to go home.

I know my father, being a deeply religious man, has a problem with the fact that Aunt Melissa divorced Jackson. But she seems very happy now, so who am I to judge? From what she says, Jackson is happily remarried as well, and she's friends with his new wife. The birthday party tonight is for one of her daughters. I know she has three. I haven't met any of them yet.

Aunt Melissa loops her arm through mine on her left side, and Declan's on her right. "I have the best-looking, and tallest, dates here."

She's right about the tallest. Declan must be at least six feet, four inches, and I've got two inches on him.

Declan grabs Jade's arm on the other side and we make our way to the party.

I walk into the ballroom and am in complete and total shock. It's enormous. The decorations are like nothing I've ever seen. It's got a club vibe, with several bars, sofas, a huge, illuminated dance floor, and a band on a big platform. It looks like there are over three-hundred people here. Reagan must be a popular woman.

As soon as we walk in, Aunt Melissa spots my cousins, and we make our way over to them. I haven't met their wives yet. I'm excited for that.

Aunt Melissa tried to get us all together a few times, but I kept my job as a waiter on the weekends just in case my training didn't go well at Jackson's company, Knight Investments. Once I realized how well it was going, I gave the restaurant my notice. Today was my last day.

Jade mentions seeing friends from work and leaves us

to talk to them. She has an internship at Reagan's company.

My cousins all man-hug me hello. I meet Payton's pretty wife, Kylie, and then Hayden's adorably pregnant wife, Jessica.

Trevor then introduces me to his wife, Cassandra. I knew ahead of time that she's much older than him. What I wasn't prepared for is how attractive she is. I understand the appeal. She's gorgeous, with dark hair and the lightest blue eyes I've ever seen.

She shakes my hand and looks me up and down. "Wow, aren't you a tall drink of hotness. The single ladies will be all over your sexy self tonight."

My eyes widen as I look over at Trevor. He starts laughing.

Melissa cuts in and kisses Cassandra on the cheek. "You're only allowed one man under thirty in my family, and you've already met your quota."

Cassandra laughs. "Fair enough."

They smile at each other in a familiar way. Trevor did once mention that Cassandra and Aunt Melissa are very good friends. It's crazy to me that they're about the same age.

She introduces me to her sister, Beth. Apparently, they work together at a big law firm. They look a lot alike with their dark hair and ice-blue eyes, though Beth does seem much younger than Cassandra.

We chat for a little bit. They're all very nice and funny.

It's clear that Cassandra needs a refill on her drink. I wouldn't mind one of my own. I grab her glass. "Would you like a refill, ma'am?"

She smiles. "Yes. Thank you. Tito's on the rocks. And don't ever fucking call me ma'am again. I'm not eighty."

I smile. "I call all women, ma'am. It has nothing to do with age."

"Not this woman. Cassandra is just fine."

I nod at her and turn to Aunt Melissa. "Can I get you something?"

Before she can answer, Declan interrupts, "I'll get hers. I need a drink too."

Declan and I make our way over to one of the massive bars. There are three bartenders just at this one. It looks like each of the two other bars have just as many bartenders. It's crazy. All this for a birthday party? I feel out of my depth.

Declan orders Cassandra's drink, a Patron on the rocks for Melissa, and a light beer for himself. He points to me, asking for my order.

I ask the bartender about IPA's. We chat for a bit, and he smiles at my deep beer knowledge. He tells me that he has something he thinks I'll really like, but they only have it at one of the other bars. He offers to go get it while another bartender makes the rest of our drinks.

The three drinks are ready before he returns. Declan offers to bring them back to the group while I wait.

I wait a few more minutes for my beer. He eventually returns and I thank him.

With my beer in hand, I turn to head back to our group. As I'm turning, I crash into someone and the top portion of my beer splashes over the top of the bottle, right onto the woman's dress.

In a feminine voice, I hear, "Oh crap."

"I'm...I'm...I'm so sorry ma'am."

She looks up and smiles. "It's okay. Accidents happen."

I'm suddenly rendered speechless. I'm looking down at the most beautiful woman I've ever seen in my life.

She's got blonde hair, big green eyes, a cute button of a nose, full red lips, and a body I've only seen on movie stars. She has huge breasts, the tops of which I can see in her orange strapless gown. She has curvaceous hips and a tiny waist. She's tall, though I still tower over her. I honestly didn't know real-life women could look like this.

I must be standing there with my chin on the floor because she takes her finger and lifts it. She winks at me as she moves past me to the bar.

"Excuse me, sir, can I trouble you for club soda? A clumsy man spilled beer on my dress." She turns back and smiles at me. Her smile is as magnificent as the rest of her.

I touch her arm. "Excuse me, ma'am, but I know something that will work better than club soda. An old family trick." I hold out my hand for her. "Come with me."

She looks at me skeptically for a brief moment, but then takes my hand. I do my best to play it cool despite the fact that the simple act of touching her hand makes my heart beat faster.

I lead her down the hallway toward what looks like a kitchen door. When someone exits, I ask them for a cup of dishwashing soap.

While we're waiting, I ask for her name.

"I'm Skylar. What's your name?"

"My name is Lance. I'm so sorry about your dress. I'm confident I can get the stain out though."

"What makes you so sure, Lance?"

I smile. "I have three brothers and a sister. I grew up on a farm. We stained our clothes just about every day. My poor mother had to do this every night."

"A farm? I bet the skies are always clear there."

I nod, surprised at her random, yet accurate, observation. "They are."

We're standing by a huge floor to ceiling window. Skylar looks up into the sky. "It's a clear night. You can see a lot of the stars right from this spot. Way more than normal."

I nod. "I've noticed nights like this are unusual in the city. We had this nearly every night on the farm. I don't think I appreciated it as much until I moved here."

She smiles. "It's *definitely* unusual to have a night like this."

She keeps staring. I actually see tears forming in her eyes.

I point to a bright star. "I believe that's the North Star."

She nods. "It is." She moves her finger sideways. "If you follow the stars next to it down to that rectangle, you can see the entire Little Dipper." She points. "Can you see? It looks like a ladle."

I stare out the window. "Yes, I see it. It's always visible at home, but I haven't seen it since I came here."

She continues, "You know, it's surprising to be able to see it at all, especially in the city. The North Star, yes, but the rest of it is rarely seen because of dimness and pollution."

I can't help but stare at her face as she looks up at it.

She breathes, "So beautiful."

While still staring at her, I respond, "It sure is."

Her finger is still pointing, so I take it in mine and run it in a straight line down. "Follow this path with your eyes."

She does.

"Do you see it?"

I see the reaction in her gorgeous face the moment she does. She turns to me. "The Big Dipper?"

I nod. "Yes. You know, in fifty thousand years, the Big Dipper will change shape and face the opposite way."

She pinches her eyebrows together. "Hmm. I know a lot about the stars. I don't think I've ever heard that before."

I shrug my shoulders. "I minored in astronomy in college. That's where I learned everything."

She gives me a knowing smile. I have no idea why.

Before I can ask, the person with a cup of soap walks through the door and hands it to me. I thank him.

I grab for Skylar's hand again. I don't need to hold her hand, but I want to find any excuse to touch her.

She gives me another knowing smile as she wraps her delicate, soft fingers around my significantly larger hand in return.

I open a door that appears to be a bathroom, but as soon as I do, I hear moaning. I quickly close the door before Skylar sees anything. I'm pretty sure I just saw Jackson in there with a woman.

I turn to Skylar. "I think that room is being used."

She giggles. "It sounded like it." I guess she heard the moans.

I find another bathroom door. I take a quick peek before fully opening it. The room looks empty, so we walk in. It's an enormous bathroom. There's only one stall, but there are sofas and chairs. It's basically a huge lounge.

I point to one of the sofas. "Have a seat. I'm going to wet a few paper towels."

I run the towels under the faucet. I get on my knees

in front of her. I can't help but inhale deeply. She smells amazing. It's like raspberries and cake in one.

I take a breath and go to work, carefully rubbing the mark on her dress. Within minutes, the stain is gone.

I smile. "I think we got it."

She inspects my handiwork. "You certainly did. I guess you learn something new every day. Dish soap. I'll never forget that now. Thank you."

She moves her hand to my hair and fixes a seemingly stray strand.

My cock stirs and my hand starts shaking.

She tilts her head to the side. "Do I make you nervous, Lance?"

I shake my head and lie. "No, ma'am."

I stand without realizing that my cock more than stirred.

Given her current eye level, she notices it right away and I see the corners of her mouth turn up slightly.

She stands and moves her body close to mine. I swallow hard.

She runs the tips of her fingers up my arms and across my jaw. "Do I affect you, Lance?"

I nod and somehow manage to whisper, "You're the prettiest woman I've ever seen in my entire life. I can't take my eyes off you."

She smiles again as she runs her tongue along her upper lip. The simple sight of her pretty pink tongue takes my cock to full mast.

With her apparent Lance-cock radar, she looks down and notices right away.

I'm humiliated. I manage to breathe out, "I'm sorry. Sometimes he has a mind of his own. Please don't take it as anything other than a compliment."

She tilts her head to the side again and stares at me for a moment.

I have no idea what she's thinking right now. I want to kiss her, but I'm not sure she wants me to. I don't know if she's into me or horrified by my inability to maintain any self-control.

She turns and starts walking toward the door.

I guess I have my answer. I let out the breath I was holding. I wish I wasn't such a wimp. I'm going to beat myself up about this for a long time. I had the most beautiful woman in the world practically pressed up against me, and I didn't do anything about it.

She gets to the door, but she doesn't open it and she doesn't walk out. She locks it.

She turns around to face me. "I'm affected by you too, Lance." She crooks her finger in my direction. "If you want me, come and get me, big guy."

I don't hesitate this time. I take three long steps and crash my body to hers. I take her face in my hands and immediately seal my lips over hers.

She runs her fingers through the back of my hair. Our tongues enter each other's mouths at the same time, both exploring and working in perfect, practiced unison.

She tastes like a lemony vodka drink. It's sensational. I can't get enough of her.

Her long, toned, golden leg is exposed by the slit in her dress. I grab it and wrap it around my waist, keeping my hand on the back of her smooth upper thigh.

I push my hard cock onto her warm center, and she moans into my mouth.

I then run my hand up her inner thigh. I can feel her quiver at my touch. I love it.

I bring my hand higher and higher up her thigh

until I reach her center. Oh my god, she's not wearing any panties.

I'm doing my best to play it cool, but I want to just rip this dress right off her body. I'm having a visceral reaction to her, the likes of which I've never before experienced.

My cock is painfully pushing against the top of my pants, begging to be freed.

I run my fingers through her. She's as turned on as I am.

I immediately sink two fingers inside of her and she whimpers into my mouth. She's warm, soft, tight, and dripping her juices onto my hand.

Her grip on my hair tightens as she begins to move her hips and ride my fingers.

I move my lips down her neck while continuing to slide my fingers in and out of her. I slip my other hand into the top of her dress. Her tits are enormous. I grab one and knead her nipple with my fingers.

She pants and moans. She never stops moving her hips.

I shift my thumb to her clit and begin slow circles, contrasting the faster pace of my fingers inside her.

She grips my shirt and throws her head back. "Oh god, I'm coming."

She breathes heavily. I feel her walls tighten around my fingers. She yells out and shakes as the orgasm takes over her entire body. I have to hold her up so she doesn't collapse.

I watch her cheeks flush and notice her lips are swollen from our kiss. It's the hottest thing I've ever seen. I desperately want to see it again.

As soon as she begins to regain her senses, she pulls her leg down and goes right for my belt buckle. She unbuttons and unzips my pants. She immediately shoves her hand into my boxer briefs and wraps her small, soft hand around my cock.

She moves it up and down my length a few times. She looks up at me with heated eyes. "You really are a big guy."

She frees my cock, licks her lips, and sinks down to her knees. A grab her arm as our eyes meet. "You don't have to do this."

I try to help her stand, but she pulls her arm away. She gives me a surprised look. "I want to."

With that, she strokes me a few times and then runs her tongue from the base of my shaft all the way to the tip. It's officially the first time a woman's mouth has been on my cock. Roseanne never wanted either of us to engage in any oral sex and, of course, I never pressured her.

I think I'm in shock at how good this feels. I can sense an immediate shot of precum leak out of me. She runs her tongue through my slit. She then circles her lips around my tip and sucks it clean. I've never in my life felt anything better, and she's only on the tip.

While holding the base, she slowly slides more of my cock into her wet, warm mouth. I feel like my legs might give out. I have to rest my hands on the door behind her, so my knees don't actually buckle.

She must work at the circus as a sword swallower as her profession because she manages to take nearly my entire cock into her mouth. I can literally feel my tip touch the back of her throat.

I look down. The image of a woman that looks like her with my cock stuffed all the way down her throat is the greatest thing I've ever seen.

She begins to suck while moving my cock in and out

of her mouth. Her tongue is swirling everywhere. It's like she has three tongues with the amount of territory she's covering.

Any part of my cock out of her mouth is immediately touched by her wet hand.

In and out. Slow and fast. Suction and no suction. Holy shit.

At some point, she pops my cock out of her mouth. I immediately mourn the loss.

She looks up at me with lipstick-smeared, swollen lips. "Grab my hair and show me the pace you like."

I look at her and answer in all sincerity, "I like any pace that has my cock in your mouth."

She giggles as she grabs my hand and places it on her head. Thankfully, she then takes my cock back into her mouth.

I grab a fistful of her hair and start to move both her and my hips at a fast rhythm. She continues to lick and suck me, more than keeping up with my hard pace.

At some point, she moans onto my cock. She's genuinely enjoying this.

I need to shake my head a few times to make sure I'm not dreaming. If I am, I don't want to wake up.

With her other hand, she grabs my balls and squeezes them.

That's the endgame for me. My whole body is numb, with every ounce of blood now at my cock.

"Skylar, I'm coming."

"Hmm."

She doesn't make even the slightest attempt to get off me.

I can't hold it anymore. My vision is clouded with dots. I'm experiencing pleasure from my toes to my fingertips as I explode into her mouth.

It lasts shockingly long. I don't think I've ever come so hard. Thankfully I'm leaning on the wall, or my legs definitely would have given out.

I blink as my vision starts to return. Skylar's licking her lips clean as she stands.

I pull her close to me and kiss her hard, trying to express my appreciation. She kisses me back. I can taste myself on her. It's insanely hot.

My cock begins to harden again. She squeals as she feels it against her body.

She pulls her lips away, looks down, and her eyes widen. "That was a quick turnaround."

"Have you looked in a mirror lately?"

She smiles.

Just then, her phone rings in her purse.

She lets out a breath. "I need to get that."

I nod and tuck myself back in as she opens her purse and removes her phone.

"Hey."

"Sorry. I was...umm...in the bathroom. Someone spilled beer on my dress, and I was cleaning it. I'll be right there."

She ends the call and places her phone back in her purse, pulling out her lipstick.

She starts toward the door while reapplying the lipstick. "Sorry. I've got to run. I'll see you out there."

Before I can utter a word, she's gone. I'm in a state of shock that she could just leave like that after what we did together.

After a few deep breaths, I slowly make my way back to the ballroom. I spot Trevor immediately and walk over to him.

"Hey, Lance. Where have you been? My mom was freaking out that you might have left and went home."

"Uh, no. I was just in the bathroom."

He looks at me and smiles. "I bet you weren't alone."

My eyes widen. "What makes you say that?"

He laughs. "The lipstick all over your face and neck."

Crap. I didn't bother to look in the mirror before I left the bathroom.

I try to wipe it, but he grabs a napkin and does it for me.

"Thanks, man."

"No problem. Who was she?"

I can't help but smile. "The most beautiful woman I've ever seen." I look around. "She's in a long orange dress. Let me see if I can find her."

I spot her. She's standing with a group of attractive women. I point to her. "Right there."

Trevor looks and then holds his stomach and starts laughing hysterically. Cassandra looks at him like he's crazy. "What's so funny, Secretariat?"

He smiles at her. "Lance just got lucky in the bathroom with a stranger. Guess who it was?"

He nods toward the group of women, and she smirks. She turns to me. "The only single woman standing over there is Skylar." Pause. "My niece." Pause. "Trevor's stepsister."

My mouth widens in complete shock, but now both of them are doubled over in laughter. I'm not sure why this is funny.

I put my hand on Trevor's shoulder. "I'm so sorry. I didn't know."

He shrugs. "I don't care. I'm not blind. I know she's beautiful. I also know enough to know that if she wasn't into it, it wouldn't have happened. So she must be into you. You'll be the envy of every single man in this room."

Cassandra nods. "I'm glad Skylar's getting some

action. She needs it. She broke up with a long-term boyfriend nearly a year ago and hasn't dated at all. I'm not sure she even goes out anymore."

I'm pretty sure the two of them are crazy.

The music stops and one of the women standing with Skylar takes the microphone. She's holding hands with a big, muscular guy who's smiling at her like she hung all the stars in the sky.

She starts speaking. "I don't want to stop the fun for long, but I want to say a quick hello. Thank you to everyone for coming tonight to help us celebrate. This was supposed to be a wedding reception, but Carter insisted on it being a birthday party for me instead." She turns to him and smiles. "Let's just call it both and skip to the part where you kiss the bride."

She turns and wraps her arms around him. She then kisses him. *Really* kisses him, in a way I've never seen done in public. He lifts her off the ground and gives it right back to her. Everyone starts yelling and clapping. There are many catcalls and wolf whistles being thrown around.

When they're done, she pulls the microphone back to her lips and fans her face with her other hand. "Wow. I can't wait for the honeymoon." Everyone laughs. "While we're celebrating, I want to mention that it was my cousin Jade's birthday last week. Where are you, gorgeous?"

I see Jade raise her arm until she catches the attention of who I assume is Reagan. The woman then motions for Jade to come up to them, which she does.

She throws her arm around Jade. "Happy birthday, beautiful." She smiles. "She's eighteen now, gentleman, so take a number. The line is going to be long." The two of them laugh.

I can hear over-exaggerated coughing nearby.

I can't help but smile. That must be Declan. He's probably freaking out about what Reagan said.

"Eat, drink, dance, and have fun." She points to the band, and they start up again with a fast song.

Trevor grabs my arm. "Come dance with us for a song and then I'll introduce you to the rest of my family. I'd have you dance with Beth, but she twisted her ankle a few songs ago. I don't know where she went. Are you good to dance with us?" He jokes, "They do have dancing in your hometown, right?"

I subtly nod and hide my inner smile. I happen to be a fantastic dancer. I have no clue where I got it from. No one in my family can dance, but for some reason, I can.

We dance for an entire song, and I bust out all my moves.

When it's over, Trevor stares at me wide-eyed. "What the hell did I just witness? Are you secretly a professional dancer?"

I can't help grinning in glee. I always get this response from people when they see me dance.

I shrug. "I guess I got all the dancing talent in our family."

He gives me a playful scowl. "Don't worry, I've got moves where it matters most." He turns to Cassandra, "Right, Sexy?"

She gives him a condescending pat on the cheek. "You bet, Secretariat."

I don't know why she calls him that. I'm about to ask when he starts to walk toward the front of the room and motions for me to come with him.

Trevor gives Reagan a huge bear hug, lifting her off the ground. "Happy birthday, sis." They both laugh in a familiar way. They must be close.

Reagan looks me up and down. "Who's the hottie with the badass dance moves?"

I hold out my hand. "I'm Lance Remington. Thank you for having me, ma'am. Happy birthday to you."

She smiles. "My pleasure. Call me Reagan though."

No one likes to be called ma'am around here. My mother would whack me in the head if she heard me call a woman anything but ma'am.

Trevor nods toward Skylar. "It seems Lance had the good fortune of meeting Skylar earlier." He moves his eyebrows up and down in a suggestive manner.

Reagan toggles her head back and forth between Skylar and me. She smiles at Trevor. "You mean when Skylar went missing for thirty minutes and came back with messy hair and smeared lipstick?"

Trevor winks and Skylar narrows her eyes at Reagan.

I don't want Skylar to be embarrassed. "I spilled my beer on her dress. I was just using an old family trick to help her remove it. And, because it's a clear night, she gave me a lesson on the stars outside.

Reagan laughs. "I *bet* she gave you a lesson."

Yet another attractive woman sticks out her hand. It's the woman I saw in the closet with Jackson earlier. "Pay them no attention. They act like they're in junior high. I'm Darian Knight. It's nice to meet you, Lance. Are you a friend of Trevor's?"

Before I can answer, Jackson throws his arm around me. "This is Lance. Melissa's nephew. You know he's now working for us while he's in business school."

Skylar looks shocked. "You're Melissa's nephew?"

I nod. "Yes, ma'am."

Skylar and I stare at each other for a few moments before Jackson says, "Lance is doing so incredibly well, that I'm going to let him take the lead on the Bancroft proposal as his first test at Knight Investments. Skylar, I know you're doing the same for Daulton and Lawrence Holdings. I guess you two will be competing against each other for the contract."

He smiles. "This should be fun."

CHAPTER ONE

EIGHTEEN YEARS AGO

SKYLAR

"Mommy, do I look beautiful?"

She smiles at me. "Skylar, you always look beautiful."

"My date said not to wear a dress. He said to wear jeans. I think I'd look more beautiful in a dress."

Mommy shakes her head. "Skylar, clothes don't make a woman beautiful."

"What does?"

"Confidence." She tweaks my nose. "You, doll face, are smart, sweet, and confident. I think those qualities make you more beautiful than any dress would."

"Okay." I bite my lip. "Can you tell me if this sweater is pretty? I want to look pretty on my date."

She laughs. "The green color matches your eyes." She winks. "Our eyes."

I smile. Mommy and I have the same color eyes.

"Will I be as pretty as you when I grow up?"

"I think you got the best of both me and Daddy. You're very pretty. Don't ever doubt it."

I nod my head just as the doorbell rings.

I jump up and down several times. "He's here. He's here."

Mommy opens the door and Daddy is standing there with flowers smiling at me. Mommy reaches up on her tippy toes to kiss him, but he holds up his hand. "Sorry, but I have a date with Skylar tonight. I'm afraid I can't kiss another woman right now. It would be rude to my date."

Mommy and I both laugh.

Daddy walks in and hands me flowers. They're peach colored and they smell really good.

"Are you ready for our date?"

"Yes. Will you tell me where we're going?"

"Not just yet. You'll have to wait until we get there."

I start to pout, but Mommy pulls me into a hug.

"You're going to have the best time." She whispers to me, "I'm jealous of how cute your date is. I wish I had a cute date like him tonight."

I giggle.

"Would you like me to put those in water and leave them in your room while you two are out? I can put them right next to your bed."

I nod. "Yes. Thank you." I give them one last sniff before handing them off to her.

Daddy offers his arm to me. "Shall we go?"

I loop my arm through his and we walk out the door.

Mommy shouts from the door, "No motorcycles or tattoos. Be home before your curfew."

Daddy and I both laugh.

We get into his car and drive for a very long time.

"Are we almost there, Daddy?"

"Yes, doll face. Just a few more minutes."

When we arrive, it's dark outside. There aren't any lights. It's kind of scary.

"Daddy, it's really dark here."

"I know. It's okay. We need it to be dark."

He opens the trunk of the car and pulls out a big blanket and a basket. He spreads the blanket out on the grass.

He sits and then lays down. "Come lay with me." He offers me his arm to rest my head on, so I slide and lean my head back on his big arm.

"Skylar, look up."

I gasp. "Wow. There are a million stars in the sky. I don't think we have this many at our house."

"It's the same sky, the view is just better from here. That's why I brought you to this spot."

"It's so pretty."

"It is. Guess what?"

"What?"

"There are a lot more than a million stars in the sky. I don't remember the exact number, but I do know that there are ten times more stars in the sky than there are grains of sand on all the beaches on Earth."

"Wow, that's a lot of stars."

"It sure is."

"How do you know so much about stars?"

"I studied them in college. I've always loved them. If you love them too, I thought that maybe it could be something special only you and I share together. We can learn lots of fun facts about the sky and the stars."

"You mean something you won't do with Harley and Reagan?"

"Nope. Just you and me. I love the sky and I love you. There's a reason you're named Skylar after all."

I turn my head to him in shock. "I'm named after the sky?"

He nods. "You are. Your eyes sparkled just like your mom's when you were born. They looked like stars in the sky to me. I mentioned the name Skylar to your mom, and she loved it as much as I did."

"Wow. I didn't know that."

We lay there and watch the stars for a while. He teaches me a few more fun facts.

I start singing "*Twinkle Twinkle Little Star*."

He laughs. "Skylar, I'm sorry to be the one to break it to you, but stars don't really twinkle."

"They don't?"

"No. The movement of the Earth makes it look like they do, but they don't."

He points to two big stars. "Do you see how the one on the right looks so much brighter than the one on the left?"

"Yes."

"Now close your eyes. I'm going to carry you for a minute. Keep them closed. No peeking."

I shut my eyes tight. I feel him pick me up and walk for a minute or so.

"Okay, doll face, open them." I do. "Now look up at those same two stars." I do. "Do you see how the one on the left now looks brighter than the one on the right?"

"Oh wow. How did that happen?"

"All stars shine, Skylar. Some look brighter from one place, and some look brighter from another, but they all shine just the same."

We walk back to the blanket and sit. He opens the basket. There are bags of McDonald's hamburgers, french fries, and lots of different sauces he tells me to try.

"Don't tell your mother I gave this to you. If she asks, we ate chicken and vegetables."

I giggle. "Okay."

While we're eating, he starts talking about the star brightness again. "Doll face, you and your older sisters are all bright stars. You shine in different ways, and there will be times that one of you shines brighter, but you'll all have your time to shine bright. I know Harley gets a lot of attention at school, and Reagan likes to be the center of attention, but your star shines just as bright. Promise me that you'll never doubt that."

I shrug. "Okay, Daddy."

"Your Aunt Gillian and I did very well in school, and I was also a bit of a football star. I know you don't remember Uncle Declan, but he always thought our stars shined brighter, and got very sad about it. He never saw that he could shine too."

"I have an Uncle Declan?"

My daddy looks sad. "Yes. He did some bad adult things, so we don't see him anymore. Maybe one day, he'll realize that his star shines bright too, and we can see him again. That would make me happy."

"I hope so too. Is he as silly as Uncle Will?" Mommy's brother is very funny.

Daddy smiles. "Even sillier."

My mouth opens in shock. I'm not sure I know anyone sillier than Uncle Will. Then I realize I do know one person sillier than Uncle Will.

"Is he sillier than Aunt Cass?"

"No one is sillier than Aunt Cass."

I smile. That's true. My mom's best friend is the funniest person I know.

We see a flash across the sky, and he points up. "Did you see that shooting star?"

I gasp. "Wow. That's the coolest thing I've ever seen. How does that happen?"

"'I'll tell you in a second, but first make a wish. You should make a wish every time you see a shooting star."

"Is it like a birthday wish where I can't tell you or it won't come true?"

"No, you can tell me."

"I wish to be as pretty as Mommy one day."

"Skylar, you're beautiful. You and Mommy may not look a lot alike, but you're just as beautiful."

I put my head down. "Why does Harley get to look like Mommy, and I don't?"

He smiles. "You're the lucky one who looks like me."

"Reagan looks like you. More than I do."

"Do you think Reagan's pretty?"

"Duh, of course." My sister Reagan is very pretty. Everyone says so.

"She doesn't look like Mommy at all. You share Mommy's eyes. You look more like her than Reagan does."

"Wow, you're right."

"Want to know a secret?"

"Yes."

"Shooting stars aren't really stars."

"They're not?"

"No, they're meteoroids, rocks, falling into Earth's atmosphere and burning up."

"Where do they come from? Why do we make wishes when we see them?"

"There are a lot of theories about that, but I choose to believe the Greek mythological one. Basically, sometimes the gods look down at Earth. When they lean over to look, some rocks fall, causing the shooting stars. When you see a shooting star, the gods are looking and listening, so, if you make a wish, they'll help it come true."

"I like that. I'll make wishes whenever I see shooting stars."

We eat our food, talk about the stars some more, and then pack up the car.

On the way home, Daddy turns to me. "Did you like learning about the stars?"

"I *loved* it."

He smiles. "Good. Maybe every few months we can go on a date and look at the stars together."

"Can we have McDonald's?"

He laughs. "If that's what you want."

"It is. Can I have french fries with barbecue sauce?"

"You liked the barbecue sauce the best?"

I nod and he squeezes my hand. "Me too, kiddo. But we'll tell Mommy we had chicken and veggies, right?"

I smile. "Yes, I promise."

We drive home, and as we walk to the house, I reach for his hand. I always see him and Mommy holding hands. Now it's my turn.

He brings my hand to his mouth and kisses it. "I love you, Skylar."

"I love you too, Daddy."

We get to the front door, but he doesn't open it. He turns to me. "May I have permission to kiss you on the cheek?"

I giggle. "You're my daddy. You don't have to ask permission to give me a kiss."

"Tonight, I'm your date. No date should ever kiss you without asking for permission first. You'll always be the one to decide which dates get to kiss you and which don't."

"Okay. You can kiss my cheek."

He gives me a big kiss on my cheek. He then hands me a wrapped present.

My eyes widen. "For me?"

"Yes. Open it before we go inside."

I open it and it's a thick book on the stars. There's a piece of paper wedged inside it. I pull it out.

Daddy asks, "Can you read that?"
I nod.

"Look up at the stars and not down at your feet."

I move my eyes back to his. "What does that mean?"

"It means I want you to always keep your head up and be proud. Never look down. I'm going to leave you notes in that book from time to time, so be on the lookout. Keep it in your room. You can read this book every night before bedtime and learn a lot about the stars from it. Maybe my notes will help you learn some other things too."

I hug the book tight. It will be my most cherished possession.

CHAPTER TWO

PRESENT

SKYLAR

I arrive at my oldest sister Harley's house early in the morning. She asked me to come by for coffee before we both head off to work. I have no idea what she wants to talk about.

As soon as I open the door, her two-and-a-half-year-old son, Scotty, comes flying into my arms. "Aunt Skyar!" He struggles with the *L* in my name.

I lift him into my arms and give him a big kiss on his chubby little cheek. "Hey, baby boy. Do you have big kid school today?" He attends a preschool a few days a week.

He nods with enthusiasm. "I have art today. We're making robots."

"Wow. That's awesome."

He nods with wide-eyed excitement.

Harley appears. "Scotty, you need supplies for your

project. Run to the garage and grab a few boxes out of our recycling bin. I left a shopping bag for you by the garage door. Fill it with the boxes."

"Okay, Mommy."

I put him down and he sprints toward their garage at full speed.

Harley hands her daughter to me, and I pull her into my arms. She's nearly a year younger than Scotty. They had them in rapid succession.

"Can you hold her for a minute? I just need to pack their lunches. Brody will get them out of here in a few minutes and then we can talk."

"Of course I can play with my best girl, right, Ellie?" I rub her nose with mine and she giggles. She's so cute. She looks just like Harley, with dark hair and big green eyes. They both resemble my mother. Reagan and I look most alike, except her eyes are blue like my father's. She and I have at least four inches on Mom and Harley though, getting our father's height.

"Can you say Aunt Skylar?"

"Ska Ska."

I guess that will have to do for now.

Without noticing me, Brody quietly walks into the kitchen and simply stares at Harley. He's extremely tall, broad, and good-looking, with blond hair and blue eyes. He looks like the California born man that he is.

He legitimately just stands and watches her make lunch for a full minute before she notices him in the room. When she sees him, she smiles. "Hey, baby."

He moves toward her, wraps his arms around her, and gives her a deep kiss. She kisses him back for a brief moment before tapping her hand on his chest. She nods her head toward me. "Skylar's here."

He turns to me. "Good morning. I didn't see you there."

I let out a laugh. "Brody, you never see anyone but Harley when you walk into a room." He's madly in love with her.

He smiles as he kisses my cheek. "Proud of it. I have the most beautiful, perfect wife in the world."

He turns back to Harley. "I packed their bags. Are they ready otherwise? I need to drop them off and get in for surgery."

"Yep. I'm just finishing their lunches. I'll be at the hospital in about an hour. I don't have anything scheduled until late morning."

Harley and Brody are both surgeons at a nearby hospital. She's a cardiothoracic surgeon, and he's a neurosurgeon.

She turns her head toward the garage and yells, "Scotty, hurry up."

He appears with a shopping bag full of empty boxes. "I got it, Mommy."

"Good boy. Give me a big kiss." He runs to her and gives her a kiss on the lips. Their family is so perfect. I'm happy for them and envious of them all at the same time.

She hands him his lunchbox. "Give Aunt Skylar a kiss too."

He runs over to me and kisses me. He's the sweetest little boy ever. Not at all surprising given how Brody behaves. He has Brody's laid-back, loving disposition. He's going to grow up watching his father love Harley the same way our father loved our mother. Wholeheartedly and unashamedly. He'll be a better man because of it.

After our kiss, I take a quick peek inside his shopping bag of recyclables and start laughing. "Harley, you may want to check Scotty's bag before he goes."

She pinches her eyebrows in confusion as she walks over to his bag and looks in. She lets out a loud gasp and then mumbles, "Oh, shit."

She pulls one of the boxes out. "Scotty, Mommy needs this box. You can have the rest."

It's a pink box for a vibrator with a clit stimulator.

Brody and I both cover our smiles with our hands.

Scotty's little lower lip starts to quiver. Sensing he's about to have a meltdown over it, Brody grabs his hand. "Come on, bud. I have an even cooler box in my car that you can use instead. It's way better. It's for boys. That's a yucky girly box." Brody lifts his head and winks at Harley.

Scotty nods his head as the lip retracts back into place. "Yeah, I need a boy box."

Brody kisses Harley longer than is normal, and then takes Ellie from my arms. They head out the door.

Harley covers her eyes in embarrassment.

I smile. "It's not like I don't know you have toys. I'm surprised you need that though. I know you get laid on the regular."

"I do get laid on the regular. More than regular. I don't use the toys on my own, Brody likes to use them on me." She smirks as if remembering something, but then takes a breath. "Speaking of getting laid, let's talk. Have a seat. I'll grab you a coffee."

I sit at their kitchen table while she pours our coffees. She hands me mine and sits across from me.

"Sky, I'm worried about you. Have you gone on *any* dates since Jason?"

My face drops and I shake my head. "I haven't been up to it. He and I had a good thing for nearly four years. I just can't seem to get motivated, but I did hook-up at Reagan's party last weekend. That was a big step for me. It was the first time since Jason."

Her face lights up. "Reagan said she was pretty sure you did. Was it with Melissa's hot nephew?"

I nod. "Yes."

"Did you have sex with him?"

I shake my head. "No. We just fooled around in a bathroom, but it was the first time I came from someone else's hand in a year."

"Well, I guess it's a start. Are you going to see him again?"

I shake my head. "I don't think so. Not like that. I didn't know he was Melissa's nephew until after the fact. He works for Jackson. It sounds like we're going to be competing against each other for a big project. He's about to become my enemy."

She bites her lip. "That could be kind of hot."

"No, we definitely can't go there again. This is a huge project. Reagan desperately wants it. I need to prove that I can handle it in a professional manner. People at Daulton already think I have a cushy job because the CEO is my sister. I need to prove that I'm capable."

"You *are* capable. I'm sure no one doubts it." She smiles. "How was the hook-up?"

I sigh. "Good. Really good. He was so sweet. Maybe it just felt good to have a man's hands on my body. A hot man at that. It really has been a while."

"You were with Jason for a long time. You were comfortable. You need to get out there more. You won't meet anyone staying home or hanging with your family all the time. I love how much we see you, but my house isn't exactly conducive to finding single men. Neither is Mom's or Hayden's."

"I know. My friends have been begging me to go out. It's been a year since Jason and I broke up. I know it's time. I needed to nurse my broken heart, Harley. The break-up hurt me deeply."

What my friends and family still don't know is that Jason cheated on me. I loved him, but he threw our relationship away like it meant nothing. I fear that from now on I'll always have trust issues. If I'm being honest, it's made me afraid. I'm scared to be with another man. I fear that he'll hurt and betray me the way Jason did.

I decided not to tell my sisters about the cheating because they always suspected he was unfaithful to me. I didn't want an *I told you so* speech from them. It's also a little embarrassing that a man felt the need to cheat on me. I've kept the pain bottled up. They thought we amicably broke up because he was moving, and I never corrected them.

I shake those thoughts. "I think the hook up with Lance was good for me. It was the wake-up call I needed to get out there again. To know that I *want* to get out there again." That's true. I miss physical intimacy. My short encounter with Lance reminded me of that.

She smiles. "Good. This conversation was easier than I thought. I was expecting you to fight me on it."

"No fighting. If I ever want to have what you and Reagan have with Brody and Carter, and what Mom had with Dad and now Jackson, I need to put myself out there. I get it." I desperately want what all of them have.

"I'm happy to help. We can go out with you too. We finally found a regular babysitter. Jade offered to babysit too."

"I would love that. Obviously Reagan and Carter are always up for a good time. I'm sure they'd be happy to go out." Reagan and Carter can have a good time just about anywhere. Reagan has always been the life of any party, and she found a man that's the exact same. They're a perfect match.

"Very true."

She bends her head to blow on, then sip, her coffee. She looks back up with sad eyes. "I took Scotty to Dad's grave for the first time last week. His teacher asked the students if they knew why their parents chose their names, so I took him and tried to explain. He sort of got it, but thinks of Brody's dad and Jackson as his two grandpas. I told him that Jackson is a bonus grandpa, but that Scott Lawrence, not Jackson Knight, is my father. I'm not sure he really understands it yet. It kind of hit me hard that he won't ever know Dad. He'll know of him, and that he's named after him, but he won't know what a truly great man he was. He won't be able to get advice from Dad like we did."

I can't help but get choked up. "Can you believe it's been over seven years since he passed?"

She starts to tear up as well. "It's crazy. I can still hear his voice in my head at times, giving me advice. I don't think I realized how much he gave us until he passed. Now, when I encounter real-life situations, I can hear him clear as day, telling me what to do."

I nod. "I know exactly how you feel. I was talking to someone about the stars recently. It made me realize how much I've missed my nights with Dad looking at the sky. It was our thing together, and it's been totally void from my life since he died."

She looks at me with compassion. "I'll go with you sometime. Maybe you can teach Scotty all the stuff you know. Bring it full circle in the family."

I smile at the thought. "I'd like that. Maybe when he's a little older. I started at about eight years old. I haven't star gazed since my astronomy classes in college. And only once during college did I go and star gaze outside of class."

"With Jason?"

I shake my head. "No. He never understood my love for the stars. He thought it was nerdy. It was on the three-year anniversary of Dad's death. Mom was still such a mess. She had only just started leaving the house again." I sigh. "Did you know that Mom didn't make it to a single parent's weekend at college my first three years?"

She shakes her head. "I'm sorry, Sky. That sucks."

I shrug. "She was still mourning. Aunt Cass came, but

Mom didn't come until my last one during my senior year. Anyway, I went to the spot that Dad and I used to go to, and I wished on a shooting star for Dad to help Mom get better. It worked. A few weeks later she met Jackson. I believe wholeheartedly that Dad sent Jackson for her."

We both have tears trickling down our cheeks. She walks over and hugs me. "I'm so sorry I wasn't there for you. Those three years were bad for me between losing Dad, medical school, and being separated from Brody. I was so into my own shit. I was a terrible big sister to you."

I hug her back. "No, you weren't. You were a little out of it, but you've never been a bad big sister. Plus, Reagan transferred, so she was around all the time, getting us both into all kinds of trouble."

We both laugh as we pull away and wipe our tears.

"Now she's my boss and runs a billion-dollar company. Dad would be proud of her."

She gives me a small smile. "Dad would be proud of all of us."

AFTER LEAVING HARLEY'S, I make my way to work. Reagan is waiting for me in my office when I arrive.

She turns when I walk in. "Did everything go okay at Harley's?"

Clearly my sisters had a tag team plan in mind.

"If you mean, am I willing to start going out and meeting men, yes. I get it. You don't need to hit me over the head anymore."

She nods. "Good. It's been a year. You're treading in dangerous spinster territory. If I see kitty litter on an expense report, we're staging a full-blown intervention."

I roll my eyes while laughing. "I know. I assume you're happy I hooked up at your party though?"

She smiles. "Of course I'm happy. You needed to get off on something not battery operated."

I give her the finger. "Fuck you."

Though that reminds me of what happened at Harley's, and I smile. "Speaking of battery-operated toys, Scotty almost brought an empty box from one of Harley's vibrators to school today for an art project. I found it in his bag. I should have let him take it to school, so she could suffer the humiliation."

Reagan hysterically laughs as I explain to her what happened. At the end, she shakes her head. "Brody does love using toys with her."

I nod in agreement. "You have funky kinks too."

"Back at you, little sister."

I let out an exasperated breath. "Are you just in my office to harass me about dating, or is there a work-related reason?"

"I want to talk about the Bancroft project. I'm fucking thrilled that you got some ass, but if he's going to be representing Knight Investments, I need to know if it's a problem. I want this project. It's going to shape the Philly landscape for the next century. I'm honestly surprised Jackson is giving it to him, but it seems to be the case. Is this a conflict for you? Should I flip it to Dominic?"

Dominic is the other Vice President of Strategy and Operations. He's not a bad guy, but he's been circling around this project, wanting it. I can't blame him, it's one of the most coveted projects in company history.

"No, I can handle it myself. I'm sure people are surprised you're giving it to me though. He's been here much longer than I have."

"Exactly no one is surprised. Dom works mostly in acquisitions, and you in the new projects. Why do you put yourself down? You're good at what you do. Everyone sees that except you. I honestly wouldn't have delegated the project to you if I didn't think you were the right person. You know how much I want to win this one."

"Thank you. Lance won't be a problem. It was a one-time hook up. It's over. Honestly, I doubt I would have done it if I knew he was Melissa's nephew. I've already forgotten about him."

That's not entirely true. I was definitely attracted to him. It was the first time I've had any attraction to a man since Jason.

"Good. Are you ready for the pitch meeting next week? You need to demolish the competition."

"I have a few more numbers to crunch, and a few visuals to tighten with Thor, but I'm otherwise prepared. I'm just going to go through everything as many times as I can to make sure it's perfect."

She stands. "Excellent. If you need me or Carter, you know where to find us."

"On top of your desk fucking?"

She laughs as she walks out the door. She turns her head back and yells, "Sometimes it's under my desk." As she gets further away, she shouts again, "Or on my desk chair."

I swear those two get it on in the office at least once a day. I guess when you're the CEO and your husband is the president, you can do whatever you want.

They've only been married a few months though. I'm sure it's still the honeymoon phase. But, even at the beginning with Jason, I don't remember wanting him in the all-consuming way Carter and Reagan constantly want each other. They look at one another like they're going to devour the other at any moment. Given that they get off on people watching them have sex, they really don't care about how they act in front of other people, though they do at least attempt to keep it discreet in the office.

I shake thoughts of them away and sit down to work. I need to make sure this proposal is perfect.

A little while later, Dominic walks in. He's an attractive and imposing man. I don't know his precise heritage, but he looks Italian. He's got dark hair, olive skin, and big brown eyes. I'm guessing he's about ten years older than me. He should technically be senior to me, but that's not how Reagan organized things. We have the same title and simply divide the labor according to our respective areas of expertise.

I smile at him. "Hey, Dom. How are you?"

"I'm okay." He doesn't look okay. He looks beat.

"Are you sure? You don't look like it."

"Just a little personal life drama. Nothing for you to worry about. Do you have a minute?"

"Of course." I motion for him to sit, which he does. "What's up?"

"Is everything good on the Bancroft proposal? I'm happy to help."

"I think I have it under control."

"Great. I'm here if you need anything. I took a little peek in the files. Your vision is amazing. I've never seen anything quite like it. Bancroft would be crazy not to go with you."

I smile. He didn't have to say that. I appreciate it. "Thanks. I'm happy with it so far."

He places a file on my desk. I look at him in question. "What's this?"

"It was a meteorological report I had commissioned on another project before you came here. I thought it might be helpful to you in designing the locations of the outdoor spaces."

"Thank you, Dom. I'll take a look at it." I probably won't. I'm settled on the locations of the outdoor spaces.

"Good. I wanted to talk to you about my Gunnar project." The Gunnar project is an acquisition, but I know it's become a bit hostile.

"Are they still being problematic?"

"Yes, and our legal department thinks we need outside counsel to advise. Do you know anyone who works in mergers and acquisitions?"

"I do. My aunt, Cassandra Blackstone, is a partner at Cooper and Kronfeld. She runs the M&A department."

"Oh, I've heard of her. She's supposed to be the best."

I smile at that. "She is. Her sister works with them, and she's good too. Beth O'Connell is her name."

His eyes widen and his back stiffens. "I...I...I think I met Beth at your sister's party. Long dark hair and light blue eyes, right? That was her?"

I smile. "Yes, it was." He's clearly interested, though I thought he was married.

He stands, now rushing to get out of my office. "Thanks, I'll reach out to them."

There's definitely a story there.

CHAPTER THREE

FOUR MONTHS AGO

LANCE

"Son, are you ready to join your brothers and me representing your country?"

I put my fork down on my dinner plate and my shoulders sink. "Dad, we've been through this. We made a deal. I went to college in town. I've worked here for over three years. I've done everything you asked of me. Now it's time for you to support me going to business school in the city. I'm moving to Philadelphia in two months. You know this."

He exhales a disappointed breath. "Why do you feel the need to defy me?"

"Dad, this isn't about you. It's about me and the kind of life I want. I don't want military life. I don't want to live in a small town. I want to be in a city. I enjoy business. I've been told that I have the mind for it. We've been over this."

"I thought you'd outgrow this nonsense."

"It's not nonsense. It's my dream."

"Don't disrespect me, Lance."

"I'm sorry, sir, but we made a deal. I followed through on my end of the bargain. Now you need to live up to your end of things."

Mom starts tearing up. "What about Roseanne? That girl loves you so much. She wants to raise a family here. She doesn't want to live in a big, scary city."

"Mom, Roseanne and I are breaking up when I leave. You know this already. It's for the best. We want different things in life." I've felt for a long time that Roseanne and I weren't quite right together, but it's been nearly ten years. I didn't want to hurt her unnecessarily. We knew my move was the end of our relationship. I've been waiting on that to make a clean break from her.

Now tears spill from Mom's eyes. "Oh, Lance, you're leaving a wonderful woman to chase a silly dream."

"It's not silly." My family doesn't understand me at all.

Dad shakes his head. "You're upsetting your mother. I've let this go on long enough. You've refused all proper military training. I let you study business because I thought it might help you in officer's school. I even indulged your astronomy silliness. It's time for you to lead a proper life."

I can't take much more of this. I won't let him push me around like he does my three older brothers. "No, sir. We made a deal. You always say that we're nothing if not our word. In two months, I'll be starting business school in Philadelphia. I'm moving there."

He shakes his head in disgust. "I'm not paying for it."

That wasn't our deal, but I'm not sure I care anymore. "If that's what you want, fine. I'll get a job and pay my own way. I've saved a little money. Enough to get me started."

I bring my dinner dish to the sink, rinse it, and place it in the dishwasher. "Excuse me, I have plans with Roseanne tonight."

As I walk out of the room, I hear my mother say, "Maybe she can talk sense into him, Craig. I never thought he'd actually leave us. You promised he wouldn't."

"I know. It's time to take a hard line. He can't go without our money. He'll eventually see the right course."

I'm going. Why don't they get it? If I have to live on the streets and sell my blood to pay my tuition, I'm going.

I pull up to Roseanne's house in my old, blue pickup truck. I get out of the truck planning to knock on her door, but she comes running out of the house and into my arms before I approach. She gives me a big hug, and I give her one in return.

When she pulls back, she smiles. "Where are we going tonight?"

"Let's go somewhere and talk."

I help her into the car, and we drive for a bit. I eventually pull into a secluded area we've spent a lot of time in. I stop the car and put it in park.

She moves over to me, assuming we're doing what we normally do here, but I grab her wrist. "Don't. We need to talk."

It's been weeks since we've been together in that way. I can't bring myself to be like that with her anymore. My feelings have waned, and I don't think she can emotionally handle it.

She looks embarrassed. "Oh. Okay."

I take her hand in mine. "Rosie, I think it's best if I leave for Philadelphia earlier than planned. Things are getting ugly at home. My father just told me that he's not paying for school anymore, even though we made a deal. I should go and get a job to save money before school starts. And I feel like it's only prolonging the pain for you. I don't want to hurt you."

She smiles at me with hope. "Then don't leave. Stay. We can make a great life here."

I shake my head. "Rosie, you've always known what I wanted. I want to live in the city. I know you don't. I'd never ask it of you. It's time to say goodbye. I've loved our time together, but now it's time to go our separate ways. I want a different life than you. I want to free you to find someone that can give you what you want. What you deserve."

Roseanne is beautiful. I can name at least a dozen men in this town who would give anything for a chance to be with her.

She starts crying, which breaks my heart. "I don't want you to go. I know you'll miss me. You'll miss us. You'll come back. I know you will."

"I don't know anything for certain except that I'll regret it my entire life if I don't try. I'd only end up resenting you, and that's not fair." I kiss her cheek. "I'm sorry."

After a tear-filled ride back to her house, I head back to mine. I have to get out of here. If my father is cutting me off, I need to get to Philly and figure out a way to make some money. I need to take out loans to pay my tuition.

My father doesn't know it, but I want to reconnect with his sister, my Aunt Melissa. I know they don't speak, but I don't know why. She was never anything but kind to me. I know I have three cousins that live in Philly, but it's been over ten years since I've seen them. I barely remember them. I'd love to reconnect. I don't know anyone else in the city, but I sort of know them and that's a place to start.

I decide that I just need to go and make a quick, clean break.

That night, I pack my bags, throw them into the truck, and head to Philadelphia. I know this is the first day of the rest of my life.

CHAPTER FOUR

PRESENT

LANCE

I've been working with Jackson, Trevor, and Payton all day, every day, for a week. I have no idea why, but they want me to take the lead on this giant proposal. They've been inundating me with information and helping me prepare for the upcoming presentation.

At some point, Donna, Jackson's long-time assistant and the office manager, pops her head in the conference room. "Jackson, Darian is here." Donna smirks. "She brought you *lunch*." She pronounces lunch with a weird emphasis.

Trevor and Payton look at each other and roll their eyes. Jackson practically sprints out of the room without uttering a word to the rest of us.

Trevor and Payton start laughing hysterically. I look at them. "What did I miss?"

Payton responds, "Darian shows up at least once a month for some lunchtime office action. They don't hide it well."

Trevor nods in agreement. "She wears a trench coat every time. Even in the middle of summer. She's obviously got something skimpy, or nothing at all, on underneath. He won't resurface for two hours."

I smile and shake my head. "It's kind of awesome that they're so passionate at their age. I don't think I've ever even seen my parents kiss."

Trevor raises his eyebrow. "*Their age*? You do know that my wife and Darian are longtime best friends and the same age?"

I give a guilty smile. "Whoops."

Payton laughs. "Don't worry about it. You'll see my dad and Darian more than kiss at family dinners. They can't keep their hands off each other. It's nauseating."

I shake my head in disbelief, but then something occurs to me. "I thought Cassandra said Skylar was her niece. Are she and Darian friends or sisters?"

"They're best friends but are close enough that the girls call her Aunt Cass. She's not technically their aunt though. She and Darian were college roommates."

I nod in understanding.

Payton stands. "I'm running out for a bit. Are you guys good?"

"Yes, sir. I packed lunch."

Trevor laughs. "You don't need to do that. The kitchen here has a ton of food. Dad makes sure it's always full for everyone. He says it costs him less to feed everyone lunch than it does for them to leave the office for an hour every day."

"Oh. I didn't realize that. Good to know." That will save me a ton of time and money.

Trevor and I grab big platefuls of food from the kitchen and go back to the conference room to eat.

At some point I turn to him and ask, "Trevor, why is your dad trusting me with this big proposal? Don't get me wrong, I'm excited for the opportunity, but this is a major project."

He shrugs. "The team that ran the training thought highly of you. They're usually spot on at identifying those that can succeed in this business and those that likely won't. This is what my dad does. If he sees someone with potential, he likes to throw them in the deep end. I was managing skyscrapers in New York City right after I graduated business school. He likes *in the trenches* learning. He doesn't like baby steps. And yes, this is an unusually large project, but my dad has been around a long time. He doesn't feel a sense of urgency over anything anymore. Honestly, since Darian came into his life, work and this business stopped being his focal point. She's the center of his universe now."

"Does that upset you and your brothers?"

He looks surprised. "Not at all. Just the opposite. She's the best thing that's ever happened to him."

"What about your mom?"

"They were a mismatch. Darian is much better suited to him." He shrugs. "Mom's also much happier now too."

"She's definitely into Declan. He's an intense guy though."

"That's an understatement. He can be nuts, but he seems nuts for her, so it's all good. I've never seen her happier."

"I guess so."

I eat a little more of my food and then look at the piles of paperwork in front me. "Honestly, I've learned more in the past week than in all four years of college. I'm so grateful. I just hope I'll make you guys proud."

"You'll be fine. You have the mind for it. I can tell."

He takes a few bites of his sandwich. "How did you leave things with Skylar the other night?"

"I didn't get to talk to her. Your dad mentioned that we'd be competing against each other. I guess that ended whatever we briefly started. She basically ignored me the rest of the night."

He's quiet.

"What is it?"

"Skylar had a long-term boyfriend. They were together for about four years. They broke up a year ago. I haven't seen her with anyone since. She rarely goes out. I honestly think you're the first guy she's hooked up with since the breakup."

My shock must be evident on my face.

He lets out a laugh. "That good, huh?"

"I'm not really a kiss and tell kind of guy, but she's incredible. She knows what she's doing. More than I do."

"What does that mean?"

I'm sort of embarrassed to tell him this, but I do. "Well, I dated the same woman for nearly ten years. She's the only person I've been with, and she wasn't as... adventurous as Skylar."

"I have no idea what that means. Did you have sex with Skylar?"

I shake my head. "No, but...it was the first blow job I've ever received."

He spits out his food all over the table. "Are you fucking kidding me?"

I shake my head. "No. My ex wasn't into oral. I never pushed. I didn't realize until Saturday just how much I was missing out on. It was the greatest thing I've ever experienced in my life."

He starts laughing. "I bet it was. Did you reciprocate?"

"Is it weird that we're talking about this stuff? I've never talked like this with my brothers, plus, she's sort of your sister."

"It's not weird. I know you haven't been around us all together yet, but we have very open communication with Darian's girls. Everyone speaks in an uninhibited way. Reagan's one of my best friends, and she shares everything. I feel like I live her sex life with Carter in real time. We didn't know each other until we were all adults. I'm sure that's part of it. My wife also has no qualms about sharing. When you come to a family dinner, you'll see how it is."

"I think I'm afraid to come to dinner."

He smiles. "They're fun. You didn't answer my question though, did you reciprocate?"

I hem and haw for a minute. I don't love talking about this stuff, but I eventually answer, "No. I touched her first, to...umm...completion, and then she did her thing to me. As soon as that was done, her phone rang, and she walked out."

"So you've seriously never gone down on a woman?"

I shake my head.

His eyes light up. "Oh my god. This is amazing. You're a blank slate. I can be your teacher. Skylar's off limits for now because of the Bancroft project, so let's focus on other women. You need to get out there. I'm going to teach you how to handle women. I'm now your sensei. Call me Sensei Trevor."

I chuckle. "No, I'm not calling you that, but I'll take a little guidance."

"Don't worry. Sensei Trevor is on the job. We're going to get rid of the farm boy crap and make a business barracuda *and* a dominant Casanova out of you."

"What do you mean?"

"Look, I think I'm considered a nice guy, but sometimes you can't be Mr. Nice Guy. You need to know when to shelve him. I'm generally laid-back, but I'm no pushover in business or in bed. I can be demanding and tough when I need to be. You have to maneuver your way through this and learn when to switch gears. Knight Investments isn't a mom-and-pop shop in a rural town where everyone knows your name. Mr. Nice Guy doesn't get the job done in this business. Sometimes you need to go for the jugular. Sometimes bravado matters."

I nod. "I hear you. I need to learn to shelve the nice guy sometimes and play dirty. Got it. I may need you to help me learn to do that."

He gives me a big grin. "That's what Sensei Trevor is for." He takes another bite of his food and then looks at me. "And the same thing goes in bed with smart, successful women."

"I don't understand. What does having a strong business persona have to do with women?"

He rubs his hands together in excitement. "This is going to be so much fun. It's not the law or anything, but it's been the case with every smart, successful woman I've ever had. And I've had a lot. These women maintain careful control all day long. In bed at night, they want someone to take over for them. To boss *them* around."

"Wait, what? They don't want sweet and loving? Isn't that what all women want?"

He shakes his head. "You're so lucky Sensei Trevor is here for you. It's rare any woman wants Mr. Nice Guy in bed, but certainly not powerful career women. They want to be manhandled a bit."

"Do you hurt them? I couldn't do that."

"No one gets hurt. Maybe a little spanking. Maybe a lot of spanking, but that depends on the woman. It's more about handling their bodies in a domineering manner. I promise you'll know right away if they're into it. I'm not suggesting you do anything too drastic that would actually hurt them, but trust me when I tell you, they want someone to take charge. Pin them down, flip them over, push them against the wall. Things like that."

My mind is blown right now.

"Do you at least throw in a little dirty talk?"

"Like what?"

He shakes his head. "I think I have my answer. You need to step up your game, man. *All* women like a little dirty talk. Some more than others, but they all want at least a little of it."

"What kinds of things do you say?"

"I say exactly what I'm thinking. How I'm feeling. What I want to do to them."

I run my fingers through my hair. "I'm so clueless."

"When you were with your girlfriend, weren't you manic with need?"

"Honestly, no."

"You were with the wrong girl then."

I sigh. "I know. I let it go on too long. I knew a while ago that she wasn't for me. I stayed with her out of guilt."

"I'm not going to touch that. I'll let the shrinks deal with it. What about with Skylar? How were you feeling?"

I was exactly what he said. "Manic with need."

He smiles. "The next time you feel that way, just say

what's on your mind. What you want to do to the woman you're with."

"The things going through my head weren't very gentlemanly. What if it scares them away?"

"Then you'll back off."

I let out a breath in frustration.

He puts his hand on my shoulder. "Let's work on some of the other stuff. We know you need to learn how to better take charge in the boardroom and the bedroom. Let's start with the boardroom. I think it will be easier for you."

He spends the rest of lunch reviewing the way I need to conduct myself around our competitors at the pitch meeting. Apparently, I have to be an egomaniacal asshole.

CHAPTER FIVE

SKYLAR

It's Monday morning and I have my big presentation to Adam Bancroft, the CEO of Bancroft Development. They want to develop a skyline changing building in downtown Philadelphia. They prefer to use a Philly-based company to provide seed money, design, and project management. The top four companies in Philadelphia are all presenting, one of which will be awarded the project.

Lance and I arrive at the elevator bank at the same time. He gives me a big smile. "Good morning."

Fuck, I don't think I noticed before that he has big dimples when he smiles. I'm a sucker for dimples. They're so cute. I can't help but look him up and down. He's a very attractive man. Too bad he's off limits.

I smile back. "Good morning, Lance. Good luck today."

"Thank you. Same to you. Can we maybe grab some coffee after this meeting and talk about what happened last weekend?"

I shake my head. "That's not a good idea. It was a

mistake." His face drops. "Not that it wasn't nice, it was. But this project is a big one. We're competitors now. Anything beyond business is off the table. These things tend to get ugly. I can't let my judgment get clouded."

"I understand and agree. I just felt bad that we didn't get to talk afterward."

"There's no need. I'm a big girl. I can handle it. I'm here to fight for my company, and you for yours. This must be your first project. You have a lot to learn."

I couldn't help myself getting in that dig. He needs to know that what happened between us won't impair my judgment.

He slowly licks his lower lip. "You're pretty sure of yourself, Skylar."

"You bet I am. I crushed this. It's in the bag for me." I've learned the hard way that swagger is important in these things.

He smirks. "We've got something pretty special up our sleeves, so, game on, sweetheart."

There is nothing more degrading in business than a man calling you sweetheart. That was a purposeful direct hit. I guess the nice guy is going away and he's switching to business mode. I know exactly what he's doing. I won't let it get to me.

I hold my head up high as we exit the elevator and head to a conference room. I see Larry Clarrett of Clarrett Investments, and Matthew Anderson of Atlas Holdings already seated. Obviously, Lance is here representing Knight Investments, and I'm representing Daulton and Lawrence Holdings.

I shake Matthew's hand first. He's a decent guy. I competed against him on a few projects when I was with Knight Investments before I joined Reagan at her company. It's always a friendly competition with him, mostly because he's never beaten me out for a big project.

I offer Larry my hand next, but he refuses it. He's a

dickhead. He narrows his eyes at me. "Tell your bitch sister congrats on sleeping her way to the top. It must have been hard spending all that time on her back. Tell me, are you climbing the ladder the same way?"

Lance jumps up out of his chair and starts toward Larry. I turn to him and hold my hand up. "Don't. He's not worth it. A few years ago, Reagan stole his clothes and left him in a bar naked, with his one-inch french fry dangling. He's just bitter." I say that loud enough for everyone to hear.

I turn back to Larry. "Better to get a job on your back than on your knees like you do it. At least she got to enjoy the ride."

Matthew starts laughing. "Fuck, Clarrett, she burned you."

Larry snarls. "You're as big of a bitch as your sister."

I smile at him. "Thank you. That's a sweet compliment. It was nice of Daddy to let you play with the big kids today. I guess he doesn't want this job." I smile at Lance and Matthew. "It looks like it's down to the three of us."

I wink at Matthew and Lance while Larry stews in his seat. I sit in mine.

I lean over to Lance and whisper, "This is how these things go. You'll get used to it. Matthew happens to be one of the good guys out there. Most are like Larry."

Adam Bancroft walks in. We all shake his hand. He tells us that he'd like each of us to challenge the other proposals. He wants to expose all potential issues and he admittedly is using us for our brain power. That's fairly unusual. This is going to be a bloodbath. I couldn't be more excited for it.

Larry presents first. It's a complete and utter shitshow. Lance, Matthew, and I tear it apart. We work as a team in cutting Larry down to his true size. Every single aspect of what they're proposing is out of the realm of reason. It's like he didn't spend a minute preparing for this. I could have put together a better proposal while still in high school.

Adam clearly recognizes it. He asks Larry to leave when he's done. He doesn't bother to let him stay for the rest of the proposals. I blow Larry a kiss and give him the universal sign for a blow job on his way out. He gives me the finger.

Matthew presents next. It's a very typical Atlas proposal. It's conservative. Not at all innovative. I hate to chop Matthew down, but I do mention a few weaknesses, as respectfully as possible. Lance also notes a few deficiencies. Admittedly, one or two I hadn't noticed. I don't think we need to inflict much damage. Adam Bancroft is smart. He sees what's happening.

Lance is next. He does a fantastic job. I know it's his first proposal, but it doesn't show. Jackson, Trevor, and Payton prepared him well. I'm not surprised. It's innovative in a totally different way than mine. I do challenge him in a few areas, but he responds more than adequately.

I present last, laying out our vision with virtual models. I'm proud of what I put together. It's different and forward thinking.

I can tell Adam likes it too. He turns his head to Matthew and Lance for them to challenge any of the plans. Matthew holds his hands up like he's got nothing.

Lance clears his throat. He pulls out a file and holds it up. "Well, Mr. Bancroft, we commissioned a meteorologic report. All of Ms. Lawrence's balconies are on the west side of the building. Our reports suggest wanting to limit weather related exposure on the west side. It makes much more sense to set that up on the east side. There's better protection from the elements."

I shake my head. "We're in Philadelphia, not North Dakota."

"Certainly, but why take the risk? That's why we put our outdoor open areas on the east side. No one likes ice damming in the winter. It's a nightmare that could eventually lead to structural issues."

I challenge him right back. "Our research suggests most people enjoy outdoor spaces in the early and mid-afternoons. The west side will have the better sun. The east side will have very limited sun in the afternoons."

Lance shrugs. "That's a fair point. Most people I know try to stay out of the sun though." He adds sarcastically, "But the business suit wearing sunbathers will undoubtedly like your vision." He turns to Adam. "Mr. Bancroft, do you often sunbathe in your business suit during the business day, or do you stay in the shade?"

Adam chuckles. "Absolutely the shade."

I need to save face here. "If that's what you want, we can make some small changes with our engineers and architects. This is a relatively minor item in the grand scheme." I then redirect the conversation to the more substantive aspects of my proposal. Adam seems to like it.

We all walk out at the same time. Matthew excuses himself to go to the restroom, leaving Lance and I to enter the elevator together.

He leans against the wall. He's trying to hide his smile, but the dimples on his cheeks give him away. I hate those dimples.

"You haven't won anything yet, Mr. Remington. He liked my proposal a lot."

"He liked mine too, *Ms. Lawrence.*" He crosses his arms and smugly says, "Did I do okay for my *first time,* or do I still have a lot to learn?"

I narrow my eyes at his smug face. "You think you've got this in the bag, don't you?"

"I know I do. We were spot on. He loved it. Ate up every word I said."

The elevator doors open in the lobby. He motions for me to leave first, and I do. Before I exit the building, I turn back and say, "I've already won. You're just too clueless to realize it.

You should head back to the farm now." I wink at him. "Enjoy coming in second place."

When I get back to the office, my assistant tells me that Reagan wants to see me right away. I walk into my office to drop my things first. I quickly take a look through the file Dominic gave me last week. It mentions the ice damming issue. He was trying to warn me without overly inserting himself. Shit. I should have read it.

I gather myself and head down to Reagan's office. I nod at her assistant, Sheila.

"She's on a phone call, but she said to send you in right away."

"Thanks, Sheila."

I walk in. She's in front of her desk leaning against it on the phone. She holds up her finger for me to wait a minute. She says something in Mandarin. She learned the language in college. She minored in it actually. Perhaps I should have done that instead of astronomy, but it was important to me to continue learning about the stars. I know it's what my father would have wanted.

When she hangs up the phone, she raises her eyebrows. "How'd it go?"

"It went well. Clarrett crashed and burned big time. He had some choice words about you."

She lets out a laugh. "I bet he did. He's such a douchebag. Did you get in a shot about his small penis?"

"Of course I did."

"Good. What about Atlas?"

"Matthew did a decent job presenting. Their plan is just so basic and ordinary though. There's nothing special about it. I don't think Bancroft was even remotely into it."

"I figured. What about Knight Investments? Did they really send Lance to pitch this?"

I nod. "Yep. He did a good job. Their proposal was strong. Really strong."

"As strong as ours?"

"Honestly, I think Bancroft liked us both. I wouldn't be surprised if he asks for more time and more information on both."

She nods as her assistant buzzes. Reagan presses the button. "What's up, Sheila? Don't talk dirty to me, Skylar's in here." She snickers while I roll my eyes.

Sheila is completely unfazed by Reagan's immaturity. "Sorry to interrupt, but Adam Bancroft is on the line. I figured you'd want me to put him through."

"Fuck, yes. Thank you."

Reagan presses the buttons and places the telephone on speaker. "Hey, Adam. How'd it go?"

"No pleasantries, Reagan?"

"Neither of us have time for that."

He laughs. "True. I love that about you. No foreplay. I can call you and not even say hello. I can just get right into it."

"Then do it, Adam. Tell me how it went."

"Your sister is pretty sharp. She doesn't miss much. She decimated the other proposals."

"I wouldn't send some shithead lacky to you, Adam. Of course my sister's brilliant." She smiles at me. "She's related to me."

"I have to tell you, Reagan, the young guy from Knight's office was impressive too. I was pleasantly surprised."

Shit.

"So where does that leave everything?"

"To be honest, I liked how competitive he and your sister were with each other. *That* was like watching foreplay." Reagan silently laughs. "I think I can benefit from it. I'm kicking Clarrett and Atlas out of contention. I want you and Knight to fine tune everything and be back in my office in a month for a final showdown. No holds barred. Guns a-blazing. I'd pay to watch the two of them tango, or more than tango."

"You're a dick, Adam."

He laughs. "I know, it's great. When you're sitting on the most coveted piece of real estate in all of Philadelphia, you can be whatever the hell you want."

"Tell my stepdad he's going down in flames."

Adam laughs again. "I will most definitely convey the message. Have a good---"

Reagan hangs up before he can finish.

She looks at me.

I shake my head at the balls on my sister. "I can't believe you just hung up on him."

She shrugs. "He doesn't give a shit. You heard him. He doesn't care for pleasantries. He gave us the info he wanted to give, and that's it. He's going to make us all hit the four corners of Earth to make this building the biggest and best."

"That's basically what I told you would happen. I knew he liked both. I knew he'd want more information from both of us. Honestly, I think whoever he chooses, he'll still use parts of both plans."

"Well then, use what you learned from him today and make the necessary tweaks to our proposal. They're not beating us on this."

"Yes, boss."

"How was it being around Lance?"

"What do you mean?"

"I mean you were on your knees sucking his dick, like, nine days ago and now you're competing against him in the boardroom. Was it weird?"

"You really have a way with words."

"It's a gift."

"It was fine. He asked me for coffee afterward, but I told him no. We're business competitors and that's it. He was annoyingly smug after the proposals. He knew he crushed it."

"Is he still hot?"

"He didn't all of a sudden become unattractive in the course of a week. Yes, he's still hot. It doesn't matter. It was all business. That's how it will remain. He's public enemy number one now, as far as I'm concerned."

There's a loud banging noise as her office door practically breaks off the hinges as Carter comes running in, out of breath. He has a shocked look on his face.

Reagan turns her head to him. "What's wrong, baby? Are you okay? You look like you saw a ghost."

"I was looking through old photo boxes in storage downstairs. I was hoping to find a project we did years ago. I found this instead." He hands her a photograph.

She looks at it and tears start to well in her eyes.

I try to look over her shoulder but can't see. "Who's in the picture?"

She stoically hands it to me.

I look at it and then back up at her. "This is Dad. He must be in his twenties. Who's the man with him? Why was the photo here?"

Reagan's hand is over her mouth. She's speechless.

Carter answers. "That's my grandfather. I looked into it. Apparently, he gave your father the seed money for his business. He loaned it to him. He offered your father the option of a job here or a loan to start his business, and your dad took the loan. They struck up a friendship over business and motorcycles. That's my grandfather's personal garage they're standing in."

Our father always had one or two motorcycles around. He

loved them, but my mother hated them. Carter has several. He and Reagan always go for rides. She loves it.

I look at the picture again. They're in casual clothes, definitely dirty, and surrounded by bikes. Both are smiling and embracing like old friends. There's a cute kid hiding behind Carter's grandfather's leg, poking his head out smiling at the camera.

I ask Carter, "Who's the little boy?"

Reagan grabs the photo and looks at it again wide-eyed. She clearly didn't notice the little boy the first time she looked at it.

Tears start streaming down her cheeks. She looks back up at him. "Carter, is that you?"

He nods. "I must have been two or three. I don't remember the day, but that's definitely me."

He rubs Reagan's cheek with the back of his fingers, wiping her tears away.

She looks up at him and whispers, "My father met you? You met him?"

He nods as tears now pool in his eyes. "It looks like it."

Suddenly, the air in the room shifts.

They're only inches apart, breathing heavily, now staring at each other like they're about to rip one another's clothes off.

Without breaking eye contact with Carter, Reagan says, "Skylar, I honestly don't care if you're here for this or not, but it's happening in about two seconds and that door needs to be locked. So either lock it and stay for the show or lock it and leave, but just close it and lock it. *Right fucking now*."

Before I even have the chance to respond, their mouths collide, and he grabs her ass and picks her up. She wraps her arms and legs around him.

I quickly turn the lock, walk out, and close the door

behind me. I hear what's likely the contents of her desk crashing to the floor as I walk away.

I look at Sheila. "I wouldn't bother her for a while."

Sheila gives me an unimpressed look. "I know the routine. It's a daily occurrence."

I'm not sure what's more shocking, the intense passion I just witnessed which I've never had or the fact that Reagan's husband got to meet our father. She's so unbelievably lucky for that. I would give anything for the man I marry to have some connection to my father. Tears form in my eyes at the fact that it will never happen.

CHAPTER SIX

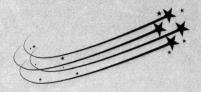

EIGHT YEARS AGO

SKYLAR

I walk out of the karate studio after my evening class. My father always insisted that my sisters and I take karate lessons for self-defense purposes. Harley and Reagan stopped when they were sixteen, but I enjoy it and have stuck with it a little longer. I probably won't be able to take it as much in college next year, but I'm almost at my black belt, and I want to see it through.

I'm heading to my car when I see my father in his.

I bend and look in his window. "Dad? What are you doing here? I have my car."

He smiles. "I know, doll face, but it's a clear night and I have chicken and vegetables in a basket in the car."

I giggle. "Did you get me an extra-large order of vegetables with barbecue sauce instead of ketchup?"

"Of course I did. It's not my first day on the job."

I get into his car, and we begin the long drive to our favorite spot. He looks over at me. "How long until your black belt test?"

"I think another month or two. I was hoping it would be before graduation, but it will be sometime during the summer."

"I'm proud of you for sticking with it. I'll never have to worry about you. You could kick my ass."

I flex and make a muscle. "I sure can." I can't. He's in great shape, being both big and strong. We both know I wouldn't stand a chance.

"What about the play? Is karate interfering with rehearsals? I know how much you love to act. I'm looking forward to seeing you as Sandy in *Grease*."

"Don't worry. I'm *hopelessly devoted* to the play. They scheduled rehearsals around my commitments. Tonight, they're rehearsing a scene I'm not in."

"Good. We have front row seats for opening night. I can't believe this is your last high school play."

"I know. It's been a fun run. Maybe I'll do a play or two in college, as long as it doesn't interfere with my business classes."

"And astronomy?"

I smile. "Definitely astronomy."

He smiles back. He's so excited that I'm planning to minor in astronomy like he did.

We get to our spot and park. He spreads out a blanket while I grab the McDonald's feast. For the past ten years, we have come here every few months and bring McDonald's when we do. We always call it chicken and vegetables, just like the first time we came here.

We eat and talk about my upcoming graduation and class schedule for college next year. When we finish the food, we lay down. I curl into the crook of his arm.

He points out a few stars, which I know, but I like how

excited he gets to point them out to me. "You know, the telescopes at school will be very high tech. You'll see so much more."

"I can't wait. It won't be the same without you though."

He squeezes me. "Thanks for saying that."

He stares up to the sky in wonderment. "I should have put a skylight in your bathroom above your tub. I know how much you like taking long baths." That's true. I love sitting in my big tub thinking or reading.

He continues, "When you're in there, you could have sat and watched the stars." He turns his head to me. "Marry a man one day who wants to give you a skylight in your bathroom so you can look at the stars."

I laugh. "Okay, that will be my top criteria when looking for a man to marry."

"I think it says a lot about a man if he wants to give you all the stars in the sky, don't you?"

"I guess. I'm a long way from that, Dad. I barely date."

"They'll be lined up for you. Trust me. You'll have your pick."

"I'm not Reagan with a different man each week."

He cringes at that thought. "That's by your choice, not for lack of effort or interest from the boys at your school. I'm not blind, Skylar. You're a beautiful woman. You attract a lot of attention. You choose not to indulge."

I suppose he's right. They do ask me out, but very few boys in my high school interest me. I go to parties, and go to all the dances, but I haven't ever dated anyone seriously. I don't know why. I simply have no interest in any of them. They're immature. People often assume I'm a flirtatious party animal like the legendary Reagan Lawrence, but I'm not. I want a man who will talk to me and get to know me, not one who only wants to do shots with me and get into my pants.

"I guess no man measures up to you, Dad. You set the bar

pretty high. It's going to take a special man to pique my interest. I want someone that looks at me the way you look at mom."

"How's that?"

Without any hesitancy, I say, "Like there's no one else in the universe."

I look up and see tears leaking out of the corner of his eyes. I pretend not to notice.

He points to nowhere in particular. "Did you know that on Uranus and Neptune, it rains diamonds?"

I smile. "That's a good one. I didn't know that. We should find a way to go there. Stake our claim. We'd be billionaires."

"I feel like I live there already. I'm surrounded by four perfect diamonds every day."

I make a gagging noise and he laughs.

"I can't believe you're going to be gone in a few months. The house will feel so empty without you."

"It's been getting emptier throughout the past few years."

"Do you miss your sisters?"

"Of course I miss them. I'm now all alone in being subjected to you and Mom pawing at each other all the time."

He pinches me and I smile. "You're a brat. I can only hope one day that you have the type of marriage we have. That a man loves you the way I love your mother."

"I know. I'm kidding. I want that too."

I look up. "I won't be far from home, Dad. My school is only thirty minutes away. You can visit whenever you want. We can still come out here sometimes to watch the stars together."

"I don't want to cramp your style. I want you to spread your wings. Did you see the note I left for you last week?"

"I did. *I know the sky is not the limit because there are footprints on the Moon.*"

"That's right. You're so smart and focused, but I love that

you also stop to smell the roses too. You have endless potential. There's no limit on what you can accomplish. I'm so proud of you."

"Thanks, Dad."

"Skylar, do you believe in bigger forces out there? Do you believe in the unexplainable?"

"You know I do."

"I think I do too. You know your mom and I met at the library, right?"

I nod. "Yes, we know the story of how you stalked her."

He smiles. "I did. I just find it strange that two people who really had no business being in the law library were there for projects at the exact same time. I thought she was already in law school. If I knew she was only a sophomore in college, I probably wouldn't have approached her. If Aunt Cass didn't make her laugh hard, I wouldn't have lifted my head to see her."

"Things happen for a reason."

"Yes, I think you're right."

He's the only one who understands this about me. My sisters laugh at it. I think my mom only tolerates it. But I do believe there are bigger forces at play out there. Dad has always supported that belief.

As we stand to pack up, at the same time we both shout, "Shooting star," as one skips across the sky.

He turns his head to me. "What did you wish for?"

"Hmmm, to marry a man just like you."

He pulls me into a hug. "I love you, Skylar."

"I love you too, Dad."

We stop to pick up my car on the way home. When we pull in the driveway, we see Aunt Cass's car is there.

We get out of our cars and head to the door. He nods toward her car. "What kind of crazy do you think we're walking into?"

"I'm guessing loud, drunk crazy."

He chuckles. "Yep, I think you're right."

We walk in the door and hear very loud laughter. I turn to Dad and we both smile that we were right.

We move toward the cackling coming from our family room. There are two empty bottles of wine on the coffee table.

Mom turns when she sees us. "There's my handsome husband." She reaches out her arms. "Come here, baby. I missed you while you were on a date with another woman."

She and Aunt Cass start giggling.

Dad shakes his head. "I think you've had enough, baby. It's late. Why don't I put you to bed?"

He bends down to help her up. She wraps her arms around his neck and loudly whispers, "Is *put in bed* code for let's get naked?"

I can't help but shake my head and smile at her. She's ridiculous.

Fortunately, Dad carries her up to bed. I plop down next to Aunt Cass.

I nudge her with my elbow. "You always get her into trouble."

"I've been doing it for twenty-seven years. It's not going to stop now."

"True. I assume you're staying over in the guestroom? We should just call it your room since you stay so often."

"Yes, but I'm not going up there for at least forty-five minutes."

I give her a knowing look.

She shrugs. "I lived with her loud ass for four years. I get it."

I can't help but let out a laugh. "Well, I'm eighteen years in. At least when Reagan and Harley lived here, I had someone to hang out with. Now they're gone and I have to hide on my own every night."

"Every night? Still?"

I nod. "Pretty much."

"Wow. Good for them. I hope you realize how lucky you are to have parents that love each other so much."

"I do. I wish she wasn't so loud, but I appreciate their marriage. We all do. It's what we all want one day. Isn't that what everyone wants?" I immediately regret my words. She's had three failed marriages.

She notices. "Don't feel bad. It's not like I didn't want it. I just never found it. I'm happy with my life though. Happiness matters the most. Are you happy, Skylar?"

"Of course. Why would you ask that?"

"You're much quieter than your sisters. Sometimes it's hard to get a read on you. You tend to keep things bottled up. You know you can always talk to me."

"I know. I'm fine. I just don't talk about myself a lot. I'm not an open book. We can't all be like Reagan."

She shivers and then smiles. "I can't even imagine a world like that."

She looks me up and down. "You're a thinker. A dreamer. Tell me what you think and dream about."

I shrug. "I guess I'm just less practical than my sisters. I don't feel like I need to be an academic overachiever like Harley. I don't feel compelled to rule the world like Reagan. I just want to be me and do my own thing. I wish on shooting stars, believing those wishes will come true. I believe in signs. I feel like the universe is always guiding us. We just need to be on the lookout."

"What kind of signs?"

"Hmmm. Like when I was deciding whether to go to college here in Philly or out of town. I was really torn. It was decision day, and I still wasn't sure. I went for a walk and saw no less than five people wearing clothes from the college here. I believe, for some reason, I'm meant to stay in town for college.

I don't know what it is yet, but I was given a sign to stay close to home."

"You're mature beyond your years."

"I'm not sure it's maturity. We just have different goals. Harley is focused on being a doctor. Reagan is all about having fun and owning a big business empire. I just want to be happy."

"Acknowledging that, and being okay with it, are the things that make you mature."

I shrug my shoulders. "Maybe."

"What about boys? Or girls? Do you date at all? I never hear anything."

I smile. "It's boys." I sigh. "I suppose that's the problem. It's boys, not men. The boys in my school like to party. I'd rather talk or lay on a blanket and watch the stars. People kind of expect me to be like Reagan, and I'm not. I'm *definitely* happy to go to a college where no one knows Reagan. Where I'm free to just be Skylar Lawrence, not Reagan Lawrence's little sister."

"I didn't realize that you felt as though she casts such a big shadow."

"Sometimes I just want my own thing."

CHAPTER SEVEN

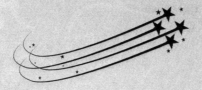

LANCE

When I got back to the office after the meeting with Bancroft last week, Jackson, Trevor, and Payton all showered me with praise. It felt good to have done a good job for them. It's not over though. We haven't won yet.

I was blown away by Skylar. She's incredibly smart. I'm going to have to up my game for the meeting next month. She had several great ideas. I may incorporate some of them with our plan. I need to prove myself and win this project at all costs.

I tried to act confident like Trevor advised. Honestly, I was feeling very confident. I could tell it ruffled her feathers, which was surprisingly fun to do. Calling her sweetheart *really* enraged her. Her cheeks got flushed like they did when she orgasmed. I may have to poke her again just to see that look on her face.

I think I'll see Skylar at Jackson's house this weekend. Admittedly, I can't wait for it. Despite being my adversary, she's still the most beautiful woman I've ever seen. Our night at Reagan's party plays on a loop in my mind.

It's lunchtime and I'm making a sandwich in the office kitchen. Trevor pokes his head in. "Are you eating in the conference room?"

"I can. What's up?"

"You have a lesson today."

"On what?"

"On pleasing a woman. If I'm going to fix you up with a few ladies. You need to be prepared. Hurry up."

I have no clue what he's up to. I finish making my sandwich and walk to the conference room.

Trevor is sitting with a bowl of grapefruits. He nods at me, "Close the door." I do.

I sit at the table. He places one grapefruit in front of me and one in front of him. I notice that a small slice is missing from each.

"What is this?"

"We're going to pretend this is a vagina. I'm going to teach you how to properly pleasure a woman with your tongue."

"Are you kidding me?"

"No. Now listen carefully. There are two types of men. One type does this simply to reciprocate to his partner and help her with her needs. They feel it's something they *have* to do. The other type *needs* to do it. Gets off on bringing so much pleasure to a woman."

"Let me guess, you're the latter."

He closes his eyes like he's reliving the pleasure. "God yes. The taste of a woman when she comes is the greatest thing a man can experience."

"Oh jeez."

"Now focus. Do you know where the clit is?"

"Trevor, I'm not an inexperienced virgin. I know how to get a woman off. I've just never done it with my mouth. My fingers and other parts are just fine at hitting the mark. More than fine."

He holds his hands up. "Okay, okay. Don't get so defensive. I'm just making sure. I need to know what I'm working with."

He uses his fingers to spread the opening in the grapefruit a bit more. "There are so many different ways to make a woman come. They're lucky for that. No two women are the same, so you need to experiment to find out what each one likes. It's pretty easy to tell by both her body's reaction and her verbal cues. You just have to pay attention."

"I understand."

He points to various spots on the grapefruit. "You've got the clit, the vaginal opening, and the anal opening."

"Hmmm. I've never done anything with the backdoor."

He sucks in a breath as though in shock. "You're missing out. You need to get on that ASAP."

"I thought most women aren't into that."

"You're wrong. Most younger women are inexperienced with it, but once they have it, they want it more and more. It's a completely different type of orgasm for them. That's why I married an older woman. She's fire. That, and she can suck a marble through a straw."

He adjusts his pants.

"Dude, I'm not sitting here with you if you start sporting wood. It's fucking uncomfortable."

He pulls out his phone and starts typing. "I'll be fine. Let me just tell Cassandra to stop by in a half hour. She'll take care of me."

I roll my eyes. I can't believe we're sitting here doing this.

After it pings, he places his phone back in his pocket. "She'll be here in twenty. Let's make this quick. Your tongue can only be in one place at a time. I would start with circles around the clit like this."

He bends his head forward and uses his tongue to rub circles at the top of the opening in the grapefruit. With his tongue still in it, he mumbles, "Some women like a pointy tongue and some like it flat. Some even like you to alternate between the two." He proceeds to demonstrate it all.

He lifts his head and wipes his chin. "You need to try everything to see what she responds to." He points to my grapefruit. "Now you give it a go."

"Are you serious?"

"Yes. Do it."

I bend my head and start tongue circles at the top of the opening.

"Good. Now go faster. Change directions. Flat tongue. Now pointy."

Like an idiot, I listen.

"Excellent. Some like it faster and some like it slower. You'll have to learn from each woman which she prefers."

I lift my head. "Are we done here?"

"Not even close. Now, you want to build them up a bit. Get them ready. Don't just throw your fingers all over the place. You want them gagging for it so that when you finally give them what they want, they can't help but explode all over your face. The buildup is incredibly important to the overall success of the operation."

"No fingers right away. Got it."

"Either no fingers or slow-moving fingers. Just don't dive right in with them. Don't go from zero to sixty in two seconds. It's very important to build them up. I can't stress this enough. Once you fully bring your fingers into play, they go nuts because they're so worked up and anticipating it."

I nod. "I think I understand."

"You can have your tongue in different places. You can go for their front and/or back openings. Then you'll use your fingers on their clit instead of inside them. Let's try both."

We both have our tongues and fingers in the grapefruit when the door opens. Payton walks in. He stops short. "What in the hell am I looking at right now?"

Trevor lifts his head. "I'm teaching Lance how to orally satisfy a woman. He's never done it before."

I smack Trevor's arm. "Don't tell people that. It's embarrassing."

We both look at Payton, anticipating a response.

He walks over to us, grabs a new grapefruit, which somehow already has a slice missing, and sits down next to us.

He says, "Lance, no two women are the same. What pleases one might not please another."

I nod. "I know. Trevor told me."

He starts licking up and down the entire opening, and mumbles, "I like to start off tasting everywhere before I commit to one location."

Trevor's eyes light up. "Yes, that's a good idea. Get a lay of the land. No pun intended." He pushes my head down. "Practice that."

We've all got our heads in the grapefruits when the

door opens again, and Jackson walks in. He stops dead in his tracks.

Trevor pops his head up. "This isn't what it looks like."

"It looks like you two are teaching Lance how to go down on a woman."

Trevor smirks. "Oh, then it's exactly what it looks like."

Jackson toggles his eyes between the three of us, and then to the remaining fruit. He walks toward the table. "You guys need to involve your lips and some suction more. Let me show you."

He tucks his tie into his shirt, grabs his own grapefruit, and sits in a chair.

"Now Lance, you have to build them up. Women need that."

"Yes, I've gathered."

"Use everything you can, even your voice."

"My voice?"

"Yes. When you make noises, your mouth and face vibrate. Women love that. Even something as simple as *hmmmm* goes a long way. Try it."

We all have our faces and fingers in our various grapefruits. We're all making unintelligible noises.

Once again, the door opens. Apparently, no one in this room has heard of a lock. Donna walks in and we all freeze.

She looks at all of us without saying a word. We lift our heads, juice dripping from our chins.

It's quiet for several long uncomfortable moments. It's like a silent stand-off.

Without saying a word, she starts to go back out through the door, but before she closes it, she pops her head back in and says, "Payton, you need to be about half an inch higher," and then she quickly leaves and closes the door.

Everyone except Payton bursts out laughing. He sulks and mumbles, "My wife is more than satisfied."

We're all still laughing.

Trevor eventually interrupts the laughter. "Back to work. Faces down. Slide your fingers in and curl them just a bit. Not too much. Feel around until you find the right spot. You'll know by her reaction."

We all have our fingers and tongues in our respective grapefruits when a flash goes off. We all jerk our heads up. Cassandra is standing there with a huge grin on her face and her phone held up taking a picture.

"Is this what guys do? Practice satisfying women in large groups?"

Trevor smiles at her. "No, Sexy. I'm just trying to share my wisdom about satisfying women with others. All for the advancement of women's pleasure. You know that's an important cause I champion."

"I see." She looks at each of us, eventually landing on Jackson. "From what I hear, I doubt your father needs any lessons in this department."

Jackson smiles. "I'm a professor at this university as well."

Cassandra laughs. She turns to Trevor. "Secretariat, I've got less than thirty minutes. Why don't we go see if you've learned any new tricks today."

Jackson shakes his head. "That's not really appropriate office behavior, Trevor."

Cassandra snorts. "Are you joking? Darian comes in here at least once a month practically naked to suck your---"

Jackson interrupts, "Okay, just go."

Trevor stands, wipes his face and hands, and starts to

make his way to the door with Cassandra. He grabs her hard around the waist, pulls her close to him, and whispers in her ear. She practically purrs.

Before they leave, I ask, "Why do you call him Secretariat?"

Jackson and Payton moan in displeasure, but Trevor and Cassandra grin from ear to ear.

She answers, "Because he's hung like a horse."

With that, they leave.

So glad I asked.

CHAPTER EIGHT

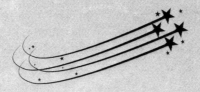

SKYLAR

It's Sunday and we have our weekly family dinner. As has mostly been the case since Declan rejoined the family, he, Melissa, and Jade are coming. My father kicked Declan out of the family when I was a baby because of his drug issues. We were only reunited with him a few months ago when he unwittingly began dating Jackson's ex-wife, Melissa. It was a shock to everyone, Declan included, when he walked through the door. Everyone has reconciled, and Declan and Melissa are now happily married.

Hayden and Jess keep a car in the city, but I don't. They live only a few minutes from me, so it makes sense for us to drive together. It's become our routine since Reagan moved in with Carter and now lives a little further from me than she did when she was single.

I'm closer to Hayden than any of my stepbrothers. He and I are about the same age, and we're the quiet ones in each of our families. We both have siblings that take up way more airspace than we do. It's been nice to have someone more like me around. I love my sisters; they're my best friends. But Hayden and I connect on a different level.

He got married earlier this year to Jessica. She's a nurse at the hospital where Harley and Brody work and is due with their first child in a few more months

"Jess, how are you feeling?"

"Like a hippo. It's getting difficult to move around."

Hayden takes her hand and kisses it. "You look beautiful, angel. You always do."

She smiles at him with so much love and affection. They have such an effortless, drama-free relationship. It's refreshing.

We arrive at the same time as Trevor and Aunt Cass. I see Lance, holding a bottle of my mom's favorite vodka, get out of their back seat. He walks around to the other side of the car and opens the other back door. An extremely attractive woman steps out.

"Do you guys know who the woman with Lance is?"

Hayden responds, "I don't know who she is, but Trevor mentioned setting up Lance on a bunch of dates. This must be one of them."

Lance offers her his arm, and they walk toward the front door.

Hayden looks back. "Is this weird for you?"

I let out a breath. "Does everyone know we hooked up?"

He and Jess smile at each other before Jess answers, "Yes. Sorry."

"Whatever. It's not weird. It's more weird to be having dinner with my current business enemy than it is a guy I kissed a few weeks ago."

Hayden turns back. "Just kissed, huh?"

He and Jess both laugh. I get out of the car. It's going to be a long fucking night.

We make our way inside. I learn that the woman with Lance is Mariana. He's very attentive to her, which I hate to admit has me a little jealous. I know I told him that we're nothing but business competitors, but I'm attracted to him and watching this isn't pleasant for me. I'd never admit that out loud to anyone though.

We all sit down for dinner. The conversation seems focused on Hayden right now. He's a pediatric resident at the same hospital where Brody and Harley are surgeons and Jess is a nurse.

Melissa asks what he's learning right now.

"I'm spending some time in radiology. I'm only supposed to be reviewing scans of kids, but we end up looking at everything. People are nuts."

Reagan asks, "How so?"

"I guess I didn't realize how many people stick things up their asses."

Aunt Cass interrupts, "What's wrong with that?"

He turns to her. "Let me clarify. I didn't realize people get off on sticking golf balls up their asses to the point where they can't find them and have to come to a hospital to have them removed."

Aunt Cass smiles. "That puts a whole new spin on *hole in one*." Per usual, Trevor laughs at everything she says.

Harley offers, "It's very dangerous. It can block the intestines and cause a rupture. I had a ton of those surgeries during my general surgery rotation. Cured meat too. For whatever reason, people like to experiment with cured meat in the back end."

Lance looks uncomfortable with the topic of conversation. He has no idea how out of hand our family dinner topics can get. If he plans on attending these weekly Sunday night dinners, he's in for a rude awakening.

Mom turns her attention to Lance, clearly noticing his discomfort. "How's the job going, Lance? Jackson has been raving about you."

Lance smiles and the dimples come out. I freakin' hate those dimples. "It's fantastic. Jackson has been amazing to me. He's given me a lot of responsibility. I'm honored. I'm learning so much from him, as well as from Trevor and Payton."

Jackson nods. "You've earned the added responsibility. You hit a grand slam with the Bancroft pitch."

I clear my throat. "Excuse me, but I was actually there. He hit no such thing. If anyone hit it out of the park, it was me. Bancroft is humoring you by giving you one last chance, but I'm the clear frontrunner."

Lance winks at me. "I know you don't believe that, sweetheart. I can admit that you did a nice job. Why can't you offer me the same?"

He's got a cocky smirk and those ugly dimples are practically begging to be punched.

"Nice? I did more than nice. Bancroft loved it. We're not losing this one, especially not to a wet behind the ears rookie like you, *sweetheart*."

Jackson holds up his hands. "Simmer down you two. All will be revealed in a few weeks. Let's keep it civilized."

Reagan says, "I agree. Jackson, like his ideas on this project, is dated. Let's not get crazy. The old man can't handle it."

She smiles at Jackson, and he jokingly scowls at her. I'm not sure how they can be so playful when there's so much on the line for both of them. Am I the only person who feels pressure on this project?

Aunt Cass, likely in an attempt to change the topic, says to her sister, Beth, "How are things going with Joseph?" Harley and Brody set Beth up with a surgeon from their hospital a few months ago. Last we heard, they had been on a few dates, though I don't remember seeing him at Reagan's party.

Beth bites her lip. "Oh, um, we broke up."

Harley says, "Oh no. I thought things were going well. What happened?"

Beth has a fearful look on her face. "I'm not sure if I should say anything. I know you work with him. I don't want to cause any problems."

Brody and Harley look at each other and then back to Beth. Harley nods. "Just tell us, we can handle it. We're all adults."

"Well...he had a bit of a fetish."

Cassandra and Trevor's eyes light up like it's Christmas morning. Trevor asks, "What kind of fetish?"

She takes a deep breath. "He has a foot fetish."

We all giggle before she continues. "He was fairly open about it early on, so I knew. He would definitely pay extra attention to my feet, which honestly wasn't so bad. I didn't mind the massages. He liked me to wear heels when we were having sex, which also wasn't a big deal. But..."

Several people shout, "But what?"

"I was checking my email on his computer one day, and I learned things about him. He not only watches an obscene amount of foot fetish porn, but he hires hookers."

Cassandra shrugs. "Oh, the dick was cheating on you? Screw him."

Beth has a pained look on her face. "Not exactly. He didn't have sex with them. He'd hire them and jerk off onto their feet."

Everyone bursts out laughing except Lance and his bimbo. They clearly don't understand what our family dinners are like. Lance looks like he's in shock, which only adds to my gratification.

Again, Mom notices Lance's discomfort and changes the topic of conversation. She turns her attention to Brody. "Harley said you took Scotty to his first baseball game the other day. How was it? She sent me a picture before you two left for the game. He looked so cute in his little hat and jersey."

Brody smiles. "He was incredibly excited. It was awesome. Though I think his favorite part was the footlong hotdog."

Trevor snickers. "*Foot*long? I bet Joseph likes those too. Maybe he'd add a few dori-*toes* or chee-*toes* too?"

He and Aunt Cass both grin. I know what this is about to start.

Reagan smacks Trevor's arm. "Cut it out. That's *toe*-tally wrong. Scotty went to his first ballgame and had a *toe*-riffic time."

Okay, that was funny. Now I'm laughing with them. I can't stop myself from joining in. "Brody, make sure you also send me the pho-*toes*. I don't want to miss any *foot*age."

Reagan nods. "Ooh. Me too. Don't get cold *feet* about it."

Beth has her head in her hands in embarrassment. Aunt Cass rubs her back. "Don't worry. You'll be back on your *feet* in no time."

Now the whole table bursts out in laughter.

Jade, never one to miss out on any fun, turns to her father. "Dad, this must have had garlic in it. Do you have any men-*toes*?"

The laughter only gets louder.

Beth looks up and smiles. "I suppose the holidays aren't far off. Maybe I'll find someone standing under the mistile-*toe*."

We're all doubled over in laughter. I notice Lance whisper something in Trevor's ear. Trevor just pats his back, likely in reassurance.

AFTER DINNER, everyone moves into the family room to talk. I decide to sit outside alone by the pool on their outdoor couches. It's beautiful out back. I love to sit here and think.

After a short while, Mom walks outside with a blanket. She lays it over me. "It's getting cold."

"Thanks, Mom."

"Can I sit with you?"

"Of course."

I lift the blanket for her to cuddle in with me. She sits and pulls me into her. She plays with my hair. "Is everything okay, doll face? You seem off kilter tonight."

I shrug. "I don't know. I guess I feel lonely."

She briefly turns her head so she's looking inside before looking back at me. "Our family is enormous. I had to buy a bigger dining room table. How could you ever feel lonely around this crew?"

"Not tonight, Mom, just in general. I've been thinking a little about Jason. I don't know if I miss him or only miss having the company. Honestly, I've been missing Dad too. Sometimes I feel like he was here just yesterday, and then it hits me that it's been over seven years since I heard his voice. Since he gave me one of his big hugs. Since we watched the stars together. Since he gave me life advice."

Tears pool in her eyes.

"I'm sorry, Mom. I don't want to upset you. We don't have to talk about him."

She shakes her head. "You should always feel comfortable talking about him. We need to keep his memory alive, and we'll do that by talking about him and telling stories. I miss him too. Every single day."

"But you have Jackson now."

"That doesn't change my love for your father. That doesn't mean I don't miss him." She places her hand over her heart. "He's a part of my soul, Skylar. There's a piece of me that's forever gone. It belongs to him and only him."

I nod. "I know, but you have someone to share your life with. I know Jackson didn't replace Dad, but he does fill some of the void."

"I understand what you're saying but know that your father is irreplaceable to me."

I smile at that. "Will you tell me about your last day with him? We've never spoken about it. I want to know what he did before he died. How he spent his last day. I know he played tennis with Alan for a little bit, but I know nothing else of that day."

I've been wanting to ask her this question for years but bringing him up in front of her doesn't always go well. For some reason, I want to know if he did something meaningful before he died. If he died happy.

She turns her head, clearly trying to collect herself. She takes a deep breath and turns back to me.

"Do you want me to shoot straight?"

That has me concerned. "Please."

"We woke up a little late. He had plans to play tennis, and I was meeting Aunt Cass for yoga and Pilates." She smiles as if remembering something happy. "But we didn't care about being late and we made love."

I can't help but let out a small laugh. Of course that would be the last thing the two of them did together. How fitting.

"As we got ready to leave, we talked about doing a little traveling once you left for school. He was looking forward to it. We made plans to have lunch after our respective morning activities. He told me he loved me, I told him that I loved him too, and then we got in our cars and left."

"The last thing you said to each other was that you loved one another?"

She nods.

"That's amazing, Mom. You're so lucky for that."

"I know I am. I'm thankful for that entire morning. It could have easily been a rushed one, but instead, we got to spend one more special morning together. What was your last conversation with him?"

"The night before was my black belt test."

She smiles. "Oh, right. I remember."

"He told me he was proud of me, and mentioned how much joy it gave him to watch me do my thing. It was a few weeks after my last play. He said that he hoped I continued both in college considering how happy they made me and how much he enjoyed watching me."

She squeezes me close. "You didn't continue either, did you?"

I shake my head. "No, I didn't. This way, he saw me at my last performance of both. It made him happy. It wouldn't be the same without him. It's lost all meaning for me since he died."

"What about your happiness? If they make you happy, you should get back into one or both of them. He'd want you to be happy, and you're not, Skylar."

"I know. For so many of the years since we lost him, I had Jason. I had Reagan too. Now they're both gone. I'm feeling a big void right now."

"Reagan isn't gone."

"I suppose. Obviously, we're together at work, but she's married and madly in love. Her evenings are filled with Carter now. It used to be me. I'm happy for her, but I'm alone. I know I have our big family. I see Hayden and Jess the most, being that they live so close. But that will change too when the baby comes." I swallow. "I don't mean to be a downer. I guess I'm just in a rut. I'll break out of it."

"Do you speak to Jason at all?"

I shake my head. "No. We haven't spoken since he left."

She has a surprised look on her face. She doesn't know about the cheating. If he hadn't cheated, I'm sure we would have kept in touch even after he left.

I continue, "He probably has a girlfriend now. He's moved on. I know it's time for me to do the same. Sometimes it's easier said than done. I really cared about him. Losing him hurt."

"I know it did, but you're so young. You need to put yourself out there. Your sisters are worried that you won't go out. Maybe you need to consider doing more of that. That's how you meet people. That's how you move on. Take it from me, I know firsthand what it's like to stay home and not live your life. I did it for several years after Dad died. I also know firsthand that wonderful things can happen if you get out and let yourself live. Look how much my life changed after I met Jackson."

I nod. She's right. "I agree. You're all one hundred percent right. I need to get out more. I'm just finding it hard to get motivated at times. Work is crazy with this big project Reagan wants. I get home and I'm exhausted. But I know if I ever want someone to come home to, I need to make a change."

We hear the door open and see Harley and Reagan walk outside. Harley asks, "Are we interrupting?"

I lift more of the blanket. "Of course not."

They both squeeze in under the blanket, the four of us now huddled tightly.

Reagan turns to me. "You look beat. Is the Bancroft thing too much?"

I shake my head. "No, not at all. I really want to get it for you. I know shaping the Philly skyline means a lot to you."

"What about you? What's it doing to you?"

"Reagan, I'm fine. The sales part will be over in a few weeks, then the fun part starts." I smile in reassurance.

"That wasn't bravado in there? You think it's ours?"

"I know it is. Don't worry. I've got this."

She looks inside and then back at me. "You don't like seeing him with another woman, do you?"

I shake my head. "I don't care what he does. He doesn't mean anything to me."

Harley and Reagan look at each other. They don't believe a word I just said.

Fortunately, Jade walks outside, ending this part of our conversation. "Can I hang with you guys? You're the fun crew."

It's a good thing Mom brought a huge, oversized blanket. Mom lifts her end and Jade slides in. Even though we only found out about Jade a little while ago, we adore her. She fits in perfectly with our family.

She not only resembles Reagan, but they also have similar personalities. She looks much older than her eighteen years, especially considering she's nearly six feet tall, though she's only a senior in high school. Reagan gave her a coveted internship in our design department, which isn't easy, but so far, she seems to be doing well.

Mom pulls her close. "How's the internship going?"

Jade's face lights up. "I love it. Not only am I learning so much, but the design department is like living in a soap opera."

Mom pinches her eyebrows together. "How so?"

"Everyone Fs on the DL. There are a million different situationships going on at all times."

Mom looks at the three of us in bewilderment. We all just shrug. We have no idea what Jade just said either. She turns back to Jade. "We have absolutely no idea what you just said. Can you translate?"

She laughs. "Can I speak freely?"

"Of course."

"F on the DL means fuck on the down low. Like, two

99

people having sex but not seeing each other. Situationship is when two people have more of a situation than an actual relationship."

Mom shakes her head. "Your generation speaks a totally different language." Mom looks at Reagan and then back at Jade. "Perhaps being in an office of adults is a little inappropriate for you."

"Aunt Darian, I can handle it."

"Well, if anything becomes too much, make sure you let Reagan or Skylar know."

"I will."

Mom looks inside. "It seems like Jackson is doing all the cleaning. I'm going to help him. You girls stay and have fun."

As she walks away, Jade yells, "Thanks for dinner. It was bussie bus."

Mom just stares at her.

Jade laughs. "Thanks for dinner. It was delicious."

"You're welcome. Thank you for the new age lingo tutorial."

Jade smiles before turning back to us. "Sorry if I interrupted you guys."

I shake my head. "You didn't. Tell us about you. Do you have a boyfriend at school?"

She scrunches her nose. "No. I don't care for high school boys. They're so immature."

Harley gives me a slight elbow to the side. "That sounds like Skylar in high school. She never dated. She didn't like how immature the boys were. She said she wanted a man, not a boy."

Jade nods. "Skylar gets it. I totally agree."

Harley rubs Jade's knee. "Don't worry, there are plenty of men out there. You'll meet so many when you go to college next year."

Jade has a surprised look on her face. "I meet plenty of

men. I just don't meet them at my school. I know I look at least twenty-five. It's never a problem. The only problem is hiding it from my dad. He's always up in my business." She winks. "But I find ways around him."

My sisters and I all look at each other with smirks. This kid is trouble.

She briefly glances inside. "Is it weird seeing your mom like that? I thought my dad and Melissa were over the top with affection, but your mom and Jackson take the cake."

We all turn and look inside. Per normal, Jackson has turned a mundane task like dishwashing into an opportunity to fondle my mom. She doesn't look remotely upset about it, leaning back into him and giving him access to her neck.

We all simultaneously shake our heads. I answer, "No, it's not weird. She was in such bad shape for so long after our dad died. We never thought we'd get her back to normal. Jackson saved her as far as we're concerned. We're not mistaken on how much she loved our father. We grew up watching a fairytale. We want our mom to be happy. Jackson makes her happy. It's that simple."

Jade stares off into space and says to no one in particular, "You're lucky. I grew up in a very different kind of fairytale. More like Grimm's original version."

CHAPTER NINE

LANCE

I had classes all day yesterday, but I'm in the office today. I'm still working to fine tune every last detail for the big meeting.

I decide to give my mother a call. It's been a while since I've spoken with her. I dial her number.

In a frantic voice, she answers, "Lance? Is everything okay?"

I swear, she thinks I'm in constant danger living in the city.

"Yes, Mom. I'm fine. How are you?"

"I'm okay. I miss you."

"I miss you too."

"Roseanne isn't doing well. I think you should come see her."

"What's the matter?"

"She's heartbroken, Lance. She loves you."

"I'm sorry she's hurting, but if I come to see her, it might give her false hope."

Mercifully, I see Trevor at my office door.

"Mom, I need to run. I'll call you in a few days."

"Please come home, Lance."

"Byc, Mom. I love you."

I hang up and let out a big breath.

Trevor sits. "Is everything okay?"

"Just my weekly dose of motherly guilt. What's up?"

He smiles. "How were things with Mariana?"

I shrug. "I don't think she's my type."

"You seemed chummy at dinner."

"Trevor, I got in your car and there was a woman sitting there. You, unbeknownst to me until it was too late, set me up on a first date at a family dinner. That's messed up."

He smirks. "You seemed to like her."

"I was being polite."

"I see. You did a good job ruffling Skylar's feathers with regard to the Bancroft project."

"I felt like a prick."

"I told you; bravado is important in these things. She has it too. The more sure of yourself and your proposal you are, the better your chances of success. I'll bet anything, she's been scrambling since dinner after seeing your confidence."

I nod. "I get it. I'm doing my best. Being cocky doesn't come naturally to me. Neither does being rude and condescending."

"No shit," he responds sarcastically.

He then drops a bag on my desk.

I look up at him. "What's this?"

"Condoms. Make sure you have at least one on you at all times. You don't want to be getting intimate with a woman only to realize you don't have one. There's nothing worse."

I shake my head. "I doubt a casual encounter is in my future. I'll wait for a woman to let me know she's into it before I just jump her bones. I think I'd prefer to get to know someone before needing one of those."

He rolls his eyes. "Sensei Trevor still has so much to teach you. Lance, women like men who take charge. If you want a woman, grab her and make your intentions known. They get off on that behavior, and you will too."

"I don't just grab attractive women. That's assault."

"Lance, if she's not into it, she'll make it known and then of course you back off. But if she's into it, you'll know right away. Her breathing will pick up, her nipples will get hard, she'll lick her lips. She'll find other subtle ways to let you know. Touching your arm, pulling you closer, moaning, rubbing her legs together, spreading her legs in invitation. Something along those lines."

I run my fingers through my hair. "I'm so fucking clueless. I don't notice any of that stuff."

He smiles. "That's why you have Sensei Trevor. I've got you, buddy. We'll make you into the Casanova I know lives within. You're starting to get it together in business. You have an inner tiger. I'm just drawing him out for you. Now we're going to focus on the ladies."

"I don't know, Trevor. It's not me."

"I have a bunch of girls I want you to try dating. Maybe you'll be into one of them."

"I don't think so, man. I'm crazy busy with school and work. I don't know if I have time for all this nonsense."

"It's not nonsense and make time. There's no harm in going on a few dates. You're in your twenties and you're a good-looking man. It's what you're supposed to do. It's healthy."

I smile at him. "You think I'm good-looking?"

"If I was a single female, I'd do you."

I laugh. "Fine. I'll go on a few dates. No bimbos. Mariana could barely put a sentence together."

He nods. "Fair enough. Now show me your latest designs on the Bancroft proposal."

I run him through everything. Afterward, he smiles. "You fucking nailed it."

SKYLAR

"Jade, these are amazing. They're perfect." We're looking at the screen of the designs she put together for the Bancroft project.

It's hard to believe she's only a senior in high school. She's really getting the hang of this. Though she's right, she looks twenty-five. Her work product and ethic make her seem more mature too. Reagan gave her a job here because she wanted to get into graphic design after college, but she spent some time with the team designing virtual models and ended up loving it. She has the eye and skill for it.

Her face lights up. "Really? I wasn't sure if you'd like them."

"You're truly talented. This is exactly the design I had in mind and tried to articulate. You captured my vision."

"Great. Do you have any modifications? Should I run it by Thor one more time to make sure there aren't any glitches?"

Thor runs our design department and is Jade's direct supervisor.

"No, you're good. Don't change a single thing." I turn off the screens. "You're really liking it here, aren't you?"

"I love it. I wish I was older so I could be here full time. I'm lucky my school is giving me some credits, so I can be here more than we thought, but I wish I was here all the time. It's so exciting."

"Is everyone treating you well?"

She nods. "Everyone is super nice, especially Carter."

I inwardly laugh. Jade doesn't hide the fact that she has a huge crush on Carter. It doesn't seem to remotely bother Reagan though. She finds it amusing.

"You do know that Carter is married and is thirty-five years old, right?"

She sighs. "I know, but he's so hot. I can still look. Just no touching." She winks at me.

I can't help but laugh at that. "I know you like older men. I'm sure you can find someone between high school age and Carter."

"Just remember, I like older guys should you have anyone in mind."

"There are a few college-aged guys working here. Have you met them?"

She shrugs. "They're okay. They've all asked me out. They're not really my type. Dominic is hot. I'm into him."

I shake my head. "Jade, Dominic is probably older than Carter. And I think he's married, though I'm not sure. Regardless, he's way too old for you."

Her face drops. "Damn it. All the hot guys are married."

I hear a noise at my door and look up to see Reagan and Carter walk into my office. Jade stares at Carter with hearts in her eyes. Carter looks unbelievably uncomfortable.

Reagan simply smirks before turning to me. "Skylar, why are you making Jade stay this late?"

I look at the clock. It's nearly eight. I gasp. "Oh my god, Jade. I'm so sorry. I didn't realize the time."

She shrugs. "It's okay. I have nothing better to do. I'm staying at Dad and Melissa's tonight. They're still in the honeymoon phase. I'm just as happy to not be there.

They're probably doing it on the kitchen table as we speak."

Everyone gets more action than me.

Reagan looks at her watch. "I have a car service picking us up. Jade, we'll drop you home. Sky, you're coming with us."

"Where are we going?"

"We're going for drinks. Maybe some dancing."

"Ugh. I'm tired. I'm just going to head home."

She shakes her head. "No, you're coming. We're meeting Collin there, and Trevor said he'd stop by for a drink or two before heading home."

Jade interrupts, "Can I come?"

Reagan shakes her head. "Sorry, kiddo. You have to be twenty-one to get in."

She mumbles. "I need a fake ID."

I begrudgingly agree to join them. We drop Jade and then head to the bar, with Reagan and Carter all over each other the whole time. It's as if their connection to the other is so strong, they don't notice that I'm here. They're lucky to have it even though it makes me feel invisible.

Collin arrives at the same time as us. Collin has been Carter's best friend since childhood. He was dating Reagan's best friend for a little while, but they broke up. Even though he's got at least eight years on me, he's a little nutty and *a lot* immature. He's extremely good-looking, but he's also a huge manwhore. He's not my type at all.

As we approach Collin, he looks at Reagan in a lascivious way. She's got her face buried in Carter's neck, so she doesn't see it, but I do. He has a thing for her. I never noticed it before. I wonder if Carter knows. He seems oblivious in this moment.

Collin clearly catches himself, and then looks me up and down. "Fuck, Skylar, you look hot in your power suit. You're like a boardroom vixen. I want you to crawl across my desk for me in slow motion."

I roll my eyes at him. "To be clear, Collin, you have zero chance of me crawling anywhere for you, and even less at seeing what's underneath this power suit, so find somewhere else to spew your bullshit."

He belly laughs, as do Carter and Reagan.

Reagan throws her arm around me, "I like when you get all spicy."

I raise an eyebrow at her, and she laughs again.

We walk in and I spot Trevor in a big booth. Seated with him is Lance and a different woman from dinner the other night. She's leaning into him. Wow, this guy gets around.

I immediately loop my arm through Collin's. He gives me a skeptical look but doesn't flinch otherwise.

Trevor stands to greet us when we arrive. He introduces Lance's friend, but I don't bother to listen for her name. I'm annoyed with him for bringing her, and myself for being so agitated by her mere presence.

Everyone drinks and chats. I can't seem to focus on any of them. Why is this bothering me so much?

"Right, Skylar?"

I turn to Reagan. "I'm sorry, what? I couldn't hear you over the music?" The music isn't really that loud. I was just watching the bimbo pawing at Lance.

She gives me a knowing look. "I was just telling Lance how you've revamped our proposal and taken it to the stratosphere."

I nod. "Yep. I can't wait to see our work come to fruition on the Philly skyline."

Trevor shakes his head and throws his arm around Lance. "Don't think so, sis. Lance just came up with something brilliant earlier today. There's no chance Bancroft doesn't go with us."

Lance turns to him and gives a conspiratorial smile and a wink. The hideous dimples come out.

"It's cool, cuz. No need to brag. She'll see soon enough. She'll be walking out of the final round with her head down and her tail between her long legs."

This fucking guy drives me nuts.

Mercifully, Lance's date asks him to dance, so they get up and leave the table.

Trevor nods in my direction. "You good, sis? You seem a little distracted tonight." He gives me a knowing grin. I hate that he can see how much Lance gets under my skin.

"I'm fantastic. I'm just excited to wipe that smug smile off his ugly face when this is over."

We turn our heads toward them on the dance floor. His date is all over him.

Trevor laughs. "He has every right to be smug. Chicks dig the farm boy. He may get more ass than I used to."

I've reached the end of my rope listening to this. I grab Collin's arm. "Let's dance."

His eyes light up. "Hell yes."

We make our way to the dance floor. Naturally, as soon as we do, a slower song begins playing.

Collin pulls me close to his body.

I mumble, "Watch it."

He smirks at me. "I know you're just trying to make Elmer Fudd jealous. Use me however you want. It might *really* get his attention if we sleep together."

I can't help but let out a laugh. "Not a fucking chance, you buffoon."

"Can't blame a guy for trying."

I imagine most women are attracted to Collin. He's very handsome. He's of Irish descent, with light eyes and skin, and darker hair. He works in construction and has the body to prove it. He's just not my type.

I look over at Lance and his woman of the day. He's got his arms around her body. She's running her hands up and down his back. He turns his head to me and gives me a self-satisfied smile.

I whisper, "Collin, kiss me."

He doesn't hesitate for a second. He immediately brings his lips to mine and slips his tongue right into my mouth.

I grab his face and kiss him back, giving as much tongue as I'm getting. I hate to admit it, but he's a good kisser. I'm sure he's had a lot of practice. I'm probably contracting a disease by simply kissing him.

By the time we come up for air, Lance and his date are gone.

Collin looks down at me wide-eyed. "Are you sure you're not down to fuck? I think we'd be pretty good together."

I shake my head. "No. Sorry. It's never happening. Let's go back to the table."

THE NEXT MORNING, I wake with a boatload of regrets. Kissing someone I'm not into isn't me. I don't know why I let Lance get under my skin. It's time to admit my feelings and then quickly get over them. It's time to focus on what's important. I need to talk to Reagan about my crush on Lance. I don't want it hurting our chances with the Bancroft project.

I decide to head over to their condo before work. I'd rather not discuss my immature, high school crush at the office.

Reagan moved into Carter's place shortly before they got married earlier this year. Carter is not only the president of a Fortune 500 company, he inherited a tremendous amount of money this year. Their penthouse is the nicest I've ever seen. It's bigger than most mansions, with large windows and amazing city views.

I have the code, so I let myself in, per normal. I head

toward their bedroom, assuming I'll wake them, but as soon as I walk in, I realize my mistake.

I'm greeted by Carter's bare ass moving on top of Reagan. An amazing ass, at that. Her legs are wrapped around him.

Not that I spend much time thinking of the two of them having sex, but to the extent I have, it's not what I'm seeing right now. This is slow, sweet, and full of love. He kisses her, tells her how beautiful she is, and how much he loves her.

Admittedly, I stand there in the door longer than I should. I know they like people watching them have sex, so I assume they won't mind.

I can't take my eyes off them. They move in perfect harmony. Her fingers toggle between being intertwined with his and running up and down his whole body. His hands don't miss a single inch of her body. It's just so perfect. They're like an instructional video for the term, *making love*.

It's been so long since I've had sex that maybe I'm misremembering, but I don't ever remember it looking quite like that. I don't remember feeling as treasured as she must be feeling right now.

As the moans get louder, I decide it's time for me to wait in the kitchen. I don't need to watch the end.

A few minutes later, I hear Reagan shout, "Skylar, you can come back now. We're done."

I walk into her room. "How'd you know I was here?"

She smiles. "The front door chimes when you open it."

"Oh." I put my head down. "Sorry."

She shrugs. "I don't care."

"There was no thought of stopping when I walked in?"

"No." She lifts the blanket slightly. "Do you want to get in?"

"Are you naked?"

"You know I am."

"I'll lay on top of the blankets."

I lay down next to her, facing both of them.

Carter sits up and stretches, the sheets pooling at his waist. We swim at Mom and Jackson's all the time, so I've seen him topless, but I never get used to it. He's enormous. He has muscles everywhere. Places I didn't know muscles existed.

I shake my head. "Carter, when do you go to the gym? You work all the time, yet you look like you work out all the time."

He smiles. "Your sister is a nympho. She's my exercise."

Reagan nods in agreement. "I guess I *am* sort of a nympho. You're a lucky man, Carter Daulton."

He leans toward her and kisses her. "I know I am." They just stare at each other for a few seconds before he sits back up. "I'm getting in the shower. Sky, either close your eyes or enjoy the show. The second show, that is."

My sister throws a pillow in my face. "Trust me, you don't want to see that monster. You can't unsee it."

Carter laughs as he stands. I do cover my face with the pillow as he makes his way to their bathroom and closes the door.

I lay back down and place the pillow under my head. She turns her head on her pillow so we're facing each other. "I can't believe you watched us have sex. That's very unlike you."

"Sorry. It's only because it wasn't what I would have expected out of you two. It was so gentle and loving. I guess I always assumed you go at it like animals."

"We do both. We had animalistic sex last night. This morning was slower. Who knows what our afternoon round will bring. He always keeps me on my toes."

I sigh. I want that too. "You're lucky."

"I know."

I briefly look toward their bathroom door. "He's so damn muscular. His muscles have muscles."

She smirks. "And you haven't even seen his biggest muscle."

We both giggle at that.

She rubs my arm. "Why are you here? Is something wrong?"

"I have to tell you something."

"Okay."

"I have a crush on Lance."

She lets out a small laugh. "Yeah, I know."

"You do?"

"Yes. It's been obvious, but never more so than last night when you kissed Collin. You don't even like him. You clearly did it because seeing Lance with that woman bothered you."

"Ugh. Why do you know that about me?"

"Because you're my best friend and I know everything about you." For some reason, hearing her say that makes me happy. I guess I miss my time with Reagan. We were together most nights until Carter came into the picture.

I turn, face the ceiling, and blow out a breath. "I don't want to fuck up the Bancroft thing. If you want to give it to Dominic, I'll understand."

"Fuck, no. This is your baby. No one is taking it from you. You've worked too hard. We're coming down the homestretch. I have a feeling everything will work out just fine. I have faith in you, sis."

She turns my head, so we're eye to eye again. "Do you want this project?"

I nod. "Very much, but I don't want to mess it up for you, and I *really* don't enjoy bickering with him. I honestly hate pushing his buttons. I don't mind doing that with assholes like Clarrett, but I don't like it with Lance."

"Then shift course. Be yourself." She smiles. "Kill him with kindness."

CHAPTER TEN

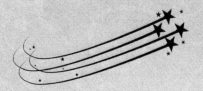

LANCE

I'm sitting at my desk with Trevor standing behind me, massaging my shoulders and humming *Eye of the Tiger*, the theme song to the *Rocky* movies.

He shouts, "Are you ready for this, big guy?"

That's what Skylar called me right before we kissed. Before her big, juicy lips...

"Are you?"

"Oh, yeah. It's in the bag."

"Sensei Trevor believes in you."

Today is the day for the Bancroft proposal. I'm more than ready for everything except seeing Skylar. Watching her kiss that guy was torture for me. I left as soon as I saw them going at it. I need to get over my crush. She's not into me. One of us is going to be disappointed today and things will probably be awkward, more awkward, for a long while. It's time to move on.

"Have you gone out on any dates in the past week?"

I shake my head. "No."

"Lance, don't you want to meet women?"

"I guess. I just haven't been into any of the women you've introduced me to."

"Do you want to know why you're not into them?"

"Enlighten me."

"Because you're totally hung up on Skylar."

I shake my head. "No, I'm not."

"You are. It's cool. I get it. You know what? I think she's hung up on you too."

"She hates me. She's into that Collin guy."

"I don't think so, but let's shelve this for later. Focus on today and then we'll worry about your love life."

I HEAD down to Bancroft's office. Skylar is sitting in the conference room alone when I arrive.

She stands when I enter and holds out her hand with a genuine smile. "Good luck today, Lance."

Our hands meet. Hers is soft. I remember it running through my hair, grabbing my shirt, wrapped around my cock.

I need to stop. Trevor was right. I'm totally hung up on her. I look her up and down. She's so fucking beautiful. How could I not be hung up on her?

She looks at me, waiting for some reply.

I manage to mumble, "Yes, you too."

"May the best woman win." She gives me a sexy smile. It's not antagonistic like our last few conversations. It's playful, and I can't help but return her playfulness with my smile.

At some point, I realize we've been staring at each other in silence for a long time. I need to say something.

"I'm sure Mr. Bancroft will have a tough decision ahead of him."

"I certainly will." We both turn to see Adam Bancroft walk in. "I've been looking forward to this day for a month."

We both shake his hand hello.

Skylar presents first. She does an incredible job. Her plan is fine-tuned and covers everything imaginable. She's left no stone unturned. Her methodology is close to perfect, and the virtual presentation is the most technologically advanced thing I've ever seen. It's like we're standing in the middle of the building seeing every small detail.

I present after her, and I think it goes well. It's hard to get a read on Adam Bancroft. He's holding his cards much closer to his chest today than he did the first time we were here.

At the end, he simply shakes our hands and tells us he'll be in touch.

Skylar and I ride the elevator together. She turns to me. "You did a great job, Lance. No one would ever guess that this is your first project."

"Thank you. Yours was amazing as well. I don't envy Mr. Bancroft having to make the decision. I imagine he can't go wrong either way."

She nods in agreement.

As we exit the elevator, I receive a text notification. I look down and see Jackson's name. I'm surprised by what I'm reading. I hold my phone up for Skylar to read it.

She reads it out loud. "Come to Reagan's office at Daulton. I'll meet you there."

She pinches her eyebrows together. "Why would you come to Daulton?"

I shrug. "I have no clue. There's only one way to find out."

We get to Daulton and Lawrence Holdings in record time, heading straight for Reagan's office. We're both anxious. When we get there, Jackson and Reagan are sitting on her sofa laughing.

When they see us, Reagan tells us to sit.

She begins, "Jackson and I have been talking. We both want our stamp on this project, and two heads are better than one. Especially when those heads belong to the two of you. We think this is what Bancroft wanted all along. The brain trust of the two best companies for the price of one. We're going to give him what he wants. This way, we all win." She turns to Jackson. "Right?"

He nods. "We do. Congratulations to both of you. You both did an incredible job, you're both going to stay on and see this project through. It will be a lot of work, and a lot of long nights, but you'll be stamping your touch on a bit of Philly history. Lance, I've spoken with your school. You'll get credits for this, so you can significantly lighten your workload at school next semester to focus on it. They were more than thrilled that one of their students was involved in this history-making project."

Skylar looks at me and then back at them. She tilts her head to the side. "When did you guys decide this? When did you discuss it with Bancroft?"

Jackson smirks at Reagan and then back at Skylar. "Why do you ask?"

"Because Lance got that text from you ten seconds after we left Bancroft. There's no way this was decided *after* the meeting today."

She's right. They knew beforehand. We went

through the crazy stress of the past few weeks for nothing.

Reagan nods at Jackson, giving him permission to say whatever he's about to say. "Reagan and I have been discussing it since the first round of presentations. We met with Bancroft three weeks ago. He insisted on it being this way though. He wanted each of you pushed to the max to come up with the best ideas possible. If it makes you feel better, he was adamant that you both work on the job to completion. That was part of our final deal. He was impressed by both of you."

Skylar turns to me and smiles. I know exactly what she's thinking. I nod my head to her in agreement with what she's about to say.

"Lance and I want big bonuses to stay on for this full job. It's a lot of work."

I nod. "I agree with Skylar. Mr. Bancroft would be mighty upset if the two of us walked from this project. It sounds like he's sold on us as a team."

Jackson and Reagan grin at each other. They both reach for envelopes on Reagan's desk and hand them to us.

Reagan says, "We had a feeling this was coming. I think you'll both be happy with the checks inside those envelopes."

Skylar stands and I quickly follow suit. "Lance and I will be in my office if you need us." She motions her head for me to follow her, which I do.

We walk down the hallway into her office. As soon as I'm through, she closes the door. "Lance, open your envelope."

We both tear into them.

I look down at my bonus check. I have to blink a few times for it to register. I whisper, "Holy shit." It's more than my annual salary. After taxes, it's just enough to pay for my tuition for both years of business school. I'll graduate debt free.

Without thinking, I scoop Skylar in my arms and spin her around. She laughs.

As soon as I place her feet back on the ground, she looks up at me. "I guess you're happy."

I look down at her close proximity to me, her body pressed against mine. I fix a stray hair of hers and whisper, "I am."

I can't help myself and rub the backs of my fingers down her soft cheek.

She leans into it for a brief moment, but then steps back. "Lance, we're going to be working together on this. I think it's best if we keep it professional."

I reluctantly nod. "Yes, of course. I want the same thing." That's a lie. I motion toward her check. "Are you happy?"

"We could probably squeeze them for more if you want."

I shake my head. "No, thanks. This covers my tuition. I'm not going to be a pig about it."

"Okay. I'm not up for squeezing my sister anyway. Why don't we start digging in. We have a lot of commonalities in our plans, but a few differences. We need to figure out which proposal we're using on various points and then consult the engineers."

"Good idea. Is there somewhere we can spread everything out?"

She nods. "Yes, we have a bunch of conference rooms. We can probably set up camp in one and leave everything. It will save us time when we meet."

That's what we do. We commandeer a conference room and set up camp.

For the next three weeks, we work Mondays, Wednesdays, and Thursdays together. I have classes Tuesdays and Fridays, plus she has other clients that she needs to make time for.

We often stay late, order dinner, and work through the evenings. She has a unique mind for this, and I'm learning a lot from her. Other than a few laughs here and there, our relationship is completely professional.

I haven't seen any sign from her that she wants anything else. In fairness, I'm not giving anything away either. It's a Herculean effort on my part because I'm completely enamored with her. I find it hard to return home at night with her scent on my clothing.

SKYLAR

It's a Tuesday and I'm having dinner at Jess and Hayden's apartment. I tend to have a weekday dinner with them at least once a week. I can't cook, but Jess is an amazing chef. I love having a homemade meal here. It's usually takeout for me when I'm alone.

"Oh my god, Jess, this lasagna might be the best you've ever made and is definitely the best I've ever had."

She smiles. "Thank you. I'm telling my mother you said that. She doesn't think I can cook."

"What? She's crazy. You're legitimately the best cook I know." I point at her. "Don't tell my mom I said that." She laughs.

Hayden smiles at her. "I told you so. I don't know why you let her get in your head."

"She's been doing it for over twenty-six years. It's not going to stop now."

Jess stands. Hayden helps her do so. She turns her head to me. "Sorry, I need to pee for the thousandth time today."

Jess leaves to go to the bathroom. I look at Hayden. "What's that about with her mother?"

He rolls his eyes. "Her mom is so damn hard on her. She always has been. If it's not her cooking, it's her being a nurse or her being overweight..."

"Overweight? She's pregnant."

"Before the pregnancy."

"She weighs, like, eleven pounds. I can normally fit her in my pocket." Non-pregnant Jess can't weigh more than a hundred and ten pounds. Even pregnant, I probably still outweigh her, though I must have eight inches on her.

He shrugs. "She was much heavier when she was younger. Her mom really messed with her head. And now that she's pregnant, her mom is telling her not to get heavy again. I'm always complimenting her, but she puts herself down. I hate it. I wish she saw what I see in her."

I didn't know any of that. In my mind, Jess and Hayden have no issues and are drama free.

Jess returns to the table. I look down at her plate. I realize that she's eaten maybe two bites of her dinner. Hayden notices too. "Angel, eat some more. The baby needs it."

Jess sighs. "Ugh, I can't. Eating after three gives me heartburn all night. I swear I've been eating. I just can't eat at night, or I won't be able to sleep."

"Just a few bites. For the baby."

She begrudgingly agrees to two more bites. Hayden is clearly unhappy about it.

There's definitely tension between the two of them over her eating.

I help myself to seconds. "Jess, I think your mom is missing out on your greatness. It's her loss. This is the best meal I've had in weeks. Lance and I order takeout constantly. I'm so sick of it."

Hayden smirks. "Oh, right. You're working *with*, not *against*, Lance right now. How's that going?"

"It's fine. We work well together."

He raises his eyebrows. "Just work?"

"Yes, just work." It's all work. Lance is mechanical. All business, all the time. We barely converse other than work related items. I imagine he's anxious to get done each night so he can return to the bevy of women Trevor loves to tell me about.

"Do you still have a crush on him?" Hayden smiles and Jess giggles.

"I don't, and never did, have a crush on him." I totally do. I can't help it. He's so good-looking. He doesn't smile much when we're together, but on the rare occasion when he does, his dimples come out and I melt. And he smells good. It's not fake cologne like most men wear. It's just natural and so uniquely him. I remember how good he tasted when we kissed, and...

"...my dad."

"Umm. Sorry I missed that?"

"Thinking about Lance?"

"No, wiseass, work."

"Sure. I was saying that your mom has gotten really into pickleball, and now she's got my dad playing."

"Oh shit. Her playing anything competitive is a recipe for disaster."

They both laugh. They know I'm right. They see her at family Thanksgiving Day football games. She turns it into a blood sport. She's psychotically competitive when it comes to sports.

"He said they love it. They play doubles. It's probably just an excuse for him to see her in tight clothes and chest bump her."

I can't help but laugh out loud at that. "True. Any excuse for him to touch her. I thought it would die down after a few years, but I think it's getting worse."

He nods. "It's definitely worse. I think I saw his hand under her shirt at dinner last Sunday."

Jess grabs his hand. "I hope we're like that when we're in our fifties."

I sigh. I just hope I have someone by the time I'm fifty.

CHAPTER ELEVEN

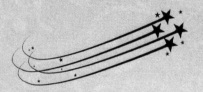

LANCE

Weeks. We've been working side by side for weeks and she hasn't so much as looked my way. I think I'm unhealthily obsessed with her.

She said business only, and boy did she mean it. All we do is work on this project.

It's late on a Thursday night. She and I are working in our home away from home, Daulton conference room three. The office is otherwise empty.

I'm in my suit pants and my button-down shirt with the sleeves rolled up. My suit jacket and tie are draped over one of the chairs.

We've been strategizing for hours. Maybe it's more like she's been strategizing for hours. I can't focus on anything but her tonight.

She's sitting on the conference table, and I'm in one of the big leather chairs right next to her. I don't manage to hear anything she's saying. Her big, cherry-red lips are moving, but the words aren't processing for me right now. I'm just wishing those lips were on my body somewhere. Anywhere.

Her long legs are in touching distance. She's wearing a navy-blue straight skirt that hugs her sexy curves, and a white silk blouse. I think I can make out her lace bra underneath.

"Don't you agree?"

I look up at her. "Huh?"

"Did you hear a word I said?"

"Ummm, something about a property inspection."

She crosses her arms, which only lifts her big breasts. I can now see the tops of them peeking out from her shirt. "Lance, we spoke about the property inspection twenty minutes ago."

"Oh, right. Sorry."

I'm inadvertently staring at her chest. They're so perfect. I remember how full and soft they felt in my big hands. She notices me looking at them. "Lance, my eyes aren't on my nipples."

I lift my head so our eyes meet. "Sorry."

She leans over and runs her fingernails over my exposed forearm. The goosebumps that spread over my skin betray my weeks-long attempt to maintain a cold demeanor.

"Do I still affect you, Lance?"

I'm silent, but it's written all over my face. I can no longer hide it. She smirks.

She continues running her fingernails up and down my forearms. It's making my heart feel like it's beating out of my chest.

Is touching my forearm one of the signs that she's interested? I can't remember all those damn signs. My brain isn't functioning right now. It's just freaking out that she's touching me. I beg my cock to stay down and not embarrass me again.

She licks her lips. I know that was one of the signs.

"Lance, do you want to touch me? Do you want to kiss me?"

I'm sick of being a wimp in these situations. I'm sick of not taking what I need. Mostly, I'm sick of not having the woman I desperately want.

I hear Trevor's voice in my head. *Smart women like assertive men who take control. Don't be afraid to make the first move. If she's not interested, you'll know right away and can back off. But you'll never know unless you go for it.*

I stare at her with all the desire I feel burning through me. I run my fingertips along her calf and up to her inner thigh. She doesn't stop me. Without any shame I say, "I want to taste you."

Her lips part and her breathing picks up. She's not backing away. Just the opposite. She spreads her legs just enough for me to know the invitation is there.

She's given me the sign that she has interest, and I'm grabbing onto it.

I stand, open her legs a bit more, and move between them. I lift her skirt just enough so I can spread them wide and push myself closely to her.

My cock is hard, but I no longer care that she can see it. She must feel it too.

She looks up at me. Her chest is moving up and down at an increased pace.

I grab the back of her hair and pull it hard, so her face is tilted up at me. I bend down and gently bite her lower lip, stretching it until it pops out and back into place. She whimpers.

I breathe, "I need...to taste you. Now."

I place my hand on the top of her chest and slowly push her back onto the table. She willingly goes. I lift her skirt to her waist. She's wearing a red lace thong. I can't help but stare for a moment. She's a goddamn goddess.

I reach my fingers into the sides of her thong and slip it down those long, gorgeous legs of hers. I don't want to rush this. I want to savor every moment of it.

I pull her panties off, bring them to my nose, and sniff them. I close my eyes and moan in satisfaction. She whimpers again.

Tossing them to the side, I get down on my knees and roughly spread her legs as wide as they'll go.

I stare at her pussy. It's pink and perfect. She has a small, short landing strip of blonde hair a little darker than that on her head.

My hands slowly make their way up her inner thighs. I can't help but briefly think of Trevor's words again. *The first time you taste a woman, you'll know whether you're the type of man who does it because he has to, or because he needs to.*

I spread her lips and take a long, slow lick through her. I immediately know that I'm the latter.

We both moan at the same time. My eyes lift as they meet hers. "You taste perfect."

She bites her lip and I move my head back down and begin running my tongue through her folds over and over.

Her juices are flowing into my mouth. My mind is blown right now. I could come from this.

I focus my circular motions on her clit. Round and round. Sometimes I go fast, and sometimes I go slow. Her hands grip the end of the conference table and her body trembles.

She groans loudest when my tongue is pointed and moves fast, so that's what I do. Over and over. She's getting louder and louder.

Her breathing is becoming more labored. Her noises are gradually escalating. She must be getting close. I don't stop my attention on her clit, but I take two fingers and slowly slide them inside her.

Her body trembles even though I haven't otherwise moved my fingers yet. She's soft, wet, and snug around my fingers.

I start pushing them in and out. I bend them just a bit and move them around until I feel the spot that makes her scream. Fuck, I love this.

I continue moving my tongue and fingers, enjoying her quickly escalating noises. Every small adjustment does something different to her.

I hit one spot and her body jerks.

"Oh god, Lance, I'm about to come. Keep going." As if I'd ever want to stop.

Her legs start to shake and her back arches. She gives one long scream and her come floods my mouth. I lick up every tasty drop. I've never experienced anything better.

I continue my movements until I'm sure she's done, relishing the taste of everything she's offering. I look up at her and ask, "Tell me, did that feel good?"

She nods as she sits up, grabs my shirt, and pulls my mouth to hers. Her tongue immediately enters my mouth and licks all around. It's so hot that she wants to taste herself.

Just when I thought she couldn't possibly be any sexier, she sucks my tongue into her mouth, wrapping those big lips around it. I'm not sure if I'm currently in the middle of the greatest fantasy or real life.

Still on my knees, I grab her head with both hands

and kiss her back with everything I have. I'm transported back to our kiss at Reagan's party. The perfect way she kisses. The perfect way her lips fit on mine and her tongue moves through my mouth. Her incredible taste.

I feel completely out of control with desire for this woman. I need more of her. I want every part of her.

She whispers into my mouth, "Do you have a condom?"

I whisper back, "I do, but not yet."

I push her knees wide again and bring my head back down to her glistening pussy. "I want more. I need to keep tasting you."

She stays seated upright, pulling my hair and writhing through it all. This time, my tongue slides in and out of her opening and my fingers play with her clit. It's amazing how many different ways I can build her toward her orgasm. It's like a treasure map with endless routes to the gold. I want to explore every single one of them.

I wish we weren't in a conference room. I want to get her naked and get acquainted with every inch of her body.

After she comes again, she tilts her face to the ceiling and sighs loudly. She breathes, "Wow."

I can't help but smile, but I still need more. I pull a condom out of my wallet as I stand. I've never been more thankful to have one in there.

She grabs it from me and makes quick work of my belt, button, and zipper. She pulls out my cock and her eyes light up.

"Shit, I forgot how big you are. I want you. Get inside me."

No man would be unhappy about a woman saying

that. I love her sense of urgency. It's like she needs me inside her as quickly as possible. I need the same thing.

She tears open the condom and rolls it on. She starts to pull me to her entrance, but I push away her hands. I want my full fantasy of having Skylar for the first time. I've been playing this scenario out in my mind for months. I know what I want, and I'm taking it.

Without asking, I flip her over, so she's bent over the table. I've spent endless nights imagining bending her over like this. She gasps, but when I give her a hard spank, she moans. Damn, Trevor was right. She loves this. I can admit I do too. I never thought I would.

I run my fingers between her legs, through her swollen folds. She's ready and needy. I can't wait another second to be in there.

I bring my tip to her entrance and begin to enter her. I look down and watch as my cock slowly disappears inside her. I inhale a quick breath at how incredible it feels. She's wet and tight. She's sucking me in. My cock has never felt anything so good in my life.

It's not like I haven't had sex before, but the months long build up and my rabid attraction to her is making this moment all the more gratifying.

Once I'm all the way in, I give her a moment to get used to my size. I can't help but examine what's happening in front of my eyes. The most beautiful woman I've ever seen has her skirt around her waist, is bent over a table, her perfect ass is in the air, and my cock is buried in her to the hilt.

She reaches back and wiggles her hips, encouraging me to begin my movements, which I do. I start off slowly. Long, deep thrusts while grabbing her hips.

She's clawing at the table as she pushes back into me, meeting me thrust for thrust. I'm not just fucking her, we're fucking each other. I want it to last, but the sounds coming out of her are making it hard for me to maintain any control.

I lift the back of her blouse and unsnap her bra. I've spent months staring at her perfect tits. I'm not passing up an opportunity to touch them. To feel them in my hands again.

I reach both hands under her and grab onto them as I continue to move in and out of her.

I hear her mumble, "Oh god, it's been so long. So good."

I bend forward and lick up her neck until I'm next to her ear. I want to tell her exactly how I'm feeling at this moment. "You are the fucking hottest woman I've ever seen. Do you know how badly I've wanted you? How good it feels to finally be inside you and your perfect pussy?"

She doesn't turn around and slap me. Instead, she says, "Lance, keep going. Don't stop. Please don't stop." I never want to stop.

I reach down with one hand and grab a fistful of her behind. "Every single time this ass is in front of me, my cock goes crazy. This fucking perfect ass stars in my dreams. This ass and these tits." I manage to squeeze both at the same time.

I love the noises coming out of her right now. Knowing this is doing to her what it's doing to me.

I move the hand on her ass around to her clit and begin to move it the way I did when my tongue was in her.

Her legs start to shake. "Ah, right there. I'm coming, Lance."

"Fuck yes."

Her orgasm around my cock may genuinely be the

greatest pleasure I've ever known. She pulses and quivers, all while squeezing my cock. I feel the utter bliss course through my entire body as I can't help but spill myself into the condom.

When it's over, I slow my motions as we breathe heavily but are otherwise quiet.

I find myself not wanting to move, but I do eventually pull out. She stands and turns around. We're nose to nose, still silent.

I rub my thumb across her flushed face and swollen lips. I love that I did this to her. I need more of it. My thirst for her is far from quenched.

I whisper, "Get dressed. We need to get out of here. I'm not remotely done with you."

CHAPTER TWELVE

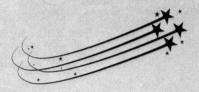

SKYLAR

The next morning at work, Reagan calls and asks me to come down to her office.

I poke my head in. "You beckoned, your highness?"

Her eyes light up. This is trouble. "I did. Close my door."

I do and she motions for me to have a seat.

"How are things going with the Bancroft project?"

"We're on schedule. Frankly, we're ahead of schedule. We've been working hard."

"It does seem that way. Lots of *long* nights. Is everything copacetic with you and the handsome Mr. Remington?"

"Yes, everything is fine. Why do you ask?" She knows something.

She clasps her hands together. "So, I was having an uneventful morning until Joe from security came by my office and completely brightened my day. He pulled up the tapes from conference room three last night."

My chin drops and my eyes widen in horror.

She simply grins from ear to ear.

She waves her hand in a dismissive manner. "Don't worry, I had the tapes wiped clean. There's no remaining evidence of my *bad, bad,* little sister. So bad that she had to be spanked." She's enjoying every minute of this.

I cross my arms. "I assume you watched the whole thing first?" She wouldn't pass up that opportunity.

"You bet your sweet ass I did...though, I guess, according to the tapes, it's more than your ass that's sweet."

I briefly place my hand over my eyes. "Ugh. Stop. This is embarrassing. I'm not like you who gets off on being watched."

"We both know you have your own kink. Does Lance know about it yet?"

"No. It's not like we're dating. I don't advertise it."

"*Yet*. You're not dating *yet*. It doesn't take a genius to see the chemistry between you two. I think you're the only ones that haven't realized the sexual tension that's been building for months."

I'm silent. I suppose she's right, but I won't give her the satisfaction.

"I'd ask how it was, but I've heard the answer with my own ears." She fans herself. "It was *hawt*. Damn!"

I can't help but smile at that. It *was* hot.

"A man that goes down on you twice before wetting his stick is a keeper."

I lean back in my chair. A little gloating is more than warranted. I nonchalantly add, "I had a good time. It continued after we left."

"I caught that at the end. I have to tell you though, his domineering demeanor was a little shocking to me. I think his whole *yes ma'am, no ma'am* crap is bullshit. He bossed your ass around like a champ. And I heard a little dirty talk in there too. Sweet farm boy has some edge between the sheets, or in your case, on top of a conference room table."

I nod. "He wasn't like that when we hooked up at your party. I had to initiate things there. He was unexpectedly different last night. It was incredible. You know it's been a long while for me. It was nice to be with someone again, especially someone so completely obsessed with my pleasure. I don't know how many orgasms I had, but it was double digits before the evening was done."

"Oh, yes! You definitely needed that. How did you leave things?"

"Well, after I woke up with his head between my legs again, he asked me out to dinner tonight."

"Ooh, he *really* likes going downtown."

"That's for sure. I don't think he's very experienced, but he's phenomenal in bed. In every aspect."

"If he's so good, what makes you think he's inexperienced?"

I bite my lip. She's not going to be happy with this answer.

"At some point we ran out of condoms. He said he's only been with one woman, his high school sweetheart. Apparently, they broke up right before he moved here."

"That means they were together for like ten years. That's a long time."

"I guess."

"I know you have an IUD. I won't give you a lecture on how dangerous it is to go bareback in a casual encounter."

I put my head down. "You're right. I got carried away by the promise of more orgasms. I was orgasm drunk."

"You may have been. Perhaps you're not at risk of disease, but you still need to be careful. I don't want to be the only Lawrence lady to not be pregnant prior to getting married."

Mom was pregnant with Harley when she got married, though I think they were trying. Harley was pregnant with Scotty at her wedding, something Brody didn't know until just after they got engaged.

"I know. You're right. I will."

"I had a copy of the video sent to your email before it was deleted. You know, maybe for the grandkids one day. You're welcome."

It's a little after six in the evening and I'm in my office, standing, reading a file, when I feel big hands snake around my waist from behind me. I jump for a moment until I realize it's Lance.

I can't help but smile and lean back into him, though he quickly turns me around, pulls me close, and, without uttering a single word, grabs my face and brings his lips to mine. I drop the papers, slide my hands around his neck, and give into the delicious kiss.

Lance kisses unlike any other man I've been with. He's in the moment and entirely focused on enjoying the connection. It never feels hurried, like it's just a steppingstone to the next activity. He savors it. I love it.

I move my tongue along his bottom lip. He slides his tongue into my mouth and turns the kiss deep and aggressive.

His big arms envelop me, pulling my body flush with his. We kiss for what is likely more than a reasonable amount of time, but neither of us seem to be willing to end it.

After several minutes, I gently pull away, a bit out of breath. "Well, hello to you too."

His dimples are in full force as his adorable face lights up. "I was thinking about doing that all day."

I can't help but run my thumb over one of his dimples. I've been wanting to explore them for months. "I hope it lived up to your expectations."

He tucks my hair behind my ear. "And then some." He

stares at me for a moment before saying, "Are you ready for dinner?"

"Yep. Let me just clean up my desk and we can head out."

I pick up the papers scattered on the floor and straighten my desk. I grab my purse and look around one last time. As soon as I make my way to the door, he reaches for my hand and leads me toward the elevator.

He looks down at me. "Did you have a good day?"

I nod. "I did. Other than my sister having watched footage of us having sex last night, it was fine."

His eyes widen. "Oh my god. I didn't think about there being cameras in the conference room. Of course there are. I'm sorry."

I shrug. "It's not a big deal. She had it erased. Being Reagan, she had to watch the full video first, but I suppose it could be worse."

We step on the elevator and start our journey down.

"Isn't it weird having your sister watch you?"

"It's not my preference." I smile and wink at him. "I think we put on a pretty good show though."

The dimples are back out. They're so damn cute.

He rubs my cheek. "The show got better and better as the night went on."

"It sure did."

He bends down and gives me a soft kiss. "Are you hungry?"

"Always."

"How does Italian sound? I need to carb load if I'm going to be spending more evenings with you."

I giggle. "That's fine. There's a good restaurant right down the street from here."

We make our way to the restaurant and the hostess shows us to a booth. I get in on one side, expecting him to take the other, but he slides in next to me, pulls me close to him, and places his hand on my thigh.

"I didn't realize that you're the touchy-feely type."

He tilts his head to the side. "Frankly, I've never been this way, but I find myself wanting to touch you all the time. I've spent the past few months dying to touch you but being unable to do so. I'm going to make up for it. Does it bother you? I'll stop if it does."

I shake my head. "No, I like it. I just need to get used to it."

I take a sip of my water. "You've been wanting to touch me this whole time? I thought you hated me."

"I needed to distance and detach myself from you. There's a difference. I've been insanely attracted to you since the second I laid eyes on you at Reagan's party. But this project was the biggest opportunity of my life, and I felt I needed to prove to Jackson and everyone at Knight Investments that I belong. That I'm not just there because Trevor and Payton are my cousins. Does that make sense?"

"Yes, I always feel the same way."

"You don't have anything to prove. You've earned your way to your position."

"Have I? My sister is the CEO. My last name is on the masthead. I went to business school and then worked for one year. I haven't earned anything."

"Well, you're very good at your job. I'm sure people recognize that."

The waitress stops at our table and introduces herself. "You two are such a cute couple. Have you been married long?"

I start to explain that we're not married, but Lance interrupts. "Our one-year anniversary is next week. One year being married to my beautiful bride. I'm a lucky man."

The waitress practically melts.

Lance gives a cocky smirk. "Actually, will you bring us a bottle of champagne? We should start celebrating early, right sweets?"

I skeptically nod at both his story and pet name.

The waitress leaves to fetch our bottle and I look at him. "Let me get this straight. This is our first date. We had sex for the first time last night. Now we've been married for a year, and I have a new pet name?"

He pulls my chin so our mouths are only a hair apart. "We had sex for the first, second, third, and fourth time last night. Fifth time this morning. You taste sweeter than anything I've ever had in my life, so *sweets* it is. And when it's a big anniversary, you always get a free dessert. I'm all about the free dessert."

He brushes his lips across mine and kisses the corner of my mouth. I suddenly find myself wishing we weren't in a crowded restaurant.

We enjoy our champagne, dinner, and conversation. We've spent so much of the past few months down each other's throats, it's nice to get to know the kind man I believe him to be.

At the end of the meal, the waitress brings us a big piece of chocolate cake with a candle. "It's on the house for the cutest couple I've ever seen. You two seem so much in love. You give me hope."

We thank her as Lance gives me a conceited smile. "I told you she'd bring us free dessert."

"She has excellent taste. Chocolate cake is my favorite. I would eat it for three meals a day if I could."

We blow out the candle. He feeds me the first bite. I mumble, "Hmm. That's good. You should have some."

I grab a forkful and offer it to him, but he grabs my face instead and kisses me with my mouth full of chocolate cake.

He slowly runs his tongue through my mouth,

undoubtedly tasting every last bit of chocolate cake in there. Again, the kiss is much longer than appropriate for our surroundings.

By the time we break free, I see the check on the table. The waitress must have come by while we were kissing.

I try to reach for it, but Lance grabs it out of my hand. I sigh. "Lance, you're a student. Let me pay."

"Absolutely not. I'm making good money, and no girlfriend of mine will ever pay for a meal."

"Lance, I'm not your girlfriend. This is our first date. And it's not the eighteen hundreds. Women pay for meals too."

"No, it's our first anniversary." He smiles but then lets out a breath. "It may be our first official date, but I've wanted you for so long. I haven't been able to look at other women since the second I met you. I want you as my girlfriend, Skylar. I've wanted it for months."

"What about Mariana? And all the other girls Trevor said you were with? The girl at the club?"

He gives me a guilty look. "Mariana was in the car when I got in. I had never met her before. I wouldn't bring a first date to a family dinner. Trevor did that. Trevor did all of them. I was never into it, and I told him so. As for the lady at the club, in all honesty, I was hoping to make you jealous. I didn't touch her or anyone else. When I tell you I've thought of nothing but you since the moment we met, I'm not exaggerating."

What? That's not what Trevor made it sound like. That asshole was definitely messing with me.

"What about Collin? You seemed...chummy with him."

I scrunch my nose. "I don't even like Collin as a person." I put my head down in shame. "Seeing you with that woman bothered me. You succeeded in making me jealous. I kissed him to get back at you. I immediately regretted it."

He lifts my hand and kisses it. "How about we agree to be

adults and not play any more childish games?"

I nod as he throws money on the table and pulls my hand. "Let's get out of here. I'm dying to taste you again. To be inside you again. I've been going nuts all day thinking about it. I had to sit at my desk all day to hide my boner."

I can't help but laugh at that. I was admittedly feeling the same way all day.

We should probably continue this conversation, but his plan sounds way better.

I take his hand and we quickly make our way out of the restaurant.

Last night we practically crashed through my door to rip each other's clothes off. Tonight, he's slow, seemingly unhurried as we travel in the elevator up to my apartment floor.

We walk down the hallway. Just as we're about to approach my door, my neighbor's door opens. My good friend Randy and his husband, Gary, walk out.

Randy smiles at me. "Hey, gorgeous. Who do we have here?"

"Randy and Gary, this is Lance. Lance, this is my favorite couple on the planet, Randy and Gary."

They both smile as Lance shakes their hands.

I notice that they're dressed nicely. "Are you guys going anywhere good?"

Their eyes light up. "Yes, we're going to Club Liberty. It just reopened after the massive renovations."

"Oh, right. Let me know how it is. Maybe we'll check it out soon."

"We? Is Lance your boyfriend?"

Before I can respond, Lance answers, "Yes."

I turn my head and give him a disapproving look.

Randy pulls me into a hug and whispers, "He's fucking hot. Good for you."

I wave as they make their way down the hallway. "Bye, boys. Have fun."

Randy turns back and winks. "You too."

As soon as we're in my apartment and the door is closed, I grab his tie and pull his lips to mine, he kisses me back, but not with the same need I felt last night.

I pull away and give him a quizzical look.

He picks up my hand and kisses under my palm. "Last night was hurried. It was months of buildup coming to a head. I want to take my time with you tonight. I want to see every inch of you. I want to touch every inch of you. I want to kiss every inch of you. I want to learn every inch of you. I want to worship every inch of you."

He runs his eyes up and down my body in a way that I know he means every word of what he just said to me. I have no clue what I'm in store for tonight, but I know it's going to be incredible.

He reaches his hand out for mine. I take it and he leads me to my bedroom. Once there, he ever so slowly removes each article of my clothing until I'm standing there completely naked and unmasked.

He runs his index finger from my neck down to my stomach. I wish he'd go further down, but he doesn't.

"You're so incredibly beautiful, Skylar. In my wildest dreams, I could never imagine anything as perfect as your body." His eyes are full of nothing but pure lust.

I breathe, "Lance, I want to see you too."

He nods as he equally slowly removes all his own clothes until he stands there naked, with nothing but giant hard-on hanging heavy between his legs.

He's the perfect male specimen. He's so tall, with broad shoulders, huge forearms and hands, a small amount of blond chest hair matching the hair on his head, with abs of steel narrowing into a huge cock that matches the rest of his flawless body. His legs are like tree trunks. They're long and thick.

I can't take my eyes off his cock, practically teasing me as it points right at me. I instinctually wrap my hand around his hardness, but he grabs my wrist and pulls it away. "Not yet. I want to learn your body."

He stands there running his eyes all over me. He doesn't touch me, he just slowly studies every part of me. I don't think I've ever felt more exposed.

I see pre-ejaculate pooling at his tip. I like that the simple act of looking at me is doing this to him.

I can't help but lick my lips, dying to taste it. He notices and the corner of his mouth raises.

He runs his finger across his tip, gathering what's there. He offers his finger to me.

I grab his hand and take his finger into my mouth, sucking on it hard and lapping it with my tongue, all without breaking eye contact with him.

I notice his breathing picks up, but otherwise, he maintains complete control.

He bends and kisses just under my ear. My whole body is immediately covered in goosebumps while my nipples pebble.

He whispers in my ear, "I learned last night how much you like to be kissed here." He kisses there again, and I shudder. "Let's find out where else you like to be kissed and touched."

He runs the backs of his fingertips down the sides of my body. When he reaches the dip in my waist, goosebumps spread again.

He smiles and gets down on his knees, peppering wet kisses along the dip in my waist. He works his way across to my stomach, finishing with one more kiss as he looks up at me with such reverence. It's so intense for the little amount of time we've intimately spent together.

He gives me a small push, encouraging me to sit on the

bed, which I do. He lifts my leg and kisses along the inside of my ankle, gradually working his way up my lower and then upper leg.

When he gets close to my center, I thrust my hips a bit, begging him to move this along.

"Soon. I promise. Lay back."

He proceeds to take no less than thirty minutes intimately acquainting himself with every single inch of my body, just as he said he would. Everywhere except where I'm now physically aching for him.

He's learned the spots that give me goosebumps, those that make me giggle, and those that make me moan.

He works his way to my breasts and grabs them with both of his big hands. "So damn perfect."

His tongue begins to circle one of my nipples. He then takes it into his warm mouth. Finally, something I can work with.

A noise I don't recognize comes out of my mouth. Thirty minutes of teasing has got me practically trembling with the need to be touched where I want him most.

He slides his big hand down my body. I'm begging to be touched. Please let him be heading there. I can't take anymore teasing. But he doesn't. He simply grabs my hip.

"Lance, if you don't touch me, I'm touching myself. I can't take anymore teasing. I need to come."

He lifts his head, and his eyes meet mine. "Yes, touch yourself. I want to watch. I want to see how you like to be touched."

I'd rather he do it, but I don't care at this point. I move my fingers down my body until they run between my folds. I gather my juices, which are extreme at this point, and bring my fingers to my clit.

He immediately slides down so that his eyes are mere inches from my fingers.

I begin slow circles.

He looks up. "Is that how you like it? Slow?"

I sigh. "I don't know anything at this moment other than I need to come."

He chuckles.

I keep moving my fingers until I feel his fingers touch mine. "Keep going, sweets. We'll do this together."

While my fingers rub my currently overly needy bundle of nerves, his fingers run through me until they're at my equally needy entrance. Please, God, let him push into me. I'm sorry for anything bad I've ever done. If he does this, I promise to be a good person for the rest of my life.

Thankfully I'm heard, because two fingers slowly enter me until they're as far as they can go. Fuck yes!

I roll my hips at the sensation. It's going to take five pumps before I come.

And then I feel his tongue sweep through me. Fuck, fuck, fuck, yes!

I lift my fingers and his tongue immediately takes their place. Slow circles working with slow, deep thrusts of his fingers.

I guess it was the long buildup, because I feel a monster tidal wave of an orgasm quickly working its way to the surface. My body feels like it's opening and something amazing is pouring out.

I'm losing all visual abilities as my whole body begins to shudder. I scream about as loud as I'm capable, as my orgasm detonates through my entire body. Every inch of me is feeling the pleasure.

He grunts into me, the vibrations causing this otherworldly orgasm to keep working its way through me.

Lance doesn't stop and neither does my orgasm. It's all-encompassing. There could be a bomb going off next to my head right now, and I don't think I'd see or notice it.

Wave after wave, it continues on, until it eventually comes to an end. His fingers remain inside me, but he kisses his way up my body.

He gets to my face, and I see those sexy dimples out as I look at his satisfied face. They're now covered in my juices, making them even hotter.

I reach my tongue out and lick over one of them.

He rasps, "You like tasting yourself on me, don't you?"

I nod, words escaping me at this moment.

He removes his fingers from my body and brings them to his mouth. He slides them in and closes his eyes in sheer and utter bliss.

When he pulls them out, he says, "I understand the appeal. I've never tasted anything better."

He then brings them down and slides them back into me. I'm overly sensitive, but he only pumps them in and out a few times before he pulls them out and slips them into my mouth. My tongue laps his fingers.

"Good, right?"

My head is spinning right now. I can't do anything but nod.

"The buildup had a nice payoff, didn't it?"

I nod again, still unable to form words. I do eloquently manage, "Hmmm."

He looks my body up and down before meeting my eyes again. "Do you want me inside you? Do you want to come again?"

That wakes my vocal cords. I breathe, "Yes. Please."

He turns my body on its side, brings his front to my back, and lifts my top leg up and over him. I feel his tip at my entrance.

I turn my head. "Did you get condoms?"

He shakes his head. "We're clean, you're on birth control, and neither of us is going to be seeing *anyone* else." The last part is said as more of a command. "I've been inside you with nothing between us. I'm not going back."

I guess I'm orgasm drunk *again* right now, because I don't bother to put up a fight. I'm desperate to get him back inside me.

He slides into my opening. I have to take a deep breath to fully take him. He's so damn big. After just a few moments, the fullness subsides and the pleasure begins to radiate all throughout my body. My fingertips and toes are all tingling at the sensation.

He grabs onto my breasts as he begins to move in and out of me. He expertly works my nipples through his big fingers. I turn my head, reach back, thread my fingers through his hair, and pull his lips to mine. I want that connection too.

My tongue enters his mouth and I realize he's right. I do get turned on by tasting myself on him. I don't remember ever feeling that way before. I think the way he so genuinely loves it makes me love it too.

While skillfully moving inside me, Lance manages to kiss, lick, and touch every single erogenous zone he spent all that time learning.

The attentiveness and adoration he showers on me and my body translates into the sex. It's like being with a familiar lover of years, who knows me perfectly, not a man who I slept with for the first time last night.

We go at it until I don't think my body is physically capable of coming again. I finally tell him to let go, and he does, deep inside my body.

As we lay there in the aftermath, he continues to touch and kiss all over my body. We're facing each other now. I tilt his head up so his eyes meet mine. "Is this how you always are in bed?" I smile. "It seems awfully time-consuming."

He flashes me the dimples. "Without sounding like an out of touch loser, I honestly didn't believe real-life women could look like you and have this body. I want to get acquainted with every part of you. Your pleasure is my pleasure. Let me worship you the way you deserve."

Fuck. This guy.

His hands still haven't left my body for a second. He rubs my leg. "Is it too much for you?"

I shake my head. "No, it's amazing."

"I need you to talk to me though, sweets. I want to know what you like and don't like. What you need and don't need. It's important to me to give you what you want."

"What about what you want?"

"Watching you come is about the most satisfying thing I've ever experienced in my life. Your lips swell and your face turns pink. It's perfection. Talk to me. Tell me your fantasies. I want to know. I want to give you everything."

"I didn't know how much I'd enjoy a slow buildup until tonight. The payoff was incredible, but..."

"But what? Tell me."

I bite my lip in hesitation. "I do sometimes enjoy a little role-play?"

He lifts his head so we're nose to nose. "Role-play? Like where you pretend to be other people?"

"Sort of. Or just dressing up and playing the role. A hot police officer frisking me. Or a doctor examining me a little too thoroughly."

He smiles in obvious shock. "For real?"

"Yes. I know it's weird. My sisters make fun of me for it, but I can't help that I like it. Maybe I miss acting. I did a lot of that when I was younger. It's fun if you really get into the part. The payoff is worth it."

"If you loved acting, why don't you do it anymore?"

I shrug. "I'd like to say it's work, but I'd be lying. I was in a play a few weeks before my father died. He sat in the front row, grinning from ear to ear. He was my biggest fan. I don't know that I could do a play without him being there for me. I don't want him to miss a performance."

"If it makes you happy, you should do it. I'm sure he'd prefer you to be happy." My mother said the same thing to me a few weeks ago.

I smile at him. "Seeing you in something like a hot fireman's costume would also make me happy."

He rubs my face. "I want to do anything that makes you smile."

He's so sweet.

We talk a little more and then fall asleep in each other's arms.

LANCE

I wake in the morning to my nose in Skylar's neck and my arm draped over her naked body. I take a deep inhale. She smells so good. The raspberries and cake aroma is quickly becoming familiar and comforting.

I stare at her. She's fast asleep, looking gorgeous. Her big lips swell in her sleep. I softly kiss them.

I remove the blanket and run my eyes all over her. She's so damn perfect.

I slide my hard body down her soft one. I spread her legs apart and look at her. So mouthwatering. I could stare at her body all day long.

I take one swipe of my tongue through her, and then a few more. It's amazing that even in her sleep, she begins to moisten. I guess I get hard in my sleep. I'm not sure why I should expect women to be any different. I love learning everything about her body.

I slide my tongue inside her entrance, and she stirs. I

AK LANDOW

lift my head up and see her sleepily smiling at me.

"Hmmm. You're spoiling me. I'm going to start expecting this as my wake-up call every morning."

Maybe I *will* wake her up this way every morning. In fact, I'm really liking the idea.

WE SPEND the entire day being lazy in bed. I've never spent a day like this in bed with a woman. It's so intimate.

We talk, we laugh, we watch movies. We order food when we're hungry. We explore each other's bodies when we want to do that.

At some point after dinner, we take a long shower together. I make love to her against the tile wall. It's perfect. She's perfect.

My boxer briefs and undershirt are the only clean things I have. We ran them through the wash today. I sit in them by her huge bay window while she finishes up in the bathroom.

She walks out in a robe looking freshly showered and freshly fucked with those flushed cheeks and puffy lips that drive me wild. She's a vision.

I hold out my arms for her. She sits between my legs and collapses back into my body. I wrap my arms around her and pull her close.

"The view of the sky from this window is amazing."

"That's why I picked this place. On a clear night, you can see the stars perfectly from here. I sit here and read or think. It makes me feel closer to my father."

"Will you tell me about him?" I only know that he died right before Skylar left for college. I've gathered that she was tight with him.

I feel her body tense.

"You don't have to."

"It's fine. Sometimes I forget that I can speak about him now. My mom struggled for a really long time after he died, years honestly, so I've gotten used to not talking about him. She couldn't handle it. But I love talking about him. His entire world revolved around me, my mom, and my sisters. He was the greatest man ever. Plain and simple. He got me in a way no one else ever has."

"How so?"

"He saw me. Really saw me. He may have been the only person that I've ever truly felt that way about. I'm different from my mom and sisters. He appreciated me for the way I am. He had this way of making me feel so special."

"You *are* special."

I look down and see her smile. "My love for the stars came from him. From the time I was about eight years old until just before he died, he and I would go to a special spot outside the city and watch the stars. We went every few months. We'd eat and talk about life. And then we'd lay and watch the stars. He always taught me fun facts. After our first-time stargazing, he gave me a huge book on the stars. He told me to read it before bed every night to learn something new. Every month he'd also leave me notes of star-related quotes that can double for life advice, or even regular life advice quotes. I have over one hundred of them in the pages of the book. I still go through them now and then. I'm sad that I won't ever get any more notes, but happy for the ones I have. They bring me peace and give me guidance when I don't feel I can go to anyone else."

I'm surprised to hear this. She seems so close to her

mom and sisters. "Why do you feel you're so different from the rest of your family?"

She shrugs. "I don't know. They're so practical, level-headed, and focused. They look forward while I look around. I've always believed there are bigger things at play, we just need to notice them."

"Like what?"

"Just small things. I almost chose a college out of state. At the last minute, I swear I saw signs telling me to stay in town, so I chose to stay here. Just before college started, my father died. I could never have left my mother and sisters those first few years. I'm so relieved I chose to stay here. Even something as simple as you spilling beer on me at Reagan's party. If we met as we likely should have, through Melissa or my stepbrothers, I'm not sure we would have ever realized our connection."

"You seem pretty focused at work though."

"I'm not a deadbeat. I want to be good at what I do. I just don't live for the thrill of the kill the way Reagan does. Harley is slightly more relaxed now, but growing up, she was all about medical school all the time. She had tunnel vision for it. She had no life outside of her academics. She blew off Brody for years because of her career. I wouldn't do that. Love and happiness are important to me. My dad understood."

I nod in understanding. "Are those his initials or yours on your backside." She has the initials *SGL* just below her panty line in the back.

"They're his. My sisters have the same tattoo." She rubs my legs. "What about you? Tell me about your family."

"I grew up with a strict military, religious family. I have three brothers and a sister. I'm the youngest.

They're all married with kids, and my brothers work with my father. It's a very small town. I, too, felt like a fish out of water. I never felt like I belonged there. I was different from everyone else. My family fought me on leaving for a long time. I had to basically sneak out in the middle of the night to make a clean break from them and my longtime girlfriend."

"She didn't know you were leaving? You didn't tell her?"

"She knew, and we talked about going our separate ways when it happened, but she never accepted it. I think she thought I was going to change my mind at the last minute and not leave. I ended up leaving early just to make it easier for everyone, especially her."

"Have you been home since you left?"

"I was in and out for my grandmother's funeral. It coincidentally was the day Aunt Melissa and Declan got married. That's why I didn't meet any of you until Reagan's party. Otherwise, no. I'm going to go home in a few weeks though. It's time for a visit."

"I guess I know why your whole family wasn't at Melissa's wedding."

"No, I doubt they were invited. Or if they were, they wouldn't have gone. They don't speak. They haven't since I was a kid. Up until a few months ago, I hadn't seen Aunt Melissa or my cousins in over ten years."

"I suppose that makes sense, being that none of you were at Trevor or Hayden's weddings. Why don't they speak?"

"I was never sure, but I gather it's about her life choices. She moved away to go to college, which no one, especially women in our town, does. She got pregnant out of wedlock. She got divorced. She just leads a different life than they do. I'm sure they don't approve."

"It sounds like you grew up in a town that hasn't moved into this century."

"That's exactly what it is. That's exactly why I needed to leave. I'll never live there again. It's not who I am."

She turns her head around to look at me. "We're both the family oddballs."

I laugh. "I guess we're perfect together then."

She nods in agreement. "Do you have *any* common ground with your family?"

"The one thing my father and I did together was brew our own beer. It was our one common interest. The only time we didn't butt heads. We had a small brewing area in our basement where just he and I would spend time."

"I didn't know that people could brew their own beer."

I smile. "Yep. It's a very small operation. We'd only produce a handful of bottles at a time. But he and I would spend evenings there together. It was kind of our thing. Just him and me. That's probably the one thing I miss, besides seeing my nieces and nephews."

"It's nice to have something special with a parent that your siblings don't share, isn't it?"

"It is. My brothers and sister were never into it."

"Do you brew here? Do you have equipment here?"

I shake my head. "No, it's a little pricey for me right now. After I pay my tuition, and save a little rainy-day money, I may look into it. It would be nice to have a hobby outside of school and work. That's pretty much all I've done since I got here."

She clears her throat. "That's not all you've done."

I laugh as I kiss up her neck. "You're a pretty good hobby too."

CHAPTER THIRTEEN

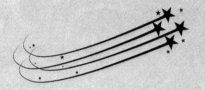

SKYLAR

It's Sunday morning. I've had the best weekend locked up with Lance. I don't want it to end, but I know it's time. He hasn't been to his apartment since Friday morning before work.

I woke up once again with his head between my legs. That's three mornings in a row. It's become a thing for him. I'm not complaining.

I walk him to the door and open it. He pulls me into a deep kiss and suddenly I *really* don't want him to leave.

"Knock, knock, neighbor."

I pull away from Lance when I hear Randy's voice. I look toward his door and he's standing there with a huge grin on his face.

He looks us up and down. I'm in nothing but a robe. I haven't worn clothes since Lance stripped me of them on Friday.

"Lance, that looks a lot like the suit you were wearing

when you arrived here on Friday. I haven't seen either of you come or go...."

I jokingly narrow my eyes at him. "Stop being a nosy neighbor, Randy. Mind your own business."

He laughs. "This nosy neighbor just bought a dozen bagels from the Yeastie Boys truck down the street. I guess you don't want any."

I point toward my kitchen. "Get your ass in my apartment. Now."

He chuckles again. "I thought so." He starts walking through my door but turns his head back. "Lance, would you like one? They're the best in Philly."

"I need to get going, but thank you. Maybe next time." He turns to me. "I'll pick you up tonight. We can drive to your mom and Jackson's together."

"Oh, I usually ride with Hayden and Jess."

"Not anymore. I'll see you at six."

He kisses me one last time and leaves.

Randy and I walk into my apartment and I close the door. He immediately turns to me. "Was that a thirty-six-hour date?"

I can't help but shrug and give a coy smile. "I guess it was."

"Were you vertical for any of it?"

I giggle. "Yes, we did it once standing in the shower."

Now it's his turn to let out a big laugh. "Good for you. It's been a long time."

"Yes, it has. Where's Gary? Tell him to come over."

"He's at a spin class. He's burning off the carbs and I'm putting them on."

I break off a piece of the warm, fresh from the oven bagel and pop it into my mouth. "I guess that's why you work so well."

"It seems like you and mister tall, blond, hot, and dimpled work pretty well together."

I moan. "Those fucking dimples will be the death of me."

"Oh god, I get it. I want to lick them."

"I did lick them. They're yummy. Just like the rest of him."

He smiles. "I'm happy for you, kiddo. You deserve someone special in your life. He doesn't look like he's going away anytime soon. He looks at you like you're his next meal."

"He does?"

Randy nods. "Most definitely. Then he bossed you around about driving with him tonight. Wow. That was hot."

"He's incredibly sweet and thoughtful on a day-to-day basis, but then with me, he's a little more dominant and possessive. I think I like how he can be both."

"That's the best type, sweetie."

LANCE PICKS me up to drive us to Mom and Jackson's house for our Sunday family dinner. He holds my hand the entire way there, constantly pulling it to his mouth for kisses. He's so loving. Jason was never this overtly affectionate with me. At least not all the time like Lance seems to be.

I turn to him. "Are we telling everyone about us? It seems kind of soon. I'm not sure what we are. Maybe we should wait." I'm nervous and rambling.

He turns to me. "We're together. It's that simple. I'm not hiding it. Now that I've touched you, I'll never make it through an evening without my hands on your body. We're telling them."

"What happened to the sweet, polite Lance?"

"Ma'am, I'm not hiding it. Now that I've touched you, I'll never make it through an evening without my hands on your sweet as apple pie body. We're telling them, sweets."

I giggle. "That's much better."

We arrive at the same time as the food delivery. I help Mom place everything on the table and we sit. I'm next to both Aunt Cass and Lance.

Aunt Cass leans over and whispers, "You look like you finally got laid. It's about time."

I turn to her and whisper, "How do you know?"

"I have a sexth sense. I always know when people are getting it good. You know that."

I think she legitimately has this superpower. She always seems to know when people are having sex.

She stares down at my thigh which I realize has Lance's hand on it. She gives me a knowing wink.

Lance clears his throats. "Everyone, can I have your attention?"

Oh boy. Why is he making a spectacle of this? I hate being the center of attention.

He lifts my hand and kisses it. "Skylar and I are dating. We just wanted you all to know."

The entire table legitimately erupts in cheers. Every single person. Reagan and Jackson clink glasses. I'm both stunned and confused by the whole scene.

Reagan and Harley hold out their hands. Trevor and Hayden reach into their pockets and then slap one-hundred-dollar bills in Harley and Reagan's hands.

I look at them. "Did you guys place bets on whether Lance and I would get together?"

Trevor raises an eyebrow. "No, of course not. That's insane."

I relax my shoulders. "Good, I'm glad. That would have been ridiculous."

"We *all* knew you were getting together. Every single person in this room knew that. We placed the bets on the timing. Hayden and I thought it would take Lance much longer to work up the balls to go for it. Reagan and Harley thought it would happen sooner rather than later. I guess you made the first move, Skylar?"

Lance shoves Trevor's shoulder. "No, asshole, she didn't."

Trevor laughs as he throws his arm around Lance. "Sensei Trevor is proud of his student."

I have no idea what that means. I'm sure I don't want to know.

I look at Jackson and Reagan. "What was with the glass clinking?"

Jackson gives me a guilty look. Mom just smiles and shakes her head.

Jackson turns to Reagan and then back at me. "Reagan and I felt like the Bancroft competition was hindering you two getting together, so we may have at least partially joined forces to eliminate that obstacle for the both of you."

I sit there in complete shock. "You two manipulated a billion-dollar deal so that Lance and I would start dating?"

They smile at each other. Reagan shrugs. "That, and it's more fun to do this project together. We'll *all* be a part of Philadelphia history. And from what I saw from the footage of conference room three the other night, it was well worth it."

"Reagan! Not here. Not now." I plead with my over-sharing sister to shut her mouth.

Trevor snaps his head to Reagan. "What footage? What happened in conference room three? I want to see it."

Reagan smiles, "I got to see Lance making the first move." She fans herself. "And it was hot, hot, hot. Good for you, Lance." She winks at him.

Trevor and Payton high five each other.

I cover my eyes in mortification. Lance simply smiles and kisses my cheek.

As EXPECTED, my sisters pull me aside right after dinner. Harley elbows me. "Where have you been *all* weekend?"

"I was...umm...busy."

Reagan shakes her head. "Busy getting busy?"

"Isn't this what you two wanted?"

Reagan nods. "Hell yes, it's what we wanted. How was it? As hot as the first night?"

Harley narrows her eyes at Reagan. "Why do you have details I don't have? I want to be updated immediately."

Reagan gives me a pleading look.

I roll my eyes. "Fine, just tell her."

Reagan practically jumps up and down with glee. "The two of them were working in one of our conference rooms on Thursday night. She touched him, then he started rubbing his hand on her leg. Then she opened her legs in obvious invitation and it was game on."

"I did not open my legs in invitation."

"Yes, you did." Maybe I did. "He pushed her onto the table and went down on her. After she came, he went down on her *again*."

"Twice in a row?"

Reagan nods. "Yes. And then she tried to immediately have sex with him, but he flipped her over, spanked her ass, and fucked her hard from behind. He added a little dirty talk too."

I shake my head at her dramatics.

"Lance did that? The same Lance that's over there?" She points to him.

"He did. Then they left and had sex at her place all night. In the morning, he woke her with his head back between her legs. He picked her up at the office on Friday night. That's the last I heard from her until tonight."

I roll my eyes. "Thank you for summarizing my sex life with such detail and colorful commentary."

"You're welcome. What happened from Friday night until now?"

"We had a nice dinner on Friday and then he came over." I mumble, "And didn't leave until this morning."

Harley moves her head closer to me. "This morning, as in two days later?"

I give a slight nod in confirmation.

"And what was it that you two managed to do all that time?"

"Ummm...we got to know each other."

Reagan smiles. "How many times did you *get to know each other*?" She air quotes the last three words.

I shrug. "I don't know. A lot."

They both laugh and high five. What's with all the high fiving in this family over my love life?

Reagan asks, "Did he go down on you again?"

Now it's my turn to smile. "Yes, several times. And he woke me up both mornings doing it again."

"Is it good?"

I let out a breath. "Yes. *Really* good. He's very into my body. He loves taking his time with everything. He's super into my pleasure and drawing it out. It's a whole thing for him. We go at it for hours."

Reagan appears to run her eyes up and down Lance. She turns back to me. "Does he have a big dick?"

We all now turn our heads to look at Lance. I smile at the thought of his naked body. "He's the biggest man in a room full of big men. He has shoulders like a linebacker and hands bigger than our DDD boobs. Does he appear to be the type of man who's hung like a pimple?"

They both laugh.

I smile while continuing to undress Lance with my eyes. He catches me staring and smiles back. Without looking away, I say, "He's definitely got a Big Dipper."

LANCE

As soon as dinner's over, Trevor, Payton, and Hayden corner me. Trevor places his hand on my shoulder. "We don't want a full description, because it's Skylar, but tell us how it all started."

"Not a chance. I won't disrespect her by giving you guys any details."

Trevor nods his head toward Skylar, Reagan, and Harley. "What do you think is happening over there? She's giving them all the dirty details right now. The three of them have no secrets. They probably know the size of your dick. We're not asking for dirty details. Just tell us how it all started."

I run my fingers through my hair as I blow out a breath. "We were working late, and I couldn't focus on anything but her. She's so goddamn perfect. I made a move, and she was receptive to it. Very receptive."

He smiles. "Did you make Sensei Trevor proud?"

I roll my eyes but nod. "She's a happy woman. I'm not saying anything else."

He smiles, but Hayden roughly grabs my shoulder and has an over-exaggerated scowl on his face. "If you hurt her, we'll hunt you and kill you."

I let out a laugh. "I won't hurt her."

Trevor whispers, "Did you add a little dirty talk?"

I turn toward her. She and I make eye contact. She gives me a subtle smile. She's so beautiful. I can't help but smile back at both Trevor's question and Skylar's beauty.

Trevor pulls me from my thoughts. "Oh my god. He's

already completely fallen for her. Look at him. He's grinning like a lovesick puppy."

"No, I'm not." I might be.

CHAPTER FOURTEEN

SKYLAR

I'm home with a glass of wine, sitting on my couch. I love what I do, but sometimes it's exhausting.

It's been a long few days of work. Lance and I aren't getting as much done as we used to, though we're painfully aware of the cameras now. It's stolen kisses, subtle touches, and a lot more smiles.

There's rarely a moment when we're together that he doesn't touch me. He doesn't play games. He doesn't play hard to get. He's passionate about me, and makes it clear every second we're together. He makes me feel cherished in a way I haven't for a very long time.

Lance said he needed to stay home and study, so I won't see him tonight. I find myself wanting to be with him. I'd rather he was sitting here with me. We've been together for a week and I'm already missing him when we're not together. I can admit that I'm totally whipped.

There's an unusually loud banging noise at my door. It

sounds like someone is pounding their fists as hard as possible on it.

I start walking toward the door when I hear a deep voice yell, "Police, open up. Now "

I start to internally freak out. What do the police want with me?

I open the door and am immediately relieved and excited by what I see. It's Lance in a full-fledged cop uniform, including a hat and aviator sunglasses. It's snug on his big body and fits him in all the right places. I feel my cheeks flushing at the simple sight of him like this. He notices and the corner of his mouth raises.

My chin must drop too because he reaches his finger out and lifts it. He doesn't break character otherwise.

In a deep, authoritative voice, he says, "Ma'am, we have a problem."

I play my part. "I can't imagine what it could be, officer. I'm a very good girl. How can I help you?"

"I'm sorry to bother you, but we've received a reliable tip that you're a drug mule. I'm afraid I'm going to have to check your body thoroughly. *Very* thoroughly."

I can't help but smile as I open the door wider. "I don't think you'll find anything, but I understand that you need to do your job. Come in."

He stalks in and closes the door behind him. "Ma'am, I need you to face the wall with your palms flat and your hands placed high on the wall where I can see them."

I love that he's getting into his character and staying there.

I walk over to the closest wall and do as he instructed. I may even stick my ass out a little. Maybe.

I catch him staring at my ass and wink at him.

He grabs my chin and jerks my face toward the wall.

"Ma'am, I need you to face forward and spread your legs

please." I do, but he uses his knee to roughly spread them even wider.

He frisks me, moving his hands down the sides of my body. Down the sides of my breasts, down my waist, over my hips, and down my legs. I can hear his breathing pick up.

"You'll have to excuse me ma'am, but I've been instructed to make this comprehensive."

"I understand, officer. I know you're just doing your job."

He moves his hand around to the front of my body and feels my entire top half, spending a little extra time on my breasts.

I can't help the smile on my face.

In a deep voice, he says, "I'm going to check under your sweater now."

He slowly slides his hands under my sweater and up my bare stomach. I can feel his erection on my ass. I wiggle a little and he freezes.

"Ma'am, I'm going to have to ask you to remain still so I can do my job."

I breathe, "Yes, sir."

He pulls the cups of my bra down and more than carefully examines every inch of my breasts. My nipples may now have actual fingerprints on them.

He slides his hands out, grabs my hips, and turns me around. "Ma'am, now I have to do a visual inspection."

I lift my arms and he removes my sweater. He licks his lips as he unfastens my bra letting it drop to the floor.

His fingertips slowly trace around my breasts, gradually making their way to my nipples, which have completely hardened. I can see him biting the inside of his cheek, desperately trying to maintain control.

I look down. His erection is fully straining against his slightly too tight pants. I'm aching to rub it, but I stay in character.

He removes his hat and sunglasses and gets down on his knees. "I'll need to taste to make sure no illegal substance traces were left behind."

I smile. "I understand, officer. Do what you need to do."

With that, he grabs one of my breasts and slowly circles it with his warm, wet tongue. His lips encapsulate my nipple as he sucks it into his mouth. With his heavenly lips, he increases the suction on my nipple to the edge of that pleasure-pain point.

I moan and can't help but run my fingers through his hair.

He grabs my wrists hard and pins them to the wall. "Ma'am, keep your hands back here. I'll restrain you if I have to."

If they weren't already, my panties are completely soaked now.

He moves his fingers down to my jeans, unbuttons the top button, and unzips them. He slips his fingers in by my hips and pulls them down and off.

He dusts his fingers over my panty-covered pussy, undoubtedly noticing how wet it is. I see his internal struggle over breaking character.

He subtly brings his nose close to my center and inhales deeply. His hands ball into fists as he battles to maintain control.

I love the sight of this big, gorgeous man on his knees in front of me, trying to please me by staying in his character, but equally struggling with not taking what he wants from my body.

He's got me completely ravenous for him right now. All without having touched me where I'm aching for him.

He looks up and whispers, "I need to be thorough."

I nod as he slides my panties down my legs. I now stand there completely naked.

"Spread your legs for me."

I do.

"I need to check inside you for the drugs."

I bite my lip in anticipation of him being inside of me. I desperately want it.

He slowly traces two fingers up my inner thigh and then through my folds. His breathing picks up. I can see his cock twitching in his pants.

He takes a few deep breaths before sinking those long, thick fingers straight into me. I'm so ready for him. They easily slide right in.

I nearly collapse from the sensation.

In and out. In and out. Deeper and deeper.

I can feel my inner walls already trembling and squeezing his fingers. I can see in his face that he feels it too.

He looks up at me. "I need to do a taste test here too. Just to make sure there were no illegal substances in here earlier."

"Yes, you should. You need to be comprehensive. I wouldn't want you to get into trouble with your boss."

He spreads my lips and runs his tongue through me. This time, he moans.

I have to lean back against the wall, or I don't think I would be capable of standing anymore.

He slides his fingers back into me as he focuses his tongue on my sensitive bundle of nerves. Slow, methodical circles. No one does this better than Lance. He's certainly practiced enough on me in the past week.

He throws one of my legs over his shoulder, burying his face deep in me. I move my hips as I ride his face.

The buildup was too much for me. I'm quickly brought to the edge. Embarrassingly so.

I'm moaning and panting. I have to place my hands on his shoulders to remain upright.

I somehow manage to say, "Officer, have you found anything yet?"

Though his fingers keep moving, he lifts his mouth from my pussy and looks up at me with lust-filled eyes and juice-covered lips. "I've found everything I've ever wanted."

His words and the look of utter bliss I see in his face right now sets me off. I yell out as my orgasm completely overtakes my body. He has to hold me up. I can't possibly stand on my own any longer.

He quickly moves his mouth back to my clit and sucks hard, causing my orgasm to continue rolling on, seemingly unending.

I shout, "Oh god, Lance. It's too good."

He keeps sucking and pushing into me, ensuring it lasts and that I enjoy every second of it.

When it's over, I blink and look down at him. He looks like he just came, even though I know he didn't. I'm overcome with emotion at how much he truly enjoys my pleasure.

I breathe out, "Officer, I don't want you to get into trouble. Make sure you check *all* of my holes."

And just like that, he completely snaps. He growls as he rips, literally rips, open his shirt. He stands, quickly unbuckles his belt, unbuttons his pants, pulls down his zipper, pulls out his fully hardened big cock, lifts me, wraps my legs around him, and impales me in one hard thrust.

I yell out, "Ah, Lance."

He pushes us against the wall at the same time his mouth takes mine in a deep, hot, wet kiss. His tongue plunders into my mouth as his cock begins pounding into me. I move my tongue into his mouth, tasting myself on his tongue.

He's driving into me at a hard, frenzied pace. He's normally so methodical, but not right now. He's out of control in a way I haven't ever seen from him. It's hot as hell. I love that I made him feel this way.

My back is rubbing hard against the wall. I have no doubt

I'll have bruises in the morning. I don't care. The pleasure outweighs the pain.

I can feel his cock legitimately pulsating inside me. He's deeper in my body than anyone or anything has ever been before. I'm feeling just as frantic with need for him. My hands slide under his shirt as I scrape my nails down his back, undoubtedly marking him.

He has one hand on my ass and the other on one of my breasts. He sucks on my neck. "You're so fucking hot, I can't manage myself right now."

"Oh god, Lance. You're so deep. Stay there. Don't stop."

"God, Skylar, I want to get deeper. I need it. I need you."

Our hands and mouths are everywhere on each other. His lips. His teeth. His tongue. They're all over my body. We're both completely animalistic in our fucking right now. We've crossed way over the other side of controlled. I've never felt this frantic with need for another person. I've never felt so carnally wanted.

I feel one of his fingers on my ass slip closer to my back entrance. He's never attempted to go there before, but he clearly is now.

The extreme wetness of my pussy is dripping that way. He gathers some of my juices and slowly slips his finger deep inside of me. As soon as he does, my vision turns to a kaleidoscope of colors. My whole body convulses as an explosive orgasm rockets through me. I have no control over my shaking body right now. All I can do is grab onto the remnants of his shirt and hang on for the wild ride.

I barely hear Lance grunting, "Oh fuck, Skylar. I can't hold on." He pushes his cock and his finger in deep as he comes inside me while tightly squeezing me.

He gradually begins to slow his pace. We're both breathing loudly as we attempt to regain our senses. His forehead is pressed to mine. He breathes out, "That. Was. Incredible."

"Hmm. It was." I look at his torn shirt. "I hope that wasn't a rental."

He lets out a laugh. "It was. I guess I'm not getting my security deposit back."

We both smile, still forehead to forehead.

He softly kisses me. "Okay, you were right. The buildup of the role-play thing is hot. I've never considered it before, but I like it. I'm game for more."

I kiss up his neck. "If it's half as good as that, I agree."

AFTER ANOTHER ROUND, we collapse onto my bed completely spent. We lay on our sides, gazing at each other, while his fingertips are gently running up and down my bare hip.

When he's with me, I always have one hundred percent of his attention. He reminds me of my father in that regard. Despite having my mom and three daughters, he always gave us each his undivided attention when spending time alone with us. I miss my one-on-one time with him the most. I miss talking to him. I miss him giving me advice and telling me fun facts about the stars and space. I know he didn't do that with my sisters. It was just our special thing. It's hard for me to see it as anything more than a sign that Lance knows and loves astronomy too.

Lance's attention is always intense. It's like he studies me. He wants to learn everything about me.

He squeezes my exposed hip. "Will you tell me some of your other role-play fantasies?"

I shrug. "I don't know. I guess normal ones. Nurse, doctor, fireman, French maid, dirty secretary." I smirk. "I may have one or two of those costumes around here somewhere."

He smiles. "I bet you wear them well. I can't wait to see you in them."

He rubs his thumb on my face. "What's your deepest, darkest role-play fantasy? Something you've never done and have never shared with anyone else? I want to know."

I bite my lip, contemplating telling him. "It's kind of embarrassing. It's dark."

His eyes widen. "Tell me. I genuinely want to know. I promise I won't judge." He tucks some loose hair behind my ear. "I just want to know everything about you."

I know he means that.

I bury my head in his chest, so I don't have to look at him when I tell him. "I've kind of always wanted to do an intruder role-play."

"What does that mean?"

I look up at him. "I mean, a man breaking in during the night and having his wicked way with me. I know it's fucked up, but it's not real, just a consensual fake situation. A *hot*, fake situation."

"What would you want him to do? How wicked?"

I bury my head again. "*Very* wicked. Anything he wants. I'd even be into him being a little rough and dangerous with me."

I feel him harden against me. I'm not sure how it's physically possible for him to be hard again after the evening we've had, but he is. What I said turned him on.

I look up. "You're into it?"

He wraps his arms around me and pulls me as close as possible to him. "I'm into anything that turns you on and makes you happy." He rubs my face. "Anything that makes your face flush like this. The way you look when you're aroused and when you come is the air I need to breathe. I want to see it on you as much as possible."

I reach my head up and bring my lips to his. I whisper into his lips, "You're so good to me."

He rolls us over and wiggles his way between my legs. I spread them wide as he brings his tip to my entrance. He peppers kisses up my neck. "I can be better. I think I need to search you again."

I moan as he slides in deep. "Yes, that's a good idea."

CHAPTER FIFTEEN

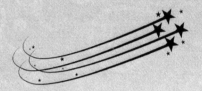

LANCE

Skylar and I have had an amazing few weeks in our little bubble. We get to work together at least two or three days a week on the Bancroft project, so we're together during the day. We then spend almost every night in one of our beds, usually hers. Her place is much bigger and much nicer than mine, so it makes more sense to stay there.

At dinner last week, Darian asked us to play pickleball with her and Jackson this weekend. Even though I have no idea what it is, I agreed. I want to get to know Darian better and I want her to get to know me too. It's difficult at the big family meals.

We're driving to the pickleball club that Darian and Jackson belong to. I turn to Skylar. "Can you explain pickleball?"

She smiles. "It's like a mix of tennis and Ping-Pong. It's paddles and a hollow ball, like Ping-Pong, but you're on a mini-tennis court. Your height and wingspan will be an advantage. There will be a few young people there, but the club is mostly people over fifty, and several over seventy. Just know that my mom was a former college athlete. She's insanely competitive. She takes it extremely seriously."

"Should I let her win?"

"You may not be letting her do anything. She's legitimately a good athlete."

We arrive and head to our respective locker rooms. I find Jackson in the men's locker room. We get changed. I brought athletic shorts and a T-shirt. Jackson is wearing the same, but some of the other men are in full-fledged tennis outfits like this is a professional sport.

We leave the locker room and sit at a small table while we wait for the girls.

He nods his head at me. "How are things with Skylar?"

I smile at the mention of her name. "Amazing. She's incredible."

"Good answer."

I look around. Skylar was right. It's definitely predominantly an over fifty crowd. Some are *way* over fifty.

A much older man shakes Jackson's hand. Jackson smiles at him. "Good to see you out here, Harry."

"When you're eighty-six, it's good to be seen at all."

Jackson laughs. "Harry, you'll outlive all of us."

"Getting old isn't so bad when you consider the alternative."

Jackson and I both laugh at that one.

Harry looks around. "Is your hotsie totsie wife with you? She gets my heart rate up without even having to run around the court. Looking at her is my cardio for the day."

Jackson and I turn and smile at each other. Jackson looks back at Harry. "She does the same thing to me, Harry. Every single day. She'll be out in a minute."

"Oh good. I'll tell the boys we've got some eye candy out here today."

Harry leaves and Jackson just shakes his head. "I suppose I hope I'm still alive and able to look when I'm his age."

The women's locker room door opens, and Skylar and Darian walk out. They're both in short tennis skirts and tight tank tops. It's honestly as if they're walking in slow motion. Every single head, men's and women's, turns to watch them.

I see where Skylar gets her flawless figure. She has several inches on Darian, but they have all the curves in all the same places.

Jackson stands and practically sprints the last few feet to Darian. "You look amazing, sugar."

She narrows her eyes at him. "You can't touch me when we're playing. You need to take it seriously or I'm dumping you as my partner for the upcoming tournament."

He places his hands on her hips. "I'll behave." He turns and winks at me.

They make their way over to the court. Skylar looks up at me. "He's going to fondle her the whole time."

I let out a laugh. "I don't blame him. You both look amazing." I rub my hands up and down her body. "I may be fondling you too."

She gives me a sexy smile. "Behave yourself."

I pull her body close to mine so she can feel what she does to me. "If I behave, can I fuck you while you wear that skirt later?"

Her breathing picks up. She leans into my body and pulls my face to hers. She traces my lips with her tongue.

Before we can kiss, we hear Darian yell, "You're going to give the people here a stroke. Let's start before all the crazies get here and commandeer the courts." She mumbles, "I'm surrounded by a bunch of horndogs."

Skylar and I smile at each other. She looks down. "Are you going to play with that monster sticking out?"

I follow her gaze. She's right. I can't go anywhere right now. She moves closer and discreetly slips her hand into my shorts.

I suck in a breath. "What are you doing?"

"I'm pulling it through your waistband, so your shorts aren't as tented."

"You touching him isn't helping my situation."

She smiles, though she does manage to pull him up and through my waistband.

She looks down. "Don't lift your shirt. Your dick is several inches above the waistband."

Staring down at it, her breathing picks up. She bites her lip and her cheeks flush. She's turned on too.

I wrap my hand around her ponytail and tilt her head so she's looking at me. "If I were to slip my hand under your skirt right now, what would I find?"

She lets out a small moan, but before she can answer, Darian yells again. "Erma is circling our court like a vulture. Get over here."

I whisper, "We'll continue this later."

She nods as I turn her around. "Walk in front of me for a second. Not too close though. Don't touch me. Then he'll never go down."

We walk toward the court. She purposefully sways her ass.

I loudly whisper out, "That's mean."

She giggles.

I finally get him down. It's not easy with Skylar dressed that way. I had to think of every unappealing thing I've ever come across in my life. The rat my brothers put in my sister's bed, the old man ass I once saw at the gym, and what it was like sharing a bathroom with my brothers growing up. I'm still traumatized from grabbing towels that were crusty. To this day, I carefully inspect all towels before using them.

We start playing. I think I'm picking up the game easily. Skylar was right, my height and wingspan are a huge advantage.

Darian yells, "Jackson, you're not going deep enough."

He mumbles, "That's not what you were screaming last night."

Skylar and I smile at each other. The two of them are hysterical.

Skylar was also right about Jackson. He makes sure to touch Darian between each point, sometimes in the middle of a point. She's getting frustrated.

"Jackson! You can only touch me when we win the point. And if we win the game..." She then whispers something in his ear before biting it. His eyes pop open wide.

I turn to Skylar. She just shakes her head. "Welcome to my world. My mother is the biggest perv of anyone."

I can't help but laugh.

After that, Jackson plays like a man possessed. It's almost comical what she does to him, though I find their relationship to be endearing.

We rotate around to different opponents. I hear Darian and old man Harry arguing on the court next to us over whether balls are in or out.

When it's over, Darian suggests that Jackson and Skylar go grab our lunch so she and I can talk.

When they walk away, Darian turns to me. "Lance, we don't have much time before they'll be back. Can I be frank with you?"

"Please do."

"I know everyone in the family is thrilled that you and Skylar are dating. Clearly, they're all fans of yours. You certainly seem very sweet, and Skylar is the happiest I've seen her in a very long time."

I can't help but smile at that.

She continues, "But in all honesty, what worries me is what will happen if this doesn't work out. You'll always be Melissa's nephew, meaning you'll always be around. That could be difficult for the both of you."

I nod. "Yes, ma'am. I understand. All I can tell you is that my intentions are honorable. I adore her. I have since the second I met her. I'm not planning on going anywhere anytime soon."

She nods. "I assume you two do a lot of talking. She's very introspective. She's a thinker. She believes that everything happens for a reason."

"I know. Sometimes she feels a little like an outcast in your family because of it."

"Is that what she's told you?"

I nod. "Yes, ma'am. We have that in common. I'm very different from my own family."

"Lance, call me Darian. Ma'am makes me feel as old as Erma."

"I'll try."

"Are you close with your family?"

"I'd like to think I am. The love is certainly there. They just had trouble understanding why I wanted to move away. They still struggle with it."

"I see. Skylar tends to bottle things inside. It's hard to get her to open up to me. She was very close with her father. She talked to him more than anyone. I'd like to think she knows she can talk to me and her sisters, but I know she holds back. She bottles her pain."

"She's filled me in on her relationship with him."

"I'm glad to hear that. I think for a long time, she relied on her ex-boyfriend. When they broke up, she really clammed up. I see her coming back out of her shell a bit with you."

I can't help but smile again. "I'm thrilled to hear that. Ma'am..."

She narrows her eyes at me.

"...Darian. We're genuinely happy together. It hasn't been long, but I'm already thinking long-term. I want to take her home with me to meet my family. I can't sit here and promise forever at this moment, but I don't see any reason why things would change for us. No matter what, her happiness will always be a priority for me."

Before Darian can respond, Jackson and Skylar return, ending our conversation.

SKYLAR

It's Lance's birthday today. In true Lance fashion, he doesn't want anyone knowing and he wants to be low key about it. He did happily agree to go out with my sisters and their husbands tonight. We've decided to go to the recently renovated Club Liberty.

Before we leave to meet them, I pull out a few big, heavy, wrapped boxes. His eyes widen. "What's all this?"

"Your birthday present."

He sighs. "I told you to keep it low key."

"I haven't told anyone it's your birthday, per your request, but there's no way I wasn't buying you a gift." I give him a puppy dog face. "Please, I'm so excited to give this to you." I'm practically jumping up and down with excitement.

I see the dimples appear. I know he's at least a little excited. Who wouldn't be excited for a birthday present?

"Fine. It better not be extravagant."

I mumble, "Maybe a little bit."

He opens the boxes. As soon as he realizes what it is, he sighs. "Skylar, I can't accept this. It's too much."

I look down at all the equipment he needs to brew his own beer. I wrap my arms around his neck, and he pulls me close. I get on my tippy-toes and softly kiss his lips. "Let me give this to you. I have nowhere to spend the crazy amount of money my sister insists on paying me. It will genuinely make me happy to see you enjoy it." I smile. "It's for me, not you. Besides, I want to know if you're good at it. I need to taste your product."

He sucks on my lower lip. "You often taste my product."

I giggle. "Not as much as you taste mine."

He picks me up and carries me to the bedroom. "How about I taste it now to thank you for an amazing gift."

"Deal."

A LITTLE WHILE later we're all sitting in a booth at Club Liberty with drinks. Reagan asks, "Lance, did you know that Brody and Harley met at this club?"

He nods. "Skylar mentioned it." He turns to Harley and Brody. "You must be excited to be back here."

Reagan smiles. "They exchanged fluids on the roof without bothering to exchange names."

Harley smacks her arm. "That's not true. He gave me his name. I just wouldn't give him mine."

I can't help but laugh at that. It's true.

Carter pulls Reagan close. "Want to reenact it on the roof?"

Her eyes light up. "I could be talked into that."

Brody interrupts, pulling Harley tight to him. "We also got engaged on that roof. That's a special memory. And that's where she told me she was pregnant with Scotty." He turns to Carter and smiles. "If anyone will be reenacting the night we met, it will be us. Dibs on the roof."

Lance leans over and whispers, "Your family is bizarrely open about their sex lives."

I smile and whisper back, "You have no idea. Two more drinks and we'll probably catch the live show for both couples."

"Does that mean no one would care if my hands were all over you tonight?" He runs his eyes up and down my body and adjusts his pants. "That dress you're wearing is doing things to me." I'm in a tight, red, one-shouldered dress.

"Is there anything I wear that doesn't do things to you?" He has a boner twenty-four hours a day.

The dimples make an appearance. "I guess not. You're hot in everything you wear, and everything you don't wear."

He's so openly into me. He's unapologetic about it. It's nice to feel so wanted and adored. I feel the same way about him.

I'm staring at him when Reagan snaps her fingers in my face.

"Earth to Skylar."

I turn. "Sorry. What?"

"Googly eyes, let's dance."

The men stay put, but Harley, Reagan, and I dance up a storm for a few fast songs. We're having a great time. We haven't done this in so long. It feels nice to let loose and have fun with my sisters.

The boys initially didn't want to dance, but we seem to have attracted a crowd of other men around us, so now I see Brody, Carter, and Lance make their way to the dance floor.

Brody and Carter dance well, but they're not in Lance's league. I nearly forgot what a ridiculously good dancer he is. I remember seeing it at Reagan's birthday party. He has the moves of a professional.

He's moving around, so carefree, with a big smile. I can't stop watching him. I'm realizing how hard I've fallen for him in just a few weeks.

Despite moving around the dance floor like crazy, his eyes stay completely focused on me. He's dancing for me. It's as if no one else is on this floor, and that at least twenty women aren't staring at him right now like they want to devour him. He's totally unaware of them.

My sisters are on either side of me. Reagan shakes her head. "He can legitimately move."

I don't take my eyes off him. "Yes, he can."

"Do you get any Magic Mike role-play sessions? He could definitely make that happen with the way he dances."

I smile at the thought. "That's not a bad idea."

They both laugh and Harley places her arm around me. "You seem happy, Skylar."

"I *am* happy. He's so genuine and different from most men. I really like how he is with me. The way he treats me and my body."

"How's that?"

"Like I'm the only woman in the world."

The current song ends and a slow one begins. He immediately makes his way over to me and wraps his arms around me. I assume my sisters leave to dance with their husbands, but I don't notice. I just stare at Lance.

Because I physically can't help myself, I grab his head and pull his lips hard to mine, slipping my tongue into his mouth. He immediately acquiesces, slipping his tongue into mine.

We kiss as if no one else is in the room. That's exactly how it feels to be with Lance. Like no one else exists around us.

Our kiss ends, but our foreheads stay together. He breathes, "Tell me I'm not alone in feeling this, Skylar."

"You're not. I feel it too."

"Are you scared?"

I swallow. "Yes."

"Me too."

CHAPTER SIXTEEN

LANCE

The night on the dance floor last month was a defining moment for us. Not that either of us was holding back before, but we've gone full steam ahead now.

I've all but moved into her apartment. I sleep there almost every night. Most of my clothes are there. She cleared half her closet for me. Her guest room is my dedicated beer brewing room. I've enjoyed doing that again. But what I love the most is coming home to her and spending the evenings with her. I especially love our mornings together.

I haven't told her, because I know she's not one for rushing feelings, but I'm in love with her. I just want to find the right time to tell her.

I'm taking Skylar home with me today. I can't help but be a bit nervous. She's a strong, intelligent, and opinionated woman. I love that about her. I'm not sure my family will appreciate it though.

We set out on the several hour drive. I hold her hand through most of it.

At some point, she asks, "Will we stay in your old room? I can't wait to see it."

"Sweets, you know my parents are very religious, right?"

She nods.

"I don't think they'll be comfortable with us staying in the same room. In fact, I know they won't."

"Lance, we're adults. That's kind of ridiculous and dated, don't you think?"

"You're right, but I have enough issues with my parents. I can't fight them on every little thing."

She pulls her hand from mine. She takes a deep breath and looks out the window. She's silent for a bit. She's obviously upset.

At some point she turns back to me. "They're not going to like me, are they?"

I swallow. "If they don't, it won't be personal. You're a progressive woman, which I adore. They're not progressive people."

"Why am I coming with you then?"

A grab her hand again and kiss it. "Because you're important to me. Despite our differences, they're still my family and I want them to meet you."

She nods. "Okay. I'll do my best to respect their beliefs, but you know I wasn't raised to hold my tongue. Just the opposite."

I smile. "I know, sweets. I love that about you."

She gives me a sexy smile. "Does this mean we'll have to be celibate all weekend? I'm not sure you have that in you."

I wink at her. "I may have made some plans to ensure we have alone time together."

She laughs. "I bet you did. Will I get to see you do any farmer stuff? I may like that image."

I can't help but smile. "I'll see what I can do for you. It's not a huge working farm. Just a few crops and animals. My dad doesn't farm for a living."

"I know, but it's still a farm. I've never stayed on one."

I nod toward the glove compartment. "Sweets, can you open that? I left something in there for you. It's right on top."

She opens the glove compartment and pulls out the flyer I found yesterday. I see her carefully reading it. She then turns to me and pinches her eyebrows in question. "What's this about?"

"There's a play at the local community theater. I thought you might want to try out. Auditions are in a few weeks. That should give you time to learn some of the lines and do whatever is needed to prepare for it."

I see tears well in her eyes, but I want to push her on this. I think it would be helpful for her.

I squeeze her hand. "It would mean a lot to me to see you perform. I know you used to love it."

"I'd rather perform in our special way."

I smile. "I *definitely* don't want that to end, but I think this would be good for you. I'm honestly dying to see you on stage. Please just think about it. For me?"

She's quiet for a moment but then nods. "I'll think about it." She smiles. "I've done this play before. I probably don't need much rehearsal to start remembering everything."

I can see the excitement in her eyes and am happy I brought it to her attention.

We eventually roll into town. We drive through Main Street so I can show her a few of my favorite places.

We make our way out to the farm. She marvels at all the cornfields and open space. There's not much of that in Philly.

We pull into the long driveway of the house. I see both of my parents are on the porch waiting for us. I hope this goes well.

I grab our suitcases as we make our way to the door. My father shakes my hand, and my mother hugs me. She squeezes me tight and whispers how much she's missed me.

I grab Skylar's hand. "Mom, Dad, this is Skylar Lawrence. Skylar, these are my parents, Craig and Stephanie Remington."

Skylar smiles. "It's nice to finally meet you both. Lance speaks so fondly of you."

They hold out their hands, but Skylar hugs them both. I can't help but inwardly smile at the fact that Skylar's going to do this her way. I find her fortitude and strength to be among the most attractive qualities about her. I think I could use a little more of that sometimes.

With a big grin on my face, I hand my father a six-pack of beer I brewed.

He looks surprised. "This is unexpected. Did you find somewhere that allows you to brew your own beer?"

"No, sir." I pull Skylar close to me. "For my birthday, Skylar bought me all the equipment I need. I have my own little operation set up in her apartment. She has an extra room."

My father looks confused. "Wow, that's a nice gift. I can't wait to see what you created."

We go inside. Mom pours each of us a glass of lemonade. As we drink, they ask Skylar the standard questions about her family and her job. I imagine they're fairly shocked that she has such a high-powered position.

At some point, my mom encourages us to take our bags upstairs and to wash up for dinner.

"Lance, take Skylar to Lucy's old room."

"Mom, I think Skylar will stay in my room with me."

She turns white as a ghost. "Lance, that's not right. I'm sure her mother wouldn't appreciate that."

"I've stayed at her mother's house with Skylar. She'd be fine with it."

"That's not what goes on in this house, Lance. You know that."

"Well, we can always go stay in a hotel."

Skylar touches my arm and smiles at me. "It's okay. For one night, we can respect your parents' wishes."

"Are you sure?"

"Yes. Come on, let's get settled in."

I nod as we make our way upstairs. I show her my sister Lucy's old room and place her bag on the bed. "Sweets, are you sure you're okay with this? I don't want to upset you. You were upset in the car. I don't like seeing you that way."

She wraps her arms around my neck and softly kisses me. "It's fine. Thank you for trying. Thank you for caring that it bothered me in the car." She gives me a sexy smile. "I was thinking about it. Sneaking around will be kind of hot. I may be into a little forbidden fun."

I grab her waist and pull her flush to my body. I kiss up her neck. "I might like that game too."

She smiles as I take her sweet, juicy lips in mine. I deepen the kiss, tasting every perfect spot in her mouth with my tongue. She runs her fingers through my hair and whimpers.

We're both completely consumed by the kiss when we hear a knock at the bedroom door. We turn our heads and see my brother Ryan standing there with a big grin. "Sorry to interrupt, but better me than Mom."

I smile as I walk over to my brother, and we give each other big bear hugs. He lifts me up off the ground. "Good to have you home. I miss you."

I turn to Skylar. "Skylar, this is my oldest brother, Ryan. Ryan, this is my girl, Skylar."

Skylar reaches out to hug him. "Nice to meet you. I've heard so much about you."

He smiles down at her. "I've heard about you too. He said you were pretty, but I wasn't prepared for this." He looks at me while keeping his arm around Skylar. "She's way too hot for you. Maybe I should keep her for myself."

I laugh. "Well, I told you she's the hottest woman I've ever seen, so you should have been prepared. Plus, I don't think Jessica would be too happy if you came home with Skylar. Where is she?"

"She's downstairs with Mom. They're in the kitchen doing girl things."

Skylar lifts an eyebrow at Ryan. "What exactly are *girl things*?"

Ryan shrugs. "I don't know. Talking recipes and stuff like that."

I pull Skylar into an embrace. "Don't worry, sweets, I prepared them for the fact that you don't know the difference between the stove and the oven."

I laugh and she smacks my arm. "I do too. The oven is where you reheat the takeout. The stove is where I keep my mail." She smiles at me and Ryan laughs.

He leaves us so we can get ready for dinner.

We make our way downstairs to the family room. My mother must have close to a hundred family pictures in frames spread around. Skylar looks through all of them while I pour us drinks.

At some point she picks up one of the frames. I notice it's of my dad shortly after he enlisted with my uncle and Aunt Melissa. She looks at me. "Is this Melissa?"

I nod. "It is. She's probably eight or nine in that picture."

"You look so much like your father. And not that it's remotely surprising, but Melissa was a gorgeous little girl. I see so much of Hayden in her."

My mother appears from nowhere and snatches the photo out of Skylar's hand. "I forgot that was in here. We don't talk about that jezebel in this house."

Skylar pinches her eyebrows together. "Who?"

"Melissa. We don't talk about her. She's no longer a member of this family." Shit. I forgot to tell Skylar how bad it is with my mom and Aunt Melissa. She knows Aunt Melissa and my father don't speak, but my mother is venomous about her. They don't know that Skylar has any connection to her.

"Why?"

"Because she got pregnant out of wedlock to that philandering sinner, and then he had the audacity to divorce her after she raised his children for him. She gave right in and let him go. She does God knows what as she dates all types of men. It's not appropriate for a woman of her age."

I walk over to Skylar, but she holds her hand up. "Not to be disrespectful, Mrs. Remington, but you have your facts all wrong. Jackson, who's now my stepfather by the way, is one of the sweetest, kindest men I've ever met. He's not remotely a philanderer, he's not a *sinner*, and their divorce was entirely mutual. Melissa's very happily remarried now to my uncle."

"We don't care for either of them."

"You're missing out. Do you even know Melissa? Did you know that she sits on the boards of several charities dedicated toward helping women that come from abusive relationships? She also donates her time to teach foreign languages to underprivileged kids. Do you know that she's an incredible mother? Do you know that she's amazing to Lance? She includes him in every family function and helped him get a great job at Jackson's company."

My mother shakes her head. "She's..."

"Enough," my father says in a booming voice. "Steph, I haven't seen my sister in ten years because of your feelings on her actions. She's obviously close to Skylar. No need to further bash the woman when she isn't here to defend herself. Skylar is a guest in our home. This family treats guests with respect."

My brother and I look at each other and widen our eyes. That's the most information we've ever gotten on their fractured relationship. It's clear my father doesn't feel as strongly as my mother. Perhaps there's some wiggle room for a reconciliation one day.

My mother leaves the room in a huff. My father looks over to Skylar. "I'm sorry for that, Skylar. It's obvious both Jackson and Melissa mean a lot to you. She should know better than to speak poorly of them."

He then turns to me. "Is what Skylar said true? Do you spend time with my sister? Did she get you a job working for Jackson?"

I nod my head. "Yes, sir. I contacted her when I moved to town. I didn't know anyone at the time, and I wanted to connect with family in the area. She immediately took me to lunch. She offered to pay for my school tuition. I declined, but she insisted on helping me get a better job so I could pay for school. I was working in a restaurant at the time, making very little money. Not only did she help me get the job, but she also bought me several suits when I started, and she does include me in all family functions. I've spent a lot of time getting to know my cousins the past few months. They've all been like brothers to me. And Jackson has promoted me to my dream job. I work with him, Trevor, and Payton every day."

"What has she mentioned about our relationship?"

I shake my head. "She's only said that it's not her business to tell me why you don't speak. That I should talk to you. She said she'd rather spend her energy building a relationship with me now. I do spend time with her, her husband, and her stepdaughter when she's staying with them. She took me to a party for Skylar's sister right around the time school started. That's where I met Skylar. I owe my entire work and social life to Aunt Melissa."

"I assume Jackson was at this party?"

"Of course. It was for his stepdaughter."

"He and Melissa speak?"

I nod. "Not only are they friends, but Aunt Melissa spends a lot of time with his wife, Skylar's mom. They're very close."

I see the look of complete confusion on my father's face. I felt the same when I first moved into the city. We don't know any divorced couples in this town. I think we all had preconceived notions about what divorce looks like.

My mother reenters the room. "And what about your

father, Skylar? I guess your parents are...*divorced* too?" She says *divorced* as if it's a dirty word.

Tears well in Skylar's eyes. I immediately go to her side. "No, my father passed away seven and a half years ago. My mom was a widow when she met Jackson. He brought her back to life after several years of deep mourning. He treats my sisters and me as if we're his own. We adore him. And we do spend a lot of time with Melissa. Jackson and Melissa have kids and grandkids together. Divorce doesn't change that fact."

My father's head snaps to me. I see a rare show of emotion in his face. "My...my sister's a grandmother?"

I nod. "Yes, Dad. She has two granddaughters and one grandson with another on the way."

I think for the first time in my life, I see tears fall out of my father's eyes.

Skylar looks up at me with tears in hers. She whispers, "I think we should get Melissa out here. Your dad obviously misses her."

I kiss her head. "You're right. I didn't realize it until just now."

The tension filled room is broken by my other two brothers, Grant and Rich, walking in with their families. A few minutes later my sister, Lucy, and her family walk in.

All of my nieces and nephews run to hug me. They all tell me how much they've missed me. I see Skylar smiling down at the interactions.

I introduce her to everyone but know it's a lot of names to memorize. I suppose it's not surprising that she seems to learn them all right away.

My youngest niece, Giselle, clings to Skylar. She's four and is clearly enamored with my gorgeous girl. I don't blame her. I am too. At dinner, she insists on sitting next to Skylar and they whisper in each other's ears the whole time.

Our big family dinner is loud, as always. Though the topics of conversation are significantly less risqué than at dinners with Skylar's family. During last week's dinner at Darian and Jackson's, I learned that Reagan calls Carter's cock *the anaconda* because of how large it is. She just referred to it that way completely matter-of-factly at dinner, and no one acted remotely surprised. I looked at Skylar in shock, and she just smiled and whispered, "This is my family. For better or worse."

Skylar fits in well with everyone here. She's charming, funny, smart, and just being her perfect self. Unfortunately, there's a bit of tension with my mother, who remains tight-lipped throughout the meal. I sort of expected that.

My father sips his beer, the one I brewed. "Hmm. This is pretty good, Lance. What kind of hops did you put in this?"

With a hint of pride, I respond, "Chinook for the bittering, Citra for the flavoring, and a little Cascade at the end, for aroma."

His prideful look matches mine. "I might have to try that on my next batch. Maybe we can brew one before you leave. You can show me exactly what you did."

I smile. "Definitely. I'd like that."

I turn to my mother. "Mom, do you need help cleaning? I'd like to show Skylar around town."

"I don't need help, but I told Roseanne you'd stop by her house. Make sure you do that."

"Mom, why in the world would you tell her that?"

"Lance, she's your future wife. The least you can do while you're in town is to see her and spend time with her. I'm sure Skylar understands that she's just a placeholder until you come home to Rosie."

That's officially the end of my rope. I slam my hand on the table and everyone jumps. "Mom!" I point to her. "Let me be perfectly clear with you. Roseanne and I broke up. We are *never* getting back together. If I've learned anything in the past few months, it's that Roseanne was comfortable. She was never my forever. I've discovered what I do and don't want. I. Don't. Want. Roseanne. If you ever again disrespect Skylar, I will immediately pack my bags and you'll never see me again. Don't you dare spend my entire life preaching about respecting others and then take every chance you get to disrespect my guest in this house. So you understand, I feel more for her in just a few months than I did for Roseanne in the nine years we spent together."

My father puts his hand on my shoulder. "That's enough, son. Why don't you and Skylar go have some fun. I want to talk to Mom. Alone." He gives my mother a look of warning. "We'll make sure the rest of your weekend here is happy."

I turn and nod at him. We say goodbye to the rest of my family and then I grab for Skylar's hand, and we walk out the door.

We head to my car in silence. When we get in and close the doors, she takes a deep breath. "Wow, things are intense at your house. I think I have a new appreciation for what Reagan dealt with at the Daulton house for months."

I grab her face and kiss her hard. "I'm so sorry you had to endure that."

She nods. "Are you completely sure you don't still have feelings for Roseanne? You can tell me. I'd rather know than have you hide it."

I shake my head. "No. Not at all. I want to be with you." I pull her chin to me and gaze into her big green eyes. "Only you."

She nods. "Okay."

I start the car and we head out toward the main road.

"You should have told me just how bad your family and Melissa's fractured relationship is. Your mom hates her and Jackson so much. And you should have told them about my connection. They clearly had no idea."

"I know. You're right. I honestly didn't think about it. I should have prepared you and them. I'm sorry."

"You know, I really think it's all your mother. Your father still obviously cares about Melissa. Maybe we can help them mend fences."

"I never realized it until tonight. He's never talked about it much other than to say that she's chosen a different path from this family. I don't think I ever understood exactly what that meant. I agree. He clearly misses her."

Skylar nods. "He got pretty emotional when he found out that she has grandkids. It was heartbreaking."

I squeeze her hand and smile. "How about a break from all this? Should we go have a little fun?"

She smiles. "Hell, yes. Where to?"

I wink. "I've been dying to take you somewhere. I won't say where. You have to see it to understand it."

I drive us through a heavily wooded area until we reach a clearing up high on a hill. I get out of the car and grab a blanket from the trunk.

Skylar exits the car and looks around. "Where are we? It's so quiet and secluded. It looks like an old-fashioned makeout place. Or a scene from a horror movie."

I laugh. "I won't lie. Teens definitely come up here to make out, but look up." I point toward the sky.

She looks up and she gasps. "Oh my god, Lance, this is amazing."

It's the highest point in the town. The skies are almost always clear. You can see the stars so perfectly out here.

I lay the blanket out for us to sit.

She leans into me. "This is incredible. It reminds me of nights with my dad. This place is so much like where he took me to look at the stars. That's where he taught me everything. It's among my favorite memories of him. It's probably what I miss the most. This is the first time I've star-gazed like this with someone else since he passed."

I can't help but smile at that.

She softly kisses my lips. "Thanks for bringing me here. I love it. It's perfect."

"Of course." I pull her hand. "Let's lay down. We can stare up at them as long as you want."

We do. She lays on my arm and we stare at all the stars.

I turn to look at her. "Tell me one of the fun facts your dad shared with you."

She gives me a big smile. "Hmm. There are a lot. I guess one that I particularly like is that space is only about sixty-two miles from us right now. If we could drive there, it would take us less than an hour."

"Really? I didn't know it was that close."

She nods. "Yep. So close, yet so far away. Now you tell me a fun fact."

"Hmm. Stars don't actually twinkle. It just looks like they do because the earth is moving."

"Yes, my dad told me that when I was little and

started singing 'Twinkle Twinkle Little Star.' I choose not to believe that one though. Tell me something else."

"Let me think of something obscure." I pause for a moment as I search my memory bank. "Ooh. I've got one. We know more about the Moon and Mars than we do about our own oceans."

She looks at me and smiles. "Really? I didn't know that."

"Yep. We've fully mapped the surface of Mars and the Moon, but we haven't even mapped ten percent of the ocean floor."

"Tell me another."

I laugh. "I'm not an endless wealth of information."

She pouts. "Please. Just one more."

"Okay. Last one." I think for a moment. "On Uranus and Neptune, it rains diamonds."

She sits up and turns to me.

I sit up and rub away the tears trickling down her cheeks. "What's wrong?"

"That's the last space fact my dad told me before he died. On our last night looking at the stars together. He told me he felt like he lived on Uranus and Neptune because my mom, my sisters, and me were his diamonds." She looks down. "I know it sounds cheesy, but it was sweet when he said it. I know he believed it too."

I lift her chin so we're looking at each other. "It doesn't sound cheesy. It sounds really nice. Since meeting you, I understand where he's coming from."

I pause for a moment and stare at her. She's looking up at the stars with such love and hope. "Skylar?"

She brings her head back down and looks at me with those big, beautiful eyes. "Yes?"

I rub her face with the back of my hand. "I love you. I'm in love with you."

She leans forward and kisses me again. She whispers, "Thank you."

She throws her leg over my body, straddling me. She grabs my face, so we're eye to eye. "I don't know if I'm ready to say it back yet. I was with someone for four years, and I thought I loved him."

She's quiet for a moment, as if in pain.

I rub her back. "What is it, sweets?"

"I've never told another soul this, but Jason cheated on me at the end. That's why we don't speak." I squeeze her tight. "The last time we were together, he told me. I kicked him out of my apartment and haven't spoken to him since."

"You didn't tell anyone, not even your sisters?"

She shakes her head. "No."

"Why didn't you tell them? You three are so close."

"I was ashamed. Like I did something wrong to make him want to cheat on me. Men don't cheat on my sisters. Just me. I love them, but they're overbearing at times. I didn't want questions or constant comments or any jokes about it, which Reagan would eventually have made."

I shake my head. "I don't think she'd do that to you. And the cheating speaks to his character, not yours. You have nothing to be ashamed about."

"On some level I know that, but it damaged me. It broke something in me. I decided not to share it with anyone."

"Why are you sharing it with me now?"

"The past few months with you have me confused as to whether I truly loved him or not. I feel so strongly for you. Our connection has been fast and fierce. It's different from the slower burn I had with him. It's had me questioning my past. Maybe I don't know what love looks like or maybe I just haven't gotten there yet. I don't want to say it again until I'm a hundred percent sure. The next time I say it, I want it to be forever. I need to wait until I know without a doubt. Is that okay?"

I can't deny that it hurts to tell someone you love them and not have them tell you back, but I certainly won't force her. On some level, I can relate. I told Roseanne I loved her too, and I know now that I didn't. Not the way I love Skylar.

I rub my hands up and down her back. "Of course. I know if I'm ever lucky enough for you to say it to me, you'll really mean it. I didn't say it just to hear it back. It's what I'm feeling, and I wanted you to know."

She smiles as she wraps her arms around me. "Thank you for understanding."

"Tell me how it's damaged you." That statement has me concerned.

"I think all this time I was under the impression that I would have trust issues with men. I kept telling myself that was the reason I didn't date for so long. I lost all faith in men. But I do trust you, Lance. That's not an issue for me. I think I don't trust myself and my judgment anymore. That's where I'm damaged. Does that make sense?"

"If it makes you feel better, I think you're perfect."

She rubs my face with her fingertips. "You make me feel better than I've felt in a really long time. You're fixing something inside of me that I feared was forever broken. I meant what I said. Thank you for loving me."

She brings her lips to mine. The kiss starts off soft. I love kissing her. I love being surrounded by her scent and taste. I love when she runs her tongue along my lips. It means she wants to deepen the kiss. As soon as she does, we both instinctually open our mouths. My cock immediately hardens. She grinds her hips onto me as soon as she feels it.

She pulls her mouth away and lifts my shirt over my head. She traces her fingertips over my chest and abs. Without looking up at me, she says, "You have the sexiest body."

She kisses her way down my chest and abs and starts to unbutton my pants.

I rub my pinkie through her waistband. "Let me take care of you first."

She reaches her hand into my jeans and begins rubbing my boxer brief covered cock. "Lance, you spend half your life with your face buried between my legs. Let me do this for you. I want to pleasure you too."

"Sweets, the look on your face when you come is just about the most pleasurable thing I've ever experienced. I crave it. I'm addicted to it."

She stands and gives me a sexy smirk. "Can I suggest a compromise?"

I smile back. "I didn't realize we're in the boardroom, Ms. Lawrence. What do you have in mind? I may be willing to negotiate a little."

She slowly undresses until she's standing there completely naked. I rub my hand up her leg. "You have such a perfect body. I've never seen anything more beautiful."

Her entire body flushes at my words. I love it.

"Lay down."

I do. She walks behind me and places her knees on either side of my head, facing down my body. She leans forward and slides down my boxer briefs, pulling my cock out and into her soft, warm hand.

Forget the stars in the sky, I currently have the best

view on this planet. Skylar's perfect, glistening, pink pussy.

I pull her down and take my first lick of her just as she takes hers of me.

AN HOUR LATER, we're walking into the Main Street Tavern arm in arm. We're smiling and kissing as we walk through the door.

She says into my lips, "Is it weird that I love kissing you after you've gone down on me? There's something so intimate and erotic about it. And considering how much you go down on me, if I didn't, I'd never be able to kiss you."

I smile into her lips. "Skylar is my favorite dessert flavor. I don't blame you at all."

She giggles.

"It's a good thing you're tall, sweets. I don't think I could physically do what we just did with any other woman."

"What do you mean?"

"I'm six feet, six inches. I'm a long man. If it were a normal-sized woman leaning over me, with her mouth on me, I'd be licking her kneecaps."

She starts hysterically laughing. "I never thought of that. I wonder how it works for Brody and Harley. She's tiny."

She rubs my face. "I guess we fit together well, don't we? I love that you're so big. I love that you can pick me up and toss me around. A *normal*-sized man can't do that with me."

She runs her eyes down my body to just below my belt. "You're definitely not *normal*-sized."

We both smile as we kiss again.

A familiar female voice breaks us from our bubble. "Lance? Is that you?"

I turn my head and see Roseanne standing there. She has tears stinging her eyes.

"Hey, Rosie. It's good to see you." I give her a small smile. "You look great."

She swallows hard. I know her well enough to know that she's hurting and is trying to put on a brave face right now. "Thank you."

She pauses for a moment. "Is this your...your girlfriend?"

I nod. "Yes. This is Skylar. Skylar, this is Roseanne."

Skylar holds out her hand. "It's a pleasure to meet you. I've heard so many nice things about you." Roseanne shakes it.

Skylar rubs my arm. "I see your brother shooting pool. I'm going to join him so you two can speak alone."

I look at her in question. She mouths, "Talk to her."

I kiss her cheek and whisper in her ear, "I love you."

She walks over to Ryan at the pool table. Within seconds, he's laughing. She makes everyone around her happy. I can't help but watch her.

"Lance."

Shit. I was just staring at Skylar. I'm such a dick.

"Sorry, Rosie." I motion for her to take a seat at the bar. "Can I get you a drink?"

She shakes her head. "No, I'm okay. I just stopped by for a burger on my way home from work. I was just about to leave when I saw you walk in."

I see the longtime bartender approach us. "Hey, Theo. How are you?"

He smiles at me. "I'm good. It's great to see you, Lance. Are you moving back home?"

I shake my head. "No, just visiting. Can I get my usual and a lemon drop martini for my girl?"

"Sure thing, Lance."

Roseanne gives me a half smile. "She's very pretty."

I nod. "She is. How have you been?"

She shrugs. "I'm okay. I thought I'd hear from you more. Honestly, I was hoping you'd realize what you were missing and move back home."

I give her a sad smile. "Rosie, that's not going to happen. I always told you that I wanted city life. I'm happy living there. I'm...I'm happy with Skylar."

She nods. "I see it. I saw the way you looked at her when you two walked in. In nine years, I don't think you ever looked at me that way."

I grab her hand. "Rosie, I'll always care about you. What you and I shared was special. We had all our firsts together. That's a bond that can never be broken. I want you to find someone that looks at you that same way. That loves you the way you deserve. You're a wonderful person. There's so much to love."

"But *you* don't love me."

"Not like that. I'm so sorry. You're going to find someone one day and you'll realize that what we shared was special, but not forever. It was young and amazing, but we both grew out of it and needed someone different. Someone that wants the same future."

"Is she your forever?"

I look over at Skylar smiling and laughing with Ryan. My heart swells and I know the true answer. "She is."

"She's very lucky."

Theo hands me my beer and places the martini in front of Roseanne. She slides it over to me and looks at Theo. "I'm not his girl anymore."

She stands and kisses my cheek. "Bye, Lance." She turns and walks out the door.

I feel terrible, but I think she needed that final closure to move on.

I grab the drinks and make my way over to the pool table. I quietly place them on the ledge and wrap my arms around Skylar from behind. I nuzzle into her and kiss her neck.

"Hmm. Don't tell Lance, but your lips feel good."

I turn her around in my arms and she smiles. She feigns shock. "Oh, Lance. I didn't realize it was you."

"Let me remind you." I pull her tight to my body and kiss the hell out of her.

She wraps her arms around my neck and kisses me back. I hear whistling from other people standing around, but I just don't care.

When she moans into my mouth, I just about lose it, but my brother clears his throat.

We break the kiss and look at him. He smiles. "This should be an interesting night in Mom's house. You know she's going to stand guard all night."

"We'll behave, right Lance?" She gives me a wink and a conspiratorial smile.

I smile back at her. "We sure will."

My brother whistles. "Glad I'm not sleeping there tonight."

I give Skylar her drink and we have fun shooting pool.

At some point when Skylar is talking to someone else, my brother nudges me. "You need to tone it down, man. Mom will legitimately flip if she catches you in Skylar's bed."

I shake my head. "I just don't care, Ry. Look at her." We both stare at Skylar laughing with a woman she just met. She's so damn beautiful. "I can't and won't keep my hands off her. Mom and Dad don't control me anymore. I've broken free of this town and their rules. I make good money. They don't pull my purse-strings anymore. I respect them, but I don't live in their house, and I don't subscribe to their way of life. It's pretty liberating. You should try it."

"Fuck you, Lance. They don't control me, but I live in the same town as them. I work with Dad. Mom cares for my kids. I can't just disrespect them like you can. I wouldn't want to."

"I don't think me trying to make it on my own and living my dream, not theirs, is being disrespectful. I love my life in the city. I love school. I love my job. And I love Skylar. There's nothing Mom and Dad can say that will change any of that."

"A blind man can see that you're in love with her. Does she love you?"

"I don't know. She hasn't said so."

He puts his hand on my shoulder. "Take some advice from your big brother. Tone it down. You guys come from different worlds. She's amazing, but things could go sideways. I don't want to see you hurt."

CHAPTER SEVENTEEN

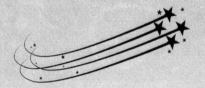

SKYLAR

I awaken to the familiar feeling of Lance's head between my legs. Maybe a day will come where this has worn out its welcome, but I'm most definitely not there yet.

I blink a few times. It's still dark out.

I sleepily whisper, "What time is it?"

He looks up with a face covered in me. There's nothing hotter. He whispers back, "It's four in the morning. I have to get up at five to help, and I need time to sneak back into my room, but I didn't want you to miss your daily wake-up call. You can go back to sleep when I'm done."

I push his head. "Okay. Less talking."

He smiles as he drops his head and licks through me, expertly making me come in just a few minutes. He plays my body like a violin. I have to cover my mouth with a pillow throughout my entire orgasm.

I must fall back asleep quickly, because the next thing I know, it's a few hours later and bright outside.

I get dressed and go downstairs. Lance's mom is sitting in

the kitchen with a mug of coffee. I smile at her. "Good morning."

"Morning." She gives me a half smile of acknowledgement.

Lance's mom dresses demure and wears no makeup, but she's attractive in an understated way. She has light hair, like his, but she has big brown eyes. Lance has his father's dark blue eyes. He looks so much like his father. Though I did catch dimples on his mom the one time she smiled at dinner, when Lance and his father were talking about brewing beer.

I point to the nearly full coffee pot. "May I?"

She nods. I walk over to the counter, my back to her, and pour myself a cup.

"Does your mother know what you do? How you behave?"

I've had about all I can take from this woman. I take a deep breath as a turn around. "Does my mother know that her twenty-six-year-old daughter is appropriately in a physical relationship with her monogamous boyfriend? Yes. Of course she knows. My family is extremely close and open. We spend a lot of time together. She adores Lance and sees that her daughter is happy. She supports *all* aspects of our relationship wholeheartedly; she doesn't judge us."

I'm growing increasingly grateful for my mom and the type of non-judgmental, supportive family I have. I do get frustrated with them for being overbearing sometimes, but I'll take their brand of in your face love over this any day of the week.

"You're not right for him. He needs to come home. He needs to marry Roseanne. Why can't you see that? You're standing in the way of his future. His destiny."

"He's happy. Doesn't that matter to you? He loves living in the city. He loves school and his job. He and I have a healthy, wonderful relationship. He doesn't want the small town, farm lifestyle. You must recognize that?"

I see tears well in her eyes. "I don't want to lose him."

That's what this is about. It's not about me. It's about her wanting him close by. I can sympathize with that.

I sit down at the table with her and reach my hand across and grab hers. "I don't think that's going to happen. He loves you and he's such a good person. He just doesn't want to live the small-town life. Whether I'm in the picture or not, I don't think Lance will ever move back here. He's enamored with city life. That's where he wants to be."

"Cities are for sin. Look at Melissa."

"People can sin anywhere, in cities and small towns. You raised a good man. You should be proud of that. He'll be a good man wherever he lives, whether here or in the city. As for Melissa, I don't think you know her at all. You're judging her for making different decisions than you, but different doesn't mean wrong. Like Lance, she's also a good person. She and Jackson raised three incredible sons. It's a shame they don't know their aunt and uncle and the rest of their cousins. I know they would welcome you into their lives with open arms if you were willing. Jackson was an only child. The cousins here are the only ones Payton, Trevor, and Hayden have. I imagine they'd really love to get to know them. They've already become incredibly close with Lance. They honestly treat him like a brother."

Just then, Lance's father walks in. He clearly notices the tension but smiles at me, nonetheless. "Did you sleep well, Skylar?"

I return his smile. "I did, thank you. Have you seen Lance?"

"Yes, I just left him out back. He's about to take the tractor out. If you hurry, you can probably still catch him before he heads out to the fields."

"I will. Thank you."

I quickly rinse my coffee cup, run out back, and see him.

I've certainly never been into the whole farmer thing, but if I were ever considering it, now is the time.

Lance is on a tractor, in jeans, boots, a cowboy hat, and no shirt. His big muscles are sweaty and rippling. I feel like the soundtrack from *Footloose* is going to turn on at any moment.

I wave my hands until he sees me. As soon as he does, he breaks out in a big smile with those fucking delicious dimples on full display.

He takes my breath away. He's so incredibly sexy, and so incredibly unaware of it.

He cuts the engine and tips his hat to me. "Howdy, ma'am. You lookin' for a ride?"

I lick my lips. I can feel my whole body flushing. "You bet I am."

I take one step up on the tractor until we're eye to eye. "You look insanely hot right now." I run my finger along his sweaty chest and then bring it to my mouth and suck on it. "You taste insanely hot too."

His eyes light up as he runs his tongue along his lower lip. "I may know of a secluded area. It's out of sight."

"Perfect."

I quickly climb up and sit on his lap. I lean back and take in his scent. He smells like sweat and Lance. I'm a minute away from combustion. "Hurry up."

He laughs as he turns the tractor back on and we take off away from the house.

He lets me steer for a bit, which doesn't help my current situation, because when my hands are on the wheel, his are free to roam my body. Over my shirt. Under my shirt. Under my bra. Why doesn't this damn thing go faster?

I'm a wet, throbbing mess. I have to squeeze my legs

together. The vibrations of the tractor are only contributing to the stimulation.

At some point, when we're well out of sight, he stops and cuts the engine. I stand and make quick work of my shoes, socks, leggings, and panties. He laughs at my haste.

I immediately straddle his body. I start licking and kissing his neck and chest. The smell and taste of his sweat are driving me wild with need.

I breathe, "I need you inside me in the next ten seconds."

I reach down and frantically unbutton and unzip his jeans, pulling him out and stroking him.

"Sweets, let me get you ready."

"Trust me, I'm ready."

He picks me up and turns me around, so my back is to his front. I love how easily he maneuvers my body. I lift so I can bring his tip to my entrance and sink down onto him.

I lift my chin and breathe into the sky, "God, yes."

I grip the steering wheel for leverage and start moving my body on his. He grabs my hips and helps my movements. He thrusts himself up into me every time I come down on him.

My body is completely overheating with desire. I can feel myself dripping down onto him. I'm not sure why this whole scene has me riled up, but it does.

I hear him in my ear, "Your tits. I need your tits."

Without breaking stride, I remove my top and bra.

He reaches in front of me and turns the engine back on. The added vibrations cause a tingling up and down my body. I want him everywhere. I *need* him everywhere.

He grabs onto my breasts with his hands. I reach back with one hand and grab a fistful of his hair, bringing his body as close to mine as physically possible. I'm craving as much contact with him as possible. I'm ravenous for it.

He licks up my shoulder and neck and whispers in my ear. "You're so fucking beautiful. I can feel what my cock is doing

212

to you. Can you hear how turned on you are right now? Even with the engine running, I can hear and smell your arousal. It's so hot. You're so damn hot."

I have no clue what the noises are that come out of my mouth next. I mumble something about how wet I am and how sexy he is.

Lance shifts the tractor into gear, places his foot on the gas, and it starts moving. His hands are still on my breasts though.

"You steer, Sweets."

"What? I can't see straight right now."

He removes one of his hands from my breast and moves it toward the steering wheel.

I immediately grab it and put it back on me. I place my hands on the steering wheel.

"Keep touching me. Don't stop."

"I'll *never* stop touching you. Your pussy is squeezing me so hard, sweets. I won't last much longer. You feel amazing."

"I'm almost there." I white-knuckle squeeze the wheel, attempting to steer, and increase the pace of my movements on him.

The vibrations and bumps are blowing my mind. "Ah Lance, it's so good."

I feel his cock swell inside me, and that's my final undoing. I yell out into my all-encompassing orgasm at the same time he grunts into his. I literally explode onto him as he explodes into me.

He mercifully pulls his foot off the gas so I can squeeze my eyes shut to enjoy this moment of bliss.

My legs feel like Jell-O. My body nearly collapses off the tractor, but he holds me up.

No part of me wants the connection to end. I keep moving but begin to gradually slow down. We're both a sweaty, panting mess. We're sticky, covered in each other's juices.

He turns my head with both hands and moves his lips to mine, giving me a long, lazy kiss. He finishes it off by sucking on my tongue.

When our breathing returns closer to normal, we break our mouths apart. He moves his fingers down and runs them through me. He brings them back up, completely covered in my juices.

"I don't think I've ever felt you that wet. You soaked me." He licks his fingers. "Hmm. I love your taste. It's now my goal to get you that way every single day."

I nibble at his lips and smile into his mouth. "Who knew the whole farmer thing would do it for me? I might have to find some farmer porn."

He smiles. "You know, I can always dress up as a farmer for you."

"Oooh. I think I'd like that."

He stands, placing me on the tractor seat, kicks off his boots and jeans, and steps off the tractor.

What he does next makes my brain explode. He spreads my legs wide, slips his fingers in to part me, and then proceeds to lick me clean. I mean every last drop. And there was a lot.

When he's done, he lifts his head, licks his lips, and moans. Despite coming moments ago, he hardens again.

The taste of me after we had sex made him hard. I sit there, mouth wide open, barely able to comprehend what's happening.

He immediately grabs and lifts me so I'm straddling him, walking us toward a downward-sloped hill. I wrap my naked body around his.

"Where are we going?"

"There's a meadow down here. Let's rinse off before we go

back reeking of sex. It's my favorite smell, but I doubt my parents will be into it."

"You're certainly right about that. I'm a big fat sinner, bringing out the sinner in you."

"Oh crap. I guess you and my mom had words this morning. I'm sorry. I shouldn't have left you alone in the house."

"I can hold my own, Lance." I run my fingers through his hair. "I realized that she's just a mom who misses her son. My mom would hate it if one of us moved away. Yours is afraid of losing you. I told her that would never happen. You're too good of a man to walk away from his family."

He kisses my neck. "Let's stop talking about my mom while we're naked and your pussy is rubbing against my cock."

I giggle as I wiggle my hips to rub up and down that hard cock. "Are we planning another round in the water?"

He smiles. "I can't go back like this, so I guess we have to."

He carries me down and steps into the water until it comes up to just below our chests.

"Hold your breath."

I do and he quickly dunks us. As soon as we break the surface, he starts kissing me again. His lips take mine with his tongue immediately pushing into my mouth.

He's so loving and passionate. His constant need to kiss me, touch me, and be close to me is as strong as mine is for him.

I think I do love him. Maybe I should have told him last night when he told me. I can't imagine myself with anyone else. I can't imagine ever wanting anyone the way I want him. I just couldn't get the words out. I know I'm afraid of getting my heart broken again. I don't think I could come back from that.

I'm lost in my thoughts and our kiss when we hear a throat

clear. We both turn our heads and look toward the top of the hill. Ryan is standing there with a big grin.

Not that anything but my back is exposed, but Lance pulls my body tight to his making sure his big arms are covering as much of me as possible.

"Here we are, *again*. Sorry to interrupt, *again*, but Mom and Dad are looking for you."

"What do they want?"

"They know you're not getting any work done if Skylar is with you. Dad wanted to go look for you, but I offered."

"Alright. We'll be back in a bit. Thanks."

Ryan smiles but doesn't leave. "Hey, Skylar."

"Hi, Ryan. Do you want to maybe turn around and leave so we can get out?"

He gives a guilty smile. "Oh, right. Sure." He points behind him but doesn't actually turn to leave. "I'm heading out. Though I'm in dry clothes if you need someone else to hold onto."

Lance practically growls, but Ryan laughs. "I'm just kidding. Man, I've never seen you so crazy possessive. I didn't think you had it in you."

"Keep your eyes off my girl. Bye."

Ryan walks away.

"I'm sorry, sweets."

"It's okay. I kind of like when you get all possessive. It's sexy."

He looks surprised. "Is it?"

I nod. "Yes."

We get dressed and head back toward the house. Lance's father asks him to brew a little beer before we leave. I head up to shower, dress, and pack.

LANCE

My father and I walk down to the basement toward the brewing area. It hasn't changed at all since I left. In fact, it looks untouched.

"Dad, you haven't been brewing?"

He shakes his head. "I like doing it with you. I'd rather wait for your visits. It's not as fun to do alone."

Without skipping a beat, we begin our regular division of labor. It's been the same for years.

It's quiet for a bit, but he eventually breaks the silence. "You seem happy, Lance."

I smile. "I'm extremely happy. I'm enjoying school and my job. Everything is perfect. It's everything I hoped for. It's exceeded the fantasy."

"I've never thought of you as unhappy before, but seeing you this happy makes me question my actions over the past few years. Perhaps I should have supported you leaving earlier."

I nod. "I have no regrets. It all brought me to this point."

"I'm sorry that I cut off your funding. It was a mistake and petty. Give me your tuition bills. I'll take care of it."

I shake my head. "There's no need. I've already paid for this year and next."

"I thought you said you didn't accept my sister's money."

"I didn't. I secured, well... Skylar and I secured a huge project together. My bonus check for it covered everything."

His eyes widen. "Wow, Lance. That's significant money. You must be very good at what you do." He puts his hand on my shoulder. "I'm proud of you."

I don't think my father has ever uttered those words to me before. It means everything to me.

"Thanks, Dad."

"You've grown up so much. This has been good for you."

I nod, happy that he realizes it.

"And Skylar? You seem quite serious about her."

"Yes, sir. I'm very serious."

"She seems, very...strong-willed."

I can't help but smile. "Yes, sir. It's one of the things I love the most about her. You should see her in business. I learn from her constantly."

"Love? You love her?"

I nod. "Yes, sir. She's everything to me."

"I see." He's quiet for a moment. "Given how fond she is of my sister, am I correct to assume the feeling is mutual?"

"Yes. Aunt Melissa is very fond of Skylar and her two sisters."

"And they're all Jackson's stepdaughters?" He still looks surprised by all of this.

I smile. "I don't think divorce is always as bad as we've been made to believe. I don't remember much of Jackson and Aunt Melissa together, but they're both very happy now. Trevor has told me that their marriage wasn't great. Both of their marriages now are solid. Jackson is totally enamored with Skylar's mom. And Aunt Melissa's husband is obsessed with her."

"What does that mean?"

"He's very possessive of her."

I see a small smirk creep on his face. He mumbles to himself, "After all that, she ended up with a possessive man." He looks up at me. "In an unhealthy way?"

I shake my head. "Not that I've seen. It doesn't seem

to bother her at all. She's a strong woman too. She can handle herself. Maybe it's time for you to reach out to her, Dad. I think she'd like that."

He takes a deep breath. "Let me work on your mother regarding my sister and Skylar. Your mother is strong-willed just like them."

"Yes, sir."

WE GOT BACK to the city this afternoon. I'm leaving for a four-day business trip tomorrow. Jackson wants me to meet with the landowners of a large property to be developed in Chicago. I've never been there. I'm excited to see the city.

Skylar and I want to spend the night together since we won't see each other for a few days. It will be the longest we've been apart since we started dating.

She's at her mom's and Jackson's for dinner. Jade wasn't feeling great, so Aunt Melissa and Declan stayed home. I told them I'd have dinner with them tonight. I'll head over to Skylar's afterward. I want to talk to Aunt Melissa about my father.

I say hello to Jerry, the security officer in her lobby. I'm on her pre-approved list of visitors, so he lets me straight through to the elevator, which opens right into her enormous condo.

I walk in with a bottle of Patron tequila, her favorite. She smiles when she sees me. "Lance, you don't need to bring something every time you come here."

"Yes, I do. That's what you're supposed to do when someone invites you to their home."

She shakes her head. "Family doesn't have to be so

formal and proper. Speaking of family, how was your weekend? Did Skylar survive your mother?"

I can't help but chuckle. "Barely. She sticks out like a sore thumb there."

"I could have told you that. Was your mother tough on her?"

We walk through to her living room. I nod at Declan who's on the couch watching a basketball game, and he nods in return.

Aunt Melissa and I both sit. She instinctively leans back into him, and he instinctively puts his arm around her waist and pulls her close. I notice that neither of them even thought about it. It's sweet.

"She was, but Skylar can handle herself. She's not one to take it on the chin. She gave it right back to my mother. In fact," I clear my throat, "she gave it to her about you."

Aunt Melissa pinches her eyebrows together. "Me?"

Here's my opening. "Yes, you. My mother made some generally unkind references to you and living in the city. Skylar wasn't having it and sung your praises. From how you spend your time to how you raised your family. You definitely have a fan in Skylar."

Aunt Melissa smiles at that. "She has a fan in me too. You know that."

I nod and continue, "What was interesting, was that my father wasn't completely onboard with my mother. He clearly misses you. Skylar and I both think he'd like to reconcile with you. He got very emotional when I mentioned that you have grandchildren. I think I saw tears in his eyes."

"Craig Remington cried?"

"He wasn't bawling. He was emotional though. He misses you."

Tears well in her eyes. "I miss him too."

I grab her hand. "I know you do. I want to help mend fences. I'll take a ride with you out there sometime. I think you two should talk."

She slowly nods. "Maybe."

Declan pulls her tight to him and interrupts. "She's not going anywhere without me. If he hurts her or fucking disrespects her in any way, I'll deck him. I don't care if he's your father."

She rolls her eyes and then winks at me, mouthing, "You and I will go."

I can't help but smile.

CHAPTER EIGHTEEN

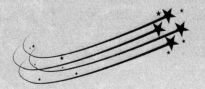

SKYLAR

I have my phone on speaker while I look through my drawers.

"Yes, Mom. Everything is fine."

"You seem distracted, doll face."

"Lance is landing any minute. I haven't seen him all week. I'm excited he's back. I missed him."

"Ah, I see. Are you going through your lingerie drawer right now deciding what to wear?"

I let out a laugh. "I find it disturbing that you know that."

Now she laughs. "I know how it works, sweetie. Have fun. Be safe."

I roll my eyes. "I will. I'll call you later...or...maybe tomorrow."

"Tomorrow is fine. Love you."

"Love you too."

I end the call and decide on a pink lace number. It's spaghetti strap, see-through, and my boobs look huge in it, but

I have a feeling he won't mind. I grab the matching see-through lace panties too.

My phone rings again. I look at the caller ID and smile. It's Lance. I accept the call. "Hey, babe."

"Hey, sweets. I just landed. Are you home?"

"Of course I'm home. I'm waiting for you."

"Okay, I should be there in about thirty minutes."

"Do you want a drink? I can open a bottle."

"I want you. I need to drink you."

I smile. "That can be arranged too."

He's going to ravage me tonight. I can't wait.

"I'll see you in a bit." He's silent for a moment. "Skylar?"

"Yes?"

"I missed you. Like *really* missed you."

I can't help but smile again. "I missed you too. Hurry so I can show you how much. I think you'll like what I'm wearing for you. It's very tiny and very see-through."

I hear him moan. "I'm going to be walking through the airport with a boner."

"I'm sure people are used to it by now. You always have a boner."

He laughs. "True. I'll see you soon."

I end the call, brush my teeth, clean up a bit, and slip into the pink lingerie. I examine myself in the mirror. I look pretty good. I think he'll be happy.

I unlock the door so he can come right in, light a bunch of candles, and lay down on the couch.

About twenty-five minutes after his call, there's a knock at the door.

In the sexist voice I can muster, I say, "Come in."

The door opens, as does my mouth. It's not Lance. It's Jason. My ex-boyfriend Jason. The man I dated for four years. The man who shattered my heart into a million pieces.

He takes a step inside, and when he sees me, his eyes widen. "Wow, that's a greeting a guy can get used to."

You can easily see every part of me in this outfit. I stand up and cross one arm over my chest and one below my waist.

"Jason? What are you doing here?"

He smiles. "I came to see you. I've missed you. I want to talk about us."

Before I can register what's happening, Lance walks through the open door. He looks at Jason and then at my state of undress. "What's going on here?"

"I...I thought he was you and told him to come in."

"Who is he?"

"Umm...this is Jason."

Jason holds out his hand. "Her boyfriend."

Lance doesn't shake his hand back.

"Jason, cut it out. This is Lance, my *actual* boyfriend."

Lance glares at Jason, and Jason glares right back. This could escalate. It won't go well for Jason. Lance has six inches and at least fifty pounds of muscle on him.

I see Lance take a breath. "I think it's time for you to leave. *My* girlfriend and I clearly have plans for the evening." He moves his eyes up and down my body and then turns his head and smirks at Jason.

Jason smirks back. "I've had those nights with her too. Four years of them. How many have you had?"

I see Lance's hands fisting. I look at him and shake my head, begging him to stay calm.

He takes another deep breath, walks over to the couch, and grabs a blanket. He wraps it around me. Something I probably should have already done myself.

Jason scoffs. "Dude, it's nothing I haven't seen before. I know firsthand the sweetness under there." He licks his lips and winks at Lance. "I've tasted it."

Oh. Shit.

Before I can remotely stop him, Lance charges at Jason and tackles him to the ground. They start trading punches.

I scream for them to stop, but no one listens. They're going at it like madmen.

They're rolling around. I don't know how to stop it.

Everything is getting knocked over. Things are breaking. I quickly move the candles out of harm's way.

I guess Randy heard the commotion because he comes running in. "Oh my." He pulls Lance off Jason.

He pushes Lance's chest. "Relax, Lance."

They're both a bloody mess, both breathing heavily, both practically snarling at the other. While Lance has a mark on his face, Jason looks like he just went ten rounds with a professional boxer.

Randy looks at me. "Baby girl, I think one of them needs to go."

I nod. Jason looks at me. "Which one of us?"

I briefly look between Lance and Jason.

"You, Jason. Just go."

"I need to talk to you. It's important."

"Fine. Text me and I'll meet you for coffee sometime. Leave. Now."

He hesitates for a moment, opening and closing his mouth a few times. "Tomorrow. I want to talk tomorrow."

"Whatever. Fine. Please go."

Mercifully, he turns and leaves.

Randy looks at me. "Are you okay in here with him?"

I nod. "Yes, thanks for the help, Randy."

Randy leaves and closes the door behind him. I quickly lock it and then approach Lance. "Are you okay?"

"I'm fine." He looks dejected. "Why was he here? Did you invite him?"

"Did I invite him here while I was waiting in lingerie for

you, knowing you were coming any minute? No, Lance. Obviously not."

"Did you know he was in town?"

"Lance, I haven't communicated with him once since the day I kicked him out of this apartment a year and a half ago. I swear to you."

I gently touch under his eye. "It's already swelling. Sit down with your head back. I'll go get you some ice."

I walk into my kitchen and gather a bag of ice. An idea occurs to me.

I quickly and quietly run into my bedroom to change.

When I return to the living room, Lance is sitting on the sofa with his head tilted back on the cushion and eyes closed.

I straddle his lap, wipe his face clean, and place the ice on his upper cheek. I pepper kisses on his neck. "I'm sorry our night was ruined. I was looking forward to it."

His eyes are still closed, but he answers, "Me too."

"I missed you this week."

"I missed you too."

"Why did you attack him?"

"He disrespected you."

"You know he *has* seen me. We were together for four years."

"I didn't like the way he said it. And I don't need to hear that. In my mind, I'm the only man that's ever seen your beautiful, naked body."

I smile as I grab his head and lift it. His eyes start to peel open. "You mean this body?"

His eyes pop wide open and he whispers, "Holy shit."

I smile as he stares at me in my very tiny, very short, very tight, naughty nurse costume.

His eyes move up and down my body as his breathing picks up and his cock immediately hardens. I love the way I affect him.

I swivel my hips and his eyes flutter.

"Tell me where it hurts, Mr. Remington, and Nurse Skylar will kiss it better."

He smiles. His dimples are out, and I know he's now putty in my hands. "Everywhere. I hurt everywhere."

I pick up his hand. "Does it hurt here?"

He nods and I kiss it.

I move to his arm. "What about here?"

He nods. I kiss my way up his arm.

I unbutton his shirt and run my fingers across his broad chest. "What about here?"

He nods again and I start peppering his chest with open mouth kisses.

I run through this same routine with a few more areas on his body. Eventually I ask, "Tell me where it hurts the most."

He smirks. "He got me right between the legs."

"Is that so?"

He nods.

"Are you shy, Mr. Remington? Should I bring in one of the male nurses to check you there?"

He shakes his head. "No, ma'am. Nurse Skylar is exactly what I need. Maybe she can help me with a sponge bath in a little while too."

I smile as I start to move down his body, but he grabs my elbow. "I think it would feel better if you weren't wearing any panties while kissing it better."

"If you think it will help."

He swallows and nods.

I stand and turn around, bending over while removing my panties. I hear him suck in a breath.

He runs his hand down my exposed ass and the back of my thigh.

I turn around.

His eyes move up my body until they land on my eyes.

"You're a real-life dream come true, Nurse Skylar." He grabs his cock through his pants and squeezes it.

He licks his lips. "Unbutton the top few buttons. I think visual stimulation helps with healing."

"I'm sorry, sir, but I'm not wearing a bra and hospital policy says that I can't reveal my breasts to patients."

"I promise I won't tell anyone. I think I need it to feel better."

I pretend to think for a moment. "Hmm. I suppose anything for the patient."

I unbutton the top few buttons and my breasts spill out.

His breathing picks up. "Nurse Skylar, I think I need them in my mouth to help with swelling."

I look down at his cock clearly straining against his pants. "Mr. Remington, they seem to be contributing to the swelling, not helping it."

He unbuttons and unzips his pants. He pulls out his gigantic cock, giving it a few long pumps. With his other hand, he crooks his finger for me to come to him. "Nurse Skylar, you're going to have to sit on this to help with the swelling."

"I need to kiss it first. I'm the nurse. I know what's best for my patient."

I get down on my knees in front of him. I bend over and give his balls an open-mouthed kiss.

He sucks in another breath through his teeth.

I slowly kiss my way up his long length, applying open-mouthed kisses the whole way.

I look up at him. "Is it starting to feel better?"

He shakes his head. "Yes, keep going."

I reach the top and kiss him there, his pre-ejaculate coating my lips. I lift my head and slowly lick my lips. "Hmm, Mr. Remington. You taste good."

He's white knuckle gripping the sofa, close to losing control. "Nurse Skylar, please."

"Please what?"

"Please suck my cock."

I lightly run my fingertips up and down his cock. "Mr. Remington, is it frustrating for me to go this slow? I can't *possibly* imagine what that's like." I can't help the small smirk on my face. I hope he now understands how hard it is at times when he slowly devours my body.

"If I promise not to go slow anymore, will you put my cock in your mouth?"

I don't bother to respond; I know he likes to savor my body. I won't take that from him. And if I'm being honest, he's right. Once he does finally touch me, I go off like a firework.

I grab the base and take him into my mouth. He lets out an audible sigh.

I feel every hard ridge and vein as I take him deep into my throat. I move him in and out, enjoying every inch with my tongue.

He gathers my hair with his hands. "Sweets, you're so fucking good at this."

His reaction is turning me on. I can feel my slickness seeping onto my thighs. I can't help but rub my legs together and let out a moan.

He notices immediately. "Nurse Skylar, touch yourself."

I don't need to be told twice. I reach down and run my hand through my folds. I'm so wet.

He moves his head so he can see what I'm doing.

"Nurse Skylar, it's time to sit on my cock and make us both all better."

I love that he stays in character.

I keep bobbing my head, but he pulls my hair until I'm off him. "Sit. On. Me. Stuff my cock into that magical pussy of yours and make everything better."

"Well, I did take an oath to give my patients whatever they need to get better."

He whispers, "Come here. I need you."

I straddle his lap again, bring his tip to my entrance, and sink down onto him.

He moans, "Oh, fuck yes."

He grabs my breasts and alternates taking each nipple into his warm mouth.

He looks up. "You've cured me."

CHAPTER NINETEEN

SKYLAR

I peel my eyes open to the morning light. Not surprising in the least, Lance is under the blankets with his mouth between my legs.

I run my fingers through his hair, letting him know I'm awake, and he picks up the pace, giving me what he knows I need.

I guess my moans are loud because I don't hear the door open. Suddenly, I see Harley and Reagan standing in my bedroom.

Even though Lance is under the blanket, it's obvious what he's doing.

Reagan smiles. "Who's under there, Skylar? Anyone we know?"

Lance pops his head out, face covered in my juices. "Who the hell else would it be?"

Reagan and Harley start laughing.

I look down at him. "Handsome, they're just messing with you. They have a deranged sense of humor."

I turn to them. "Can you two get the hell out of here so he can finish what he started?"

Harley picks up the nurse costume on the floor. "Was he in need of urgent medical care?" She smiles. "I'm a doctor. I can help if he needs it."

I yell, "Get out!"

They both giggle as they leave my bedroom and close the door behind them.

I look down at Lance and smile. "Now get back to work. You have to pay off your medical bills from last night."

He smiles back at me. "Yes, ma'am."

After he makes me come, we both get dressed and walk out of the bedroom. My apartment is completely cleaned of the mess created by the fight last night. I look at Lance in question.

He gives me a guilty smile. "I cleaned up after you went to bed. I didn't want you to have to do it in the morning."

He's so damn thoughtful. "Thank you."

We walk into my kitchen and see my sisters drinking coffee and talking.

They turn when they notice us. Reagan smiles. "Look, it's our favorite Cunnilinguist."

Harley asks, "Did you enjoy the bikini burger you had for breakfast today?"

Reagan stretches. "I hear you also like Egg McMuffs for breakfast."

Harley shakes her head. "Don't you give us any *lip* service, Lance."

Reagan shrugs. "It's cute that he likes playing in the sandbox."

Harley smiles. "Don't speak in tongues over there, Lance."

Reagan responds, "Oh stop. He likes to whistle in the weeds. There's nothing wrong with that."

Harley nods. "And worship at the altar."

Reagan rubs her tummy. "Was it yummilingus?"

I put up my hands. "Oh my god. Stop. Did you two sit out here and Google every term for him going down on me?"

They both giggle.

I shake my head. "Whatever you want to call it, Lance is a certified professional pearl diver."

Now all three of us are laughing hysterically.

Lance shakes his head. "You all have a weird relationship."

I wrap my arms around his neck. "Yes, there's a giant boundary issue in this family. You know that. You'll have to get used to it."

Reagan notices Lance's eye. "Is she into beating you in addition to dressing up?"

Lance looks at me as to how to answer her.

I softly kiss his lips. "I'll deal with them. You should get going to class."

He says his goodbyes to us and walks out the door.

After I close the door behind him, I return to the kitchen and sit with them at the table.

Reagan hands me a mug of coffee. "Does he seriously wake you up that way every single morning? I thought you were exaggerating, but maybe not."

I nod. "When we sleep together, which is almost every night, yes. It's insane. Sometimes more than once. He loves it so much." I moan. "And he's so damn good at it."

They both laugh.

"He sometimes turns down a blow job so he can go down on me instead. I've never known a man to turn down a blow job."

They look at me in disbelief.

Harley motions her head toward the door. "What was with the black eye?"

I bite my lip. "Jason showed up here last night."

Harley's chin drops. "Jason, Jason?"

"Yep."

"What did he want?"

I shrug. "I'm not a hundred percent sure. I thought it was Lance, so I let him in wearing see through lingerie. He eye-fucked me and then told me he misses me and wants to talk. Then Lance walked in. He covered me with a blanket, and Jason made some comment about his efforts being wasted since he's both seen and tasted me. Lance lost his shit and attacked Jason. They got into a fist fight before Randy broke it up. I asked Jason to leave, but he made me agree to meet him to talk before doing so."

Reagan shakes her head. "Holy shit. I guess we know where Lance got his black eye."

"Yep. Though Jason definitely got it worse. Lance is way bigger and stronger than Jason."

"Do you think he wants to get back together?"

I sigh. "I don't know. It's confusing." I choose my words carefully since they don't have the full story. "I know I made it seem mutual, but our breakup was definitely more him than me. I was willing to try the long-distance thing, but he was adamant that we should make a clean break and see other people. I don't know why he's back now. I've had months of being alone. Nearly a year. Of course he comes now when I'm happy with Lance."

I pause for a moment. "When we went to visit his family, Lance told me he loves me."

"Did you say it back?" Harley asks.

I shake my head. "No. I told him I wasn't quite ready. I told Jason I loved him. Being with Lance has made me wonder if I really did love Jason. I don't want to say it again until I'm sure. I feel like I might, but Jason coming back is messing with my head."

Reagan refills my cup and then asks, "How did Jason look? How did you react?"

"His hair isn't shaggy anymore. It's much shorter. He probably had to cut it for his job. Come to think of it, I think he was a little less muscular. I guess he doesn't have as much time to work out. But otherwise, it was Jason. He's hot. I honestly didn't have time to process anything before Lance walked in and they had it out. And then..."

Harley interrupts, "And then you had to play nurse to him."

I smile. "Yes, I did."

Reagan laughs. "You and your role-play shit. You're such a freak."

"Well then, I found my fellow freak in Lance. He's into it. *Very* into it. He showed up a few weeks ago in a tight as sin police uniform. He performed a *full* body search. It was amazing."

They both laugh.

My phone buzzes and I look down. I turn it and show the phone to my sisters.

Jason: 12:00. Our spot.

Harley asks, "Where's your spot?"

I blow out a breath. "This Italian restaurant where the waiters sing opera. We went there on our first date and loved it. We went several more times while we were dating."

Harley gives me a concerned look. "That sounds kind of romantic."

I nod. "I know. It is."

I take back my phone and type a text.

Me: Starbucks by my apartment at noon is best for me.

I show them and they nod in approval. I hear my text tone.

> Jason: Always stubborn. So sexy. Fine. Can't wait to see you and explain everything to you. xoxo

CHAPTER TWENTY

SKYLAR

I walk into Starbucks a few minutes before noon. I have mixed feelings about this meeting. I know I agreed to it last night, but something feels off about coming here. I should have told Lance. Maybe I should have brought him with me, though I don't want a public fight.

I see that Jason is already here and approach his table. He stands and hands me a drink. I look at the label. It's my favorite. He remembered.

"Thanks."

He smiles as he looks me up and down. "You're beautiful."

"Thank you." I touch his puffy, black and blue cheek. It matches his eyes and chin. "Are you okay? Does it hurt?"

"I'd take another punch from your crazy ex-boyfriend if it means you'll touch me again."

I pull my hand away like I just touched a hot iron skillet. I shouldn't have done that.

"He's not my ex-boyfriend, Jason. You are. He's my current boyfriend."

Jason smirks at me. "We'll see about that."

He points to the chair. "Have a seat. I want to talk to you."

We both sit.

I ask, "How's Bella?" Jason's sister is severely autistic. Jason is amazing with her and always cares for her. I imagine it's been difficult for her with him gone for so long.

He shrugs. "She's okay. It was hard to be away from her. She told me you visited her a few times. Thank you for doing that. It means a lot. You know how much she likes you."

I nod. "My pleasure. I adore her. We have fun together."

I pause for a moment. "Jason, tell me why we're here. I don't think we have anything to discuss. It's not like things ended well for us."

He looks at me in the eyes. "I'm coming home. I'm moving this weekend. I've missed you. I need you. I want you back."

I shake my head. "Are you nuts? We didn't part amicably, Jason. While maybe my anger has subsided, the hurt hasn't. Neither has the damage you inflicted. Why now? You know I have a boyfriend. It's serious. I care a lot about him."

"Do you love him?"

"I don't know. I might. The end of our relationship damaged me enough that I'm afraid of telling him that and risking having my heart broken again."

His face immediately turns sullen. "I'm sorry for how things ended. Perhaps I should have gone about it differently."

I'm getting angry at his cavalier attitude. I raise my voice. "Perhaps? You don't think you shit on our four-year relationship when you stuck your dick into someone else?"

He cringes at my words as he chews on his bottom lip.

He takes my hand, but I immediately pull it away. "Don't touch me. I told you never to touch me again."

He sighs. "I don't want to talk about the bad stuff. I want to talk about us and our future together."

Is he crazy? "There is no us and there is no future together. We broke up nearly a year and a half ago. You threw away a loving relationship to spend time with another woman. You moved away. Before I found out you cheated, I wanted to try a long-distance relationship, but you're the one who wanted the clean break and fresh start. Even with the cheating, you were hard to get over, Jason. I didn't date for a really long time. I didn't trust men. I didn't trust myself to adequately judge men considering I completely misjudged you. But Lance came into my life a few months ago and we're happy. He was the rainbow after a long rainstorm. He treats me like gold. I trust him. You can't expect me to drop an amazing man just because after all this time you've simply changed your mind about us or have a few regrets."

"I didn't change my mind. I never wanted to break up with you."

"I don't understand what you're saying. It was all your idea. You're very clearly the one who..."

He grabs my hand hard enough that I can't pull away. I try but it's in vain. "Skylar, I was sick."

"What do you mean you were sick?"

"Remember when I had that sore throat that wouldn't go away?"

I nod. "Yes." He must have had that sore throat for three months.

"It wasn't just a sore throat. It didn't just go away. I was diagnosed with a form of non-Hodgkin's Lymphoma. Sky, I had cancer."

Tears well in my eyes and I squeeze his hand back. "Why didn't you tell me? Are you okay?"

He nods. "I am now. That's what I've been doing for the past year and a half. I wasn't working. I didn't get a new job out of state like I told you. I was at a clinic that specializes in the rare cancer I had. I was getting treatment."

Tears break free and trickle down my cheeks. "Why...why didn't you tell me?"

"Because I knew you'd come with me to play nurse and I didn't want to do that to you. I couldn't ask you to put your life on hold to care for a man who may or may not have lived through it. I needed to let you go for your own well-being."

I'm fully sobbing now. He brings his chair over next to mine and wraps me in his arms. His touch and his scent are still so familiar and comforting. He kisses the top of my head as I sob into his chest. He whispers, "I've never stopped loving you. I never will."

He lifts my face so our eyes meet. "I didn't cheat on you, Skylar. I told you that because I thought it would help you get over our breakup more easily. You kept pushing on the long-distance thing. I panicked and needed to come up with a way for you to let me go. I was sick to my stomach hurting you, but I thought it would help you move on in the long run. I thought it would be easier for you if you hated me."

He rubs his thumbs on my cheeks. "You're the one for me. I've never for one minute believed otherwise. I was never unfaithful. I still haven't been. I let you go in case I couldn't give you everything you deserve. But I'm better now and I can. I want you back. I want to marry you. I'll do anything to make it happen."

I have no words right now. Just tears. Tears at what could have happened to him. Tears at the sacrifice he made for me. Tears for the man I thought I once loved. I'm all of a sudden uncertain if I don't still have feelings for him. I'm emotional. My head is unclear.

Eventually I look up at him. "Who took care of you? Were your parents with you?"

He shakes his head. "No, you know my mom isn't in great shape. They discussed moving everyone out there, but Bella is doing amazing at her school. She doesn't manage change well.

I wanted her to stay here. My dad needed to be around for them. They needed him more than I did."

My entire face is tear-covered. "You were alone? You went through all your treatments alone?"

He nods. "I was fine. My dad flew out every few weeks. I thought of you all the time." He smiles. "I had your pictures everywhere. The nurses made fun of me for my *Skylar shrine*."

He wipes my tears and softly kisses my lips. "I fought to get back to you. Now come back to me. Fight for me too. I love you."

My mind is a cluster of emotions. I'm sad and I'm heartbroken that he went through treatments alone. Most of all, I'm completely confused.

I look up at him. "I don't know what to do, Jason. You were such a big part of my life. There was definitely a point that I saw a future with you. When things ended the way they did, it broke my heart. It took me a long time to remotely consider being with someone else. For nearly a year I didn't go out. I didn't date. I just hung with my family. And then Lance came into my life. He's amazing. We have such a good time together. He treats me like a princess. He loves me and shows me every single day."

Jason now has tears in his eyes. "I love you too. I loved you first. I never stopped."

I shout, "I didn't know that. It's not fair for you to come back when I'm happy and fuck with my head."

"Everything I did was to protect you from hurt. I don't want to hurt you. I want to take care of you. Let me."

"I need time, Jason. I need to think about this. I need to think about what I want. Who I want."

He nods. "Okay. I understand. My instinct is to fight right now, but I want to give you the time you need. Please just give me a fair chance."

I let out a breath. "I will."

"I'm going to see Bella. Will you come with me? She asked me if she'd get to see you."

I nod. "Sure. I haven't seen her in a few months. I'll come."

We drive out to her school. It's well outside of the city. It's on a big farm. How ironic.

The kids at the school benefit from the animal therapy and participating in farming tasks.

When we arrive, Bella runs into my arms. "Skylar! I've missed you."

"I've missed you too, Bells. You look so grown up."

She smiles. "I'm almost eighteen."

"I know. How exciting."

Bella hugs Jason and then runs back to the animals.

He turns to me. "You know you're the only other person besides me that she allows to touch her. She won't even let my parents hug her."

I nod. "I remember."

"It's your kindness, Skylar. Everyone is drawn to you because of it." He rubs the back of his fingers down my cheek. I instinctually lean into it. "If possible, you've gotten more beautiful. I've missed you so much. I want to touch you so badly. I've missed the way our bodies fit together."

Tears stream down my cheeks. I've missed him too. My head is a mess.

He leans down to kiss me, but I turn my cheek.

"Jason, I can't. I think I need to go. Can you take me home?"

"Sure. Let's just stay for Bella's music class and then we can say goodbye."

We leave Bella and head back toward the city. On the ride back, he tells me a little more about his time getting treatment. My heart is legitimately breaking for the fact that he went through this all alone. He's right, I would have left everything and gone with him.

Though I tell him to just drop me, he parks a block from my building and insists on walking me to the door.

We stop outside the front steps of the building.

"Can I come up?"

I shake my head. "No, that's not a good idea."

He smiles. I used to love his boyish, cute smile. It spreads all the way to his hazel eyes. "Are you afraid you won't be able to resist me?"

I let out a small laugh. "Something like that."

He grabs my face and brings our foreheads together. "I love you. I want to make a life with you. Please let me back in."

He gives me a soft kiss on the lips. We both have tears in our eyes.

He whispers, "I'll call you later."

I nod. He turns and walks down the street. I just stand and watch him for a few moments. He was such a big part of my past. Is he part of my future too? I'm a complete mixed bag of emotions right now.

Eventually, I turn toward my building, but as I make my way up the steps to the door, I see Lance standing there with a look of pain and horror on his face. He's holding flowers. Peach-colored roses.

He drops them on the ground as tears roll down his cheeks.

I run to him, but he holds up his hands. "Don't."

I stop short. He's never once asked me not to touch him.

He takes a few breaths. "Did you sleep with him?"

I shake my head. "No, of course not. Can we please go upstairs and talk?"

"Did he...did he touch your body?"

"No. Please, we need to talk."

"Are you breaking up with me?" The look of torment on

his face right now is unbearable. It mirrors mine when Jason left.

"No. I want to explain what's happening."

"You kissed him?"

"He kissed me. Closed mouth."

"How many times?"

"Why does it matter?"

He shouts, "How many times?"

"Twice. Once at the Starbucks when I was crying, and then what you just saw."

He rubs my arm. "Why were you crying? Did he hurt you?"

His heart is breaking right now, yet he's concerned about me and my well-being.

I take his hand and he allows it this time. "No. Can we please go upstairs so I can talk to you?"

He nods his head. We walk through the lobby, ride the elevator, and walk down the hallway to my apartment in complete silence.

When we get inside, he pulls me into his arms. I immediately start crying again. He kisses my head. "Tell me what's going on, sweets. I don't understand. I thought you wanted to be with me. I thought we had something special."

I look up at him. "Jason was sick."

"What do you mean?"

"He had cancer. I didn't know. He didn't break up with me to get a new start, he broke up with me to spare me having to see him go through treatments."

He's quiet for a moment.

"You said he *had* cancer. He's healthy now?"

I nod. "Yes. He was away getting treated, but now he's healthy and is moving back here."

"And he wants you back." Said as a statement, not a question.

"That's what he told me. He said he never stopped loving me. He wants a life with me."

I see him visibly swallow.

"What do you want?"

"I'm so confused by today, Lance. Jason was such a big part of my life. I won't lie about the fact that there was a point where I thought he was my forever. My mind is a mess over the fact that he ended things to protect me, not because he didn't want to be with me anymore."

"What about the cheating?"

I shake my head. "There was no cheating. He said it thinking it would help me move on quicker."

"I see. How do you feel about everything you learned today?"

"I'm trying to process it all. It's like history has been rewritten."

"How do you feel about me?"

I rub his face. "I adore you."

"But you don't love me?"

"I don't know. I told you I want to make sure the next time I utter those words, it will be forever."

Without warning, he bends and takes my lips with his. I can't help but give in and kiss him back. He lifts me up and wraps my legs around his waist.

I run my fingers through his hair as our tongues begin to slowly explore each other's mouths. His smell and taste comfort me now. I can feel my whole body relax for the first time since I saw Jason today.

He kisses his way down my neck. "Let me make love to you. Let me show you what we have. Let me show you how much I love you."

I'm panting as he works his way down to my chest.

All of a sudden, a vision of Jason's smiling face outside pops into my head.

I place my hands on Lance's chest. "Stop. I need you to stop."

He freezes.

I hold his head until our eyes meet. Tears well in both of our eyes. "I need to get my head on straight. I need to sort through my feelings. It wouldn't be fair to either of you if I'm physical with anyone right now."

I kiss his lips one last time. "Just give me a little time, Lance. Please. Be patient with me."

He squeezes me tight. "I'm afraid to let you go. I'm afraid I'll never get to hold you again."

He places my hand over his heart. I can feel it beating at a rapid pace. "It's yours, Skylar."

We stay in a quiet embrace for a few more minutes.

Eventually, he loosens his hold and I slide down his big body.

We walk to my door hand-in-hand.

I squeeze his hand one last time. "Just give me a day or two to wrap my head around everything."

He simply nods. He doesn't say anything as he walks out the door with his head down.

CHAPTER TWENTY-ONE

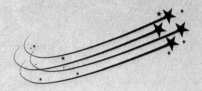

LANCE

I didn't sleep at all last night. I tossed and turned. I can't imagine my life without Skylar anymore. Her smile, her voice, her laugh, her scent, her taste. I need all of it.

I thought we had something special. Maybe I was wrong. Maybe I'm truly a naïve country boy.

I pick up my phone but it's dead. I haven't bothered to look at it in hours. I plug it in, step into the shower, and get lost in my thoughts. I let the hot water fall on my body until it runs cold.

As soon as I step out, I hear my phone ring. I pick it up and see that it's Trevor calling. I answer. "Hello."

"Finally. I've been calling you all night. Are you okay?"

"My phone was dead. I'm alright. What's up?"

"I know Jason is back in town. Skylar was a mess last night. The girls were all with her through the night."

"She's not the only one who's a mess."

"Come over."

"I don't know, man. I think I should be alone. I wouldn't be very good company right now."

"I'm not inviting you over for your charming wit. We're your family. You're upset. Get over here. I'd come to you, but the twins are sleeping, and Cassandra is with the girls."

"Okay. I'll be there soon. Can I bring something?"

"Lance, just fucking come over."

I drive to Trevor and Cassandra's house. They have a huge place just outside of the city. It's modern and decorated like it belongs in a magazine.

Trevor opens the door before I even knock. He looks at my empty hands. "You didn't bring anything? You're a guest in my home. How rude."

I give him the finger and he laughs. He waves his hand. "Come in."

As I'm walking through the door, another car pulls up. I see it's Aunt Melissa.

She runs out of her car to me. She offers me a hug and I take her up on it.

She rubs my face. "You look like you haven't slept."

"I haven't."

The three of us walk into the family room. I see a cute fluffy dog laying in his bed in the corner, barely moving.

I look at Trevor. "You have a dog? I never realized it."

He nods. "He's old. Cassandra had him for years before we got together." He turns his head toward the dog. "Aren't you, Dick?"

"Your dog's name is Dick?"

He smiles and sarcastically asks, "You've met my wife, right?"

I can only shake my head as we sit. They ask me what happened, and I give them all the details.

Trevor shrugs. "So now you just have to wait?"

"I guess. I'm honestly confused by her ability to dismiss what we share. That's what has me going back and forth between sad and angry. I fucking love her. She knows it. I've told her and now she's just tossing it aside."

Aunt Melissa asks, "Has she said that she loves you?"

I shake my head. "No. She said the next time she says it she wants it to be forever. She wants to wait until she's sure. Until it's forever. I'm pretty sure she told *Jason* she loves him. But not me. Maybe I was just a placeholder for her."

Aunt Melissa squeezes my hand. "I don't think that's how she sees it. I've watched the two of you together. She cares a lot about you."

Trevor lets out a long breath. "I saw her with Jason for three of the four years they were together. They were a nice couple, and he's a good enough guy, but she was different with you, Lance. Sometimes it's hard to get a read on Skylar because she's the quietest of the girls."

"Not with me."

He nods. "I agree. She's come out of her shell since you guys have been together. It's like we're seeing the real, confident, happy Skylar for the first time. She looks at you in a completely different way than she looked at him. Sometimes you two stare at each other like there's no one else around. Like you're communicating without talking. I know all three girls still struggle at times with losing their father, but I think it was hardest on Skylar. I think her recovery has taken the longest. I think you really helped her. She must recognize that."

Aunt Melissa looks at Trevor wide-eyed. "Who are

you? What have you done with my son? When did you become so observant? Trevor Knight, you're a bit of a romantic."

"He most certainly is."

We turn and see Cassandra walking toward us.

Trevor stands and kisses her. "I didn't think you were coming home for a while."

She rubs the side of his hair in a loving way. "It was time to come home to my family."

She turns and gives me a small smile. "I think you should check your phone, Lance. I imagine Skylar's ready to talk to you."

LAST NIGHT

SKYLAR

As soon as Lance walks out, I slide down the door and cry. I can't seem to stop crying. I sit there for what must be at least an hour trying to think, but not having any clarity.

I thought Jason was done with me, but he was just protecting me. Loving me without any regard for his own well-being.

And then there's beautiful, sweet, perfect Lance. Who loves me so wholly, so completely. Who's given me the kickstart I've been needing.

Why now? I was alone and miserable for so long.

I don't want to hurt either of them. I care so much about both of them.

I pull out my phone and dial. A familiar, soothing voice answers, "Hey."

I croak out, "Hi. Can you drive me somewhere?"

"Is everything okay?"

"No."

"I'm on my way."

Ten minutes later Hayden pulls up and I get into his car holding a big bag of things I need. He opens his arms and I sink into them.

We sit silent for a few moments before he asks, "Where to?"

"Just get on the highway. I'll show you where to go."

I tell him everything that happened on the long car ride. As always, he listens to everything I say with careful contemplation. He doesn't respond or try to tell me what to do. He allows me to talk.

When we arrive at our destination, he looks around. "This place is dark and creepy. Are you going to murder me?"

I let out a laugh. "No. This is where my father and I used to come to star gaze."

He looks up while I pull out the blanket I brought with me.

"Oh, now I get it."

I spread out the blanket and Hayden lays down. I cuddle into his arm just like I used to with my dad.

He looks down at me. "Do you want to talk more about it, or do you want to avoid it?"

"Can we talk about the stars for a little bit first? It will help me clear my head."

"Of course. I just have to keep my phone nearby. With Jess being in her third trimester, I don't like being quite this far away from her."

I gasp. "Oh my god, Hayden. I'm so sorry. You should go."

"I'm not leaving you here alone for some ax murderer. I called for reinforcements. They'll be here in thirty minutes. I'll stay until then."

"Okay. Thanks."

For the next thirty minutes, I just talk about the stars. Whether he's interested or not, he does a good job acting like he is. He's such a nice guy and such a good friend to me.

At some point we see car headlights approach and then hear car doors. I see my sisters first, then Aunt Cass, then my mom holding something I can't quite make out.

Hayden kisses my cheek. "I'm heading back to Jess. It will be okay."

I nod. "Thanks for taking me. I hope Jess is okay."

Harley and Reagan approach me first. They see the state of my face and immediately hug me.

Harley pulls back and wipes my tears. "What happened? I assume this has to do with Jason?"

I nod. "Let's sit. I'll explain everything."

Aunt Cass gives me a hug too, but when I see Mom holding the McDonald's bag, I start sobbing again. She immediately embraces me. I cry in her arms.

She rubs my back. "Oh, doll face, whatever it is will be alright. I promise."

I motion toward the bag.

She smiles. "You two thought you were so sneaky. I always knew."

I can't help but laugh through my tears. We totally thought she didn't know.

We sit and I proceed to give them all the details about Jason. I confess that, at the time, I thought he cheated on me. I tell them what he's been through, what he did to protect me, and how he now wants me back. I also tell them about Lance's reaction.

They all sit listening in stunned silence.

Harley grabs my hand. "Sky, why didn't you tell us about the breakup? How bad it was for you? I'm sick to my stomach thinking of you basically going through all of that alone."

I shrug. "I don't know. I think I was a little embarrassed that a man cheated on me. Like something was wrong with me that made him cheat. You guys knew we were planning to break up before he left, or at least he was planning it, so I just let it be."

She shakes her head. "You can't keep that stuff bottled up. It's not healthy."

Mom's eyes are full of tears. "We love you, Skylar. We're always here to support you. Let us. We'd never judge you."

I nod. Maybe I should have confided in them. Maybe it would have been easier.

She then breathes out, "Jason did something pretty special for you."

I briefly close my eyes fighting back the tears. "I know. That's what's eating me up. He sacrificed his own well-being for mine. I owe him so much."

Reagan shakes her head. "Sorry, but I'm not sure I agree with that. There's no doubt that Jason was incredibly selfless. I truly feel for him for what he went through and that he went through it alone. But it wouldn't have been your job or responsibility to be with him the past year and a half. You weren't married. Make no mistake, I agree that it's horrible that he was alone, but his family probably needed to be the ones to figure out how to be there for him, not you. They're the ones that should feel guilty, not you."

She squeezes my hand. "Skylar, while you can be appreciative that he put your needs ahead of his own, you don't owe him a life together because of it. You owe it to yourself to be true to what you want. I watched you with Jason for four years and I've seen you with Lance for the past few months. There's no comparison. You had a young, first love thing with Jason. Maybe even someone to fill a certain void in your life. You have a special, forever love thing with Lance."

I can't help the tears that break free. "Our breakup was basically fake though. It's like my feelings of the past year and a half are nullified. I did have some amount of love for him at one point. I won't discount that."

Mom asks, "Do you love Lance?"

Harley and Reagan both answer, "Yes," at the same time.

I sarcastically respond, "Thank you for telling me how I feel."

I take a breath. I've genuinely had it with the two of them and their overbearing ways. "I'm so fucking sick of you two taking over everything. I let you two do a lot for me, and often speak for me, but you won't be making this decision. It's mine and mine alone. I appreciate you being here, and your support, but you're not going to tell me how I feel or who I love. I'm more than entitled to process this as I see fit. Not you. Maybe I do belong with Lance, but I'm not impulsive. I don't rush decisions. I think about them. If I want to take a night to consider what Jason did for me, I damn well will."

With shocked faces, they both mumble their apologies.

I turn to Mom. "Lance has expressed his love for me. I haven't said it to him. I told him that the next time I say *I love you*, it will be forever. I imagine the damage left by the end of my relationship with Jason was to blame for me being trigger shy, but I'm not saying it again until end game." I pause, look up, and ask no one in particular, "Can you love two people?"

Harley quietly asks, "Can I give my opinion?"

I nod.

"I don't think so, Sky. Basically, from the moment I met Brody, I haven't remotely noticed other men. You know the years we were apart, I couldn't even bring myself to consider anything physical with another man, let alone give them my heart. It belonged to Brody from the very beginning."

Reagan nods in agreement. "Jeez, even when Carter and I

were fake dating, I didn't consider other men. Once I actually fell for him, no fucking way."

I look at Mom. "What about you? You've loved two men."

She gives me a sympathetic look. "Not while they were both available to me. I loved your father wholeheartedly. You know that. From the very beginning, I never considered another man. I don't think I've ever told you girls this, but we did spend a brief period of time apart."

We all look at each other in wide-eyed shock.

She shakes her head. "It's not what you're thinking. Not while we were married. While we were dating. I was so young when we met. He felt like he was holding me back from certain social experiences and rites of passage. He suggested we take a few months off so I could date other men to make sure he was who I wanted. It was supposed to be six months, but after two months of extreme misery for both of us, we couldn't spend any more time apart. I never had interest in dating other men, even when he asked me to."

Wow. I didn't know anything about that. Just another reason to love my selfless, perfect father.

She continues, "You girls know how hard it was for me to move on from my broken heart after he died." We all nod. "Once Jackson came into the picture, again, I never considered anyone else. While I have made space in my heart to love two men, it's not while they're both here. I don't think I could ever do that."

I nod and turn to Aunt Cass. "You're unusually quiet."

"I'm in a tough spot. I love you like a daughter, Skylar. But Lance is Trevor's cousin. They've gotten extremely close. It also took me about fifty years to fall in love, so I may not be the best source. I just want you to be happy, kiddo. You deserve it. Follow your heart. Do what makes Skylar happy, not anyone else. You always focus on other people. It's okay to do what you want."

Mom runs her fingers through my hair. "I certainly don't want to tell you how to feel, but I think you may be confusing the guilt you currently feel about what happened to Jason as something else. I completely understand that history has been rewritten and it's confusing, but whatever you went through has gotten you to this point. Your budding relationship with Lance is very real."

Harley says, "Honestly, I think you need to put all the illness guilt aside and decide how you feel for each of them. What does your gut tell you? Lie back and close your eyes."

I do.

"Don't overly think for a moment. Don't consider anyone's feelings but your own. Just feel what comes naturally and answer honestly. Think about what your future looks like. I know you want love, marriage, and a family. When you see that future scenario, who's the first person that pops into your mind? Whose face do you see alongside you?"

Lance immediately pops into my head. Without a doubt. When I see everything in my future, I see it with him. I open my eyes and whisper, "Lance."

Reagan smiles. "I'm Team Lance. You'll never find another man who wakes you up every morning with his head between your legs."

I suck in a breath. "Reagan!"

Harley and Aunt Cass giggle.

Mom tries to hide her smile. She raises her eyebrows. "*Every* morning?"

I'm silent at first but then can't fight the small smile that hits my lips. I give a quick nod.

She brings her lips together but then opens them. "Yeah, I'm not so sure I'd be willing to give that up either."

The five of us have a good laugh over it. It helps break the tension.

Mom threads her fingers through mine. "It pains me to

admit this, but Reagan's right." She winks at Reagan but then turns back to me. "You may just feel guilty for what happened to Jason. You care for him. He was a big part of your life. It's understandable. I certainly won't pretend to be inside your head or heart, but it doesn't seem like he's the one you love. He's your past. He's not your forever, is he?"

I shake my head and whisper, "No, I just hate hurting him. He was always good to me. Look at the sacrifices he made for me. He made me hate him for my betterment. He endured over a year of cancer treatment alone so that I wouldn't be inconvenienced. I just can't bring myself to kick him to the curb so callously."

"I know, doll face, but you know she's right that you don't owe him forever. It sounds like there's someone else that may be your forever. Don't forget his feelings in what went on today. I imagine he's suffering a lot right now."

She's right. I'm hurting Lance right now. That's the last thing I want to do.

We're all silent for a moment before I say, "You know, Lance reminds me so much of Dad."

Mom pinches her eyebrows together. "How so? I know he's sweet, but I imagine you mean something more than that."

"Yes. Did you know that he minored in astronomy in college?"

She smiles and shakes her head.

"He loves it as much as I do. We lay outside and watch the stars sometimes, just like I used to do with Dad." Tears start to well in her eyes. "He rattles off facts, often the exact random facts Dad shared with me, and sometimes he surprises me with new ones."

Tears stream down her cheeks.

She rubs my back. "I'm happy you have him to share that part of yourself again. I know how special that was for you."

I turn to Reagan. "You know, I'm so jealous that Dad got to meet Carter, even if Carter was only two years old and doesn't remember the encounter. It somehow feels like fate that you two ended up together. I remember thinking when we found out, I would never have that. I would never be with a man that had a connection to Dad. In some ways, it feels like I do. I know this sounds sort of weird, but sometimes I feel like Dad sent Lance to love me. I would take an obvious sign like yours, but I do love how much my conversations with him are like my special ones with Dad."

Now all five of us have tear-filled faces.

We end up talking for hours about mine and Dad's time out here. It's therapeutic for me to finally be able to speak freely about our special time together. They say they never completely understood it until tonight.

When we realize it's the middle of the night, nearly morning, they all stand to stretch.

I look up at them. "Can you guys give me a few minutes alone with my cold, soggy fries?"

Mom adds, "With disgusting barbecue sauce."

I look at her in surprise. "You know that I like barbecue sauce with my fries?"

"Skylar, I may not have fed you McDonald's like Dad, but you're my daughter and I know you pretty well."

For some reason, it makes me feel happy and loved that she knows my preferred dipping sauce. I don't ever remember her taking us to McDonald's or allowing us to eat french fries.

Mom bends and kisses my head. "We'll wait in the car. Take as long as you need." She whispers to me, "Tell him I miss him too."

I reach into the bag for the fries and pull them out along with a few packets of barbecue sauce. I pop a few in my mouth and then look up. "Dad, I miss you so much. You saw me like no one else. I feel like I've been aimlessly wandering since you left. Tell me what I should do. I need a sign from you."

I reach into my bag and carefully pull out the book he gave me. I don't want the notes he left to fall out.

I pull out a note.

I like the night. Without the dark, we'd never see the stars.

That's one of my favorites. Every single note has multiple meanings, but this, more than most. I often find myself wondering if it meant something different to him than it does to me. I wish I had asked.

I pull out another.

Do not complain beneath the stars about the lack of bright spots in your life.

I suppose he's right. I have two amazing men that love me. I'm very lucky for that.

I read a few more. No matter how many times I read them, they always carry so much meaning for me, and that meaning often changes over time. I think he knew it would.

I pull out one last note.

I love you more than all the stars in the sky.

"I love you too, Dad."

I gather my things and start toward the car. I look up one last time and see a shooting star. I close my eyes and whisper, "Please give me a clear sign that I'm making the right choice."

I look around but nothing happens.

MOM OFFERED for me to come back to her house, but I just want to go home. I'll never sleep. I want to take a long shower and then try to motivate myself to do what needs to be done. Break someone's heart. Someone I care about.

She drops me home, and when a reasonable hour hits, I head to Jason's parent's house. He's staying there until we figure things out. I think he was hoping to move in with me.

I knock on the door and his father answers. His face lights up when he sees me. "Skylar! It's so wonderful to see your face. We've missed you."

"It's good to see you too, Howard." I give him a hug.

As we pull back, he rubs my arm. "Thank you for visiting Bella. You have a special way with her."

I smile. "It was my pleasure. I'm glad she's doing so well. Is Jason around?"

"Of course. Come in. Rebecca's still asleep. Perhaps she'll wake soon. I know she'd love to see you. Jason is in the kitchen. You know where it is."

I step inside and walk through to the kitchen. I can't help but look around. I've been here so many times, but now it seems a little uncomfortable.

Jason's face lights up when he sees me. "Hey, baby girl." He wraps me in his once familiar, now foreign, arms. As soon as he does, I know I've made the right choice. I want Lance's arms around me. No one else's.

I can't help the immediate tears that sting my eyes.

I look up at him. "Can we go for a walk?"

He nods and takes my hand. As soon as we're outside, he pulls me into his arms again and moves to kiss me.

I hold up my hand to his mouth and whisper, "I can't."

His eyes widen. He's realizing that I'm not choosing him

and he's genuinely shocked. "Don't do this, Sky. We belong together. You know it."

I swallow down my emotions, trying to be strong for him. "Jason, I'm so thankful for our time together. You helped me begin to heal after losing my father. You took care of me and loved me in a way that I had been missing since he passed. I'll always be grateful to you for that. I hate what you've been through over the past year and a half. I wish you had told me. I wish I could have been there for you like you were there for me."

"Sky..."

"Let me get this out." I rub his face, still in his arms. "On some level, we did love each other. And maybe in some ways we always will. I know you were my first love..."

"But?"

I pause for a brief moment, letting it all sink in. "But you're not my last. I have to listen to my heart, and it's just taking me in a different direction. You asked me yesterday if I love him. The answer is yes. I do love him. I know he's my forever. You were my amazing past. Thank you for telling me the truth behind our breakup, because now our relationship will be remembered in such a positive way. I feel so lucky for the time we had together, but he's my future. I'm certain of that."

Tears stream down his cheeks. "Sky, I can't lose you again. I love you."

"I'm so sorry, Jason."

He pulls me close to him, and I allow it. I want to give him some comfort and closure.

As we pull back, he looks at me with a tear-stained face. "Did you see any signs? I think they'd point to me."

I smile. He knows me well. "I asked for one, but I haven't gotten it yet."

"What if it points to me?"

"I guess I'll cross that bridge when I get to it. Right now, I need to do what I feel inside. And my heart? It's taking me to Lance."

He's quiet for a few minutes. I want to give him all the time he needs to digest.

At some point he rubs his fingers over my cheek. "If he hurts you, I'll kill him."

"He won't."

I was wrong.

CHAPTER TWENTY-TWO

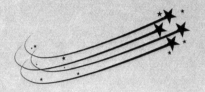

LANCE

Skylar texted asking me to come to her apartment at noon. I have no idea whether she's going to tell me she wants to be with me or if she's ending things. I have both fear and anger brewing in me.

I knock on her door, and she opens it. She smiles at me. Fuck, she's pretty. I love her. I don't know what I'll do if she ends things with me. Will I have to move away? I couldn't bear seeing her with another man.

She takes my hand, and we sit on her sofa next to each other. She doesn't let go of my hand. I find myself wondering if this is the last time I'll get to touch her. My heart hurts at the prospect. I can feel it beating hard, like it's going to jump out of my chest.

"Lance, I'm incredibly sorry about the past twenty-four hours. My head was a mess. I needed the time to think about what I want. Who I want."

Something shifts inside me at her words. She needed to think about what she wants? To think about whether or not she wants me? It's as if the past few months have meant nothing to her. He can just walk back in a year and half after hurting her and breaking her heart, and she's fucking considering taking him back. His intentions may have been noble, but he hurt her in a way that I'm incapable of doing. I'm no longer upset. I'm mad.

She leans over, brushes her lips across mine, and moves her hands up my chest. She whispers, "I've missed you, Lance. I want you. I lo..."

I put my fingers over her lips. "Don't say it. I know the next time you say it, you want it to be your forever. I don't know if I'm your forever, so I don't want you to say it to me right now."

She pulls her head back with a shocked look on her face. "What's wrong? I thought you'd be happy to hear it."

I can't help my voice raising. "What's wrong? What's wrong is that I'm in love with you. I've been in love with you for a while. I was patient while you wanted to take your time returning my feelings. You know what, Skylar? I dated someone for a long time too. Even longer than you dated him. Someone I cared deeply for. When I went home and she begged me to take her back, I didn't for one second need to think about it. I didn't have to take time to decide who I wanted. I knew exactly where my heart belonged. Don't I deserve the same treatment? Don't I deserve someone who doesn't have to think about whether they want me or some other asshole who broke her heart?"

Tears run down her cheeks. "I'm sorry I hurt you. I don't make rash, impulsive decisions. I'm a thinker. That's how I work. I was with him for four years. He helped me during a tough time in my life. Our break-up wasn't what I thought it was. I owed him a day of thought."

"What about what you owed me? The man who has given you every ounce of himself. Who holds back nothing in showing you his love. Who loves you completely without any inhibitions."

She's crying now. "I wanted to think..."

I can't help but interrupt her. "I wish you didn't have to think so hard about it. I certainly didn't."

Her lips are quivering. My instinct is to comfort her, but I don't. I'm done being Mr. Nice Guy. I'm done falling at her feet.

She swallows. "Are you ending things with me?"

I shake my head. "No, but now I need a minute. I'm not your damn puppy dog waiting for you at the door for any scraps of attention you'll throw my way. I want you to fight for me. Want me. Not have to think about it. I fucking love you. You and our future consume my thoughts. Never for one second does another woman factor into that. It's bullshit that you can't give me the same courtesy."

"I do want a future with you."

"After a day of *thinking* about it. Do you care what you put me through while you were *thinking*? It was the worst twenty-four hours of my life. I have enough self-respect not to brush it under the rug. I deserve to be treated better."

She nods. "You're right. I'm sorry. If you let me explain..."

I hold up my hand. "No. I don't want to hear excuses right now. I'm obviously hurting. Let me go and blow off some steam. I don't want to say anything I'll regret."

I stand. "I'll talk to you later. Once I sort through *my*

feelings. Because you know what Skylar? *My* feelings matter too."

I walk out the door. It hurts me to do it, but I stand by what I said. I deserve for her to treat me and love me the way I treat and love her.

———

I GET in my car and drive around aimlessly. I'm confused and mad. I'm not sure what to do with myself right now. I love her, but I hate how I was treated.

I need something positive right now. Something good. Anything that will take my mind off this pain in my chest.

I pick up my phone and dial Aunt Melissa.

She picks up immediately. "Lance? Are you okay, sweetie?"

"Honestly, I don't know. I think I'm going to take a daytrip home. Will you come with me?"

She's silent for a moment. "Lance, I want to be there for you, I really do, but I don't know if I'm ready to face my brother or that town. I haven't been there in decades."

"It's time. You'll regret it if you don't mend fences before it's too late. Please. I want to help. I need this right now. I need the distraction. I need something good in my life."

I hear her let out a breath. In a defeated, yet slightly hopeful voice, she says, "Okay. I'll come."

"Thank you. I'll be there in fifteen minutes."

I pull up to her place. She walks out hand in hand with Declan. Oh shit, I hope he's not coming. I want my dad and Aunt Melissa to make peace, not war.

She opens the car door but then turns. "I'll text you when we arrive." Phew, he's not coming.

He kisses her ridiculously hard, though she doesn't seem to mind. I don't know if he's trying to consume her or mark her. It's probably a bit of both. He doesn't remotely care that her nephew is sitting five feet away.

When they're done, he practically growls, "If anyone mistreats you, I'll take a fucking helicopter there and burn the place down."

She just shakes her head. "Okay, Neanderthal. I'll let you know if your town-burning services are required."

She slides into the car. He sticks his head inside. "Protect her or you'll have me to answer to."

I give him a big, fake smile. "You've got it, Declan."

She closes the door, and we pull away.

I turn to her. "He's crazy and obsessed with you."

The corners of her mouth raise ever so slightly as she turns and watches him as we pull away. "I know."

Jeez. She loves it. Is that what women want? Cavemen? Maybe I've been going about this the wrong way. Trevor did say that women like dominant men. Especially smart women. Maybe I need to act like psycho, demented Declan to get what I want from Skylar. Being a nice guy isn't getting me anywhere.

We talk the entire ride there. I tell her about today. She said she understands that I want to take my own step back to reflect on my mistreatment. She said she's proud of me for doing that. It makes me feel better to have someone in my corner. I've truly come to rely on her and am happy for the relationship we've formed these past few months.

I did tell my parents that I'm coming for a few hours. I decided not to give them the heads up that I'm bringing Aunt Melissa.

As always, she's dressed impeccably. She must have hated our jeans and flannel shirt hometown theoretical uniform when she was growing up.

As we drive down Main Street, I see her tense. I grab her hand. "It will be okay. While my mom may be a little tough on you, I think my dad is going to be excited. He misses you. Skylar saw it too."

She takes a long breath and nods.

I pull down the long driveway. I see Aunt Melissa's hands start to shake. She covers it with a fake smile. "This place hasn't changed in twenty years. It's amazing."

I see my parents on the porch waiting. I turn to her. "I've got your back."

She smiles. "Thank you. Lance, you're a good man. For what it's worth, I'm proud of you."

I nod in gratitude before I get out of the car first. Both of my parents smile when they see me. They can likely see a blonde woman in the passenger seat, but probably assume it's Skylar. We're a good fifty feet from the porch. I walk around and open the door for her. Aunt Melissa steps out.

My mother audibly gasps. I don't care as much about her reaction. I knew it might be negative. It's my father that I care the most about. That's the relationship that needs to heal.

Aunt Melissa and I stand there. We both look at him. No one moves for several uncomfortable seconds.

I see a single tear run down his cheek for a brief moment, and then a huge grin spreads across his face. I can't help but grin myself.

He practically sprints off the porch and to us before engulfing Melissa in a Remington-style bear hug. He lifts her off the ground and spins her around.

She laughs. It's soup for my soul. I needed this today. I can't help the tears in my eyes as I watch their reunion unfold right in front of me.

When he sets her down, he smiles at her. "Missy, somehow, I've gotten old, but you haven't aged a day in ten years. It's not fair."

She tilts her head and smiles back. "Thank you. You don't look too old, Craiginator."

He laughs at the name. "No one has called me that in nearly twenty years."

I look at them both in bewilderment. "Craiginator?"

Aunt Melissa turns to me. "Your father was completely obsessed with the movie *Terminator*. He had posters everywhere, and eventually spent a full two months talking like the Terminator. We started calling him Craiginator then, and it stuck."

I laugh. "I'm totally calling you that, Dad."

Mom makes her way down the steps. Aunt Melissa looks at her and stiffens a bit. "Hey, Steph. It's good to see you. You look well."

I have no clue what my mother is about to do, but she surprises me. She simply walks toward Aunt Melissa and reaches out for a hug, pulling an equally surprised Aunt Melissa close. "Thank you for looking after Lance. I can't tell you how much I appreciate it."

Aunt Melissa hugs her back with a bit of a shocked look on her face. "I adore him. It's my absolute pleasure. We love having him around. He's gotten quite tight with his cousins. It's been nice. He's wonderful with the little ones too. I'm sure he's had a lot of practice around here."

Dad asks, "Do you have pictures of the boys and your grandkids? I'm dying to see them."

She nods. "Of course. My husband too. Maybe you could meet him sometime."

I snort out a laugh. Declan and my parents will mix like oil and water.

Aunt Melissa jokingly narrows her eyes at me knowing what I'm thinking. I just smile back at her.

Dad turns to me. "I know you're only here for a few hours. Your brothers and sister want to see you. They're all at the park with their kids. Why don't you head down there for an hour or so and we'll get reacquainted with Missy."

I look at Aunt Melissa to make sure she's comfortable with that. She nods that she is.

"Okay. I'll see you in about an hour."

My dad mouths, "Thank you," to me as I get back in the car.

As I drive to the park, I truly smile for the first time in two days. Without thinking, I pick up my phone and start scrolling for Skylar's number. I want to tell her about this. She'll be so happy. As I get to her number on my phone, the reality of the past two days hits me, and I put my phone back down. I can't call her.

I arrive at the park. All of my nieces and nephews attack me with love. I do miss them.

I'm bent down on the ground and Giselle wraps her little arms around my neck. "Did you bring princess Skylar?"

"Why do you call her princess?"

"Because she's as pretty as a princess."

Yes, she is. "I'm sorry, sweetie. She's not with me. Maybe next time?"

"Okay. Tell her that I miss her and that her secret is still safe with me."

"I will." I tickle her and she giggles. "Any chance you'll tell me the secret? I think she'd want you to tell me."

She looks around to make sure no one else can hear her. She then moves her lips to my ear, and whispers, "She said that you're the brightest star in the sky but said I couldn't tell anyone because they may be sad that they don't shine as bright as you."

I choke up with emotion and kiss her cheek. "You're a bright star too."

She nods. "I know, princess Skylar told me."

After playing with all of them for a little bit, my siblings' spouses take the kids away, so the five of us can sit and talk.

It's Ryan, Grant, Rich, Lucy, and me. Once alone, I tell them, "I brought Aunt Melissa with me."

They all look shocked. Lucy asks, "How did Mom and Dad take it? She's not here, so either they were fine, or they killed her."

We all laugh. "Really well. Dad cried and ran to hug her. I kind of expected that. But Mom shocked me. She hugged Aunt Melissa and thanked her for taking care of me."

I tell them about the nickname, and we all get a good laugh out of it, vowing to use it moving forward. When they ask about Skylar, they can see the hurt in my face. I tell them everything that happened.

They all encourage me to follow my heart, but they're all also quick to remind me that there's a woman here in town who loves me without any doubts.

A short while later, I see Roseanne walking toward us. "Lance? I thought I saw your truck. What are you doing here?"

"I came for a quick visit. Just a daytrip."

My siblings not so subtly walk away, leaving us alone.

"That's nice." She smiles. "It's so good to see you."

"How are you doing, Rosie?"

She shrugs. "Not so great. I miss you, Lance. You're not easy to get over."

I realize Roseanne is me in my relationship with Skylar. She loves me wholeheartedly. Is Skylar like me? I loved Rosie, but always felt like something was imperfect and missing. I wonder if that's how Skylar feels about me.

She breaks my train of thought. "Are you still seeing Skylar?"

"I'm not sure. We've hit a little rough patch."

She takes my hand. "Come on. Let's go somewhere that we can be alone."

I shake my head. "I'm sorry, Rosie, but that's not a good idea. We hit a rough patch; we're not broken up. I'm not going anywhere alone with you. It wouldn't be right."

"I didn't mean for it to sound like a proposition." She rubs her stomach. "There's something I need to tell you and I don't want you hearing it from anyone but me."

AFTER A LONG DAY, Aunt Melissa and I are in the car on the way home.

She grabs my hand and squeezes it. "Thank you for today, Lance. Thank you for giving me the push I needed."

I squeeze her hand back and smile. "I needed it too. The past few days have been so emotional. I've been hurting so much. It helps to see something good come of it all."

She nods in understanding.

"Will you tell me why you stopped speaking? I have

suspicions that it's about your life choices, but no one ever told me. I'd like to know."

She nods. "I spoke with your father about it. He said that if you asked, I could give you a summary. It's mostly as you suspected. Like you, I felt like a fish out of water in that town. I wanted to get out practically as soon as I could speak. It was problematic when I left. It was *really* problematic when I got pregnant with Payton while in college, but the nail in the coffin was the divorce. You know they don't believe in it."

She takes a breath. "We did have other issues too, Lance. My father, your grandfather, used to push around my mother, your grandmother."

I turn to her in complete shock. "He beat her? He abused her?"

She shakes her head. "I never saw any beating, and I never saw evidence of it getting quite that physical. But there was shoving and a few moments that, to me, were over the line. He was also verbally abusive with her. I tried to broach the subject with my brothers and was told to mind my own business. I tried to talk to my mother about leaving, and my brothers basically accused me of wanting to break up their marriage. It was a lonely feeling."

I can see her getting emotional. I grab her hand again. "I'm so sorry."

"It made it hard to go home. Too many upsetting memories. I wouldn't bring my boys there. I didn't want them around my father. Jackson and I weren't perfect parents, and we obviously didn't have a perfect marriage, but I think we had a happy, loving home. My boys are all happy men. And while maybe Jackson wasn't perfect for me, he was a perfect father to my boys, teaching them how a woman should be treated."

That's true. I hope to be half the father Jackson is one day.

"The divide grew and grew throughout the years." She gives me a small smile. "Today your father told me I was right. That I was the only one strong enough to call out my father. He regrets not having done the same before they passed." She takes a deep breath. "It was honestly a huge burden lifted from my shoulders."

"I'm happy for you. It was clear to me when Skylar and I were home that my father wanted to reconcile. That he missed you terribly."

"I was still a little surprised at how excited your father was to see me but was truly shocked at how quickly your mother embraced me."

"Honestly, I was too. I expected him to be welcoming, but not her. Skylar did sing your praises when we visited. She really went to bat for you. Perhaps that swayed them both, especially Mom."

"Skylar's a good egg, isn't she?"

"The best."

"What are you going to do?"

"I love her. I just don't want to always be the pushover. Trevor has been telling me for months that I need to be more assertive at times. He helped me work on my business persona and it helped. He thinks I need the same in my personal life. Maybe he's right."

"What works for him might not work for you."

"Maybe. Can I ask you something that might be a little weird? A little off color?"

She laughs. "Of course. You've been to family dinners. Does it seem like there's any topic off limits?"

I can't help but smile at that. "No, I suppose you're right."

"Go ahead."

"Declan is the most assertive, possessive, domineering man I think I've ever been around in my life. He practically pisses a circle around you every time you leave the house, making sure it's known that you're his."

She smiles. "You're not wrong."

"You called him a Neanderthal earlier today, so you're clearly aware of it. Is that what women want?"

"I can only speak for myself, Lance. Am I attracted to that side of him? Honestly? Very much so. But you only see the Declan he chooses for you to see. There's more to him than the caveman. He's sweet and loving too. I do like his edge though. And I don't hate his possessive side."

She looks down and then back up at me. "I was married to Jackson, an incredibly nice man, for twenty-five years, but there was always something missing for me. Something I get from Declan. But it obviously works for Darian. She and Jackson have a happy marriage. Not every woman wants the same thing. I imagine some also like a mix of both."

"Like Trevor?"

"I would prefer not to think about how Trevor is with Cassandra, but since she has a big mouth, I would agree that Trevor appears to be a mix in terms of his public and private personas."

"Maybe Skylar needs a mix. I have to figure out some way to let her know that I won't be tossed aside like I was this week. I love her, and I don't want to let her go, but I want to be treated with respect. The same respect I give her. I love being sweet with her, but I won't be a pushover. I don't want my feelings disregarded simply because I don't bark as loud as others. Does that make sense?"

"Of course it does. Don't change who you are, Lance.

You're a sweet, kind man. It's nothing to be ashamed of. I imagine that's part of the attraction for her."

I nod more in contemplation than agreement. "I need to do something."

Before she has the chance to reply, we pull up to her building. Declan is out front and practically rips my car door from its hinges. He reminds me of the Incredible Hulk sometimes.

She calmly says, "Did you miss me, honey?" I feel like she pushes his buttons on purpose. She certainly doesn't fear him in any way. I suppose that's good.

He growls. "One text? One fucking text the whole day saying, *all good*. That's it? That's all you could send?"

She looks back at me, smiles, and winks before he picks her up. It appears rough, but he just holds her close, and I hear him whisper, "Are you okay? I was so worried about you. I love you."

She runs her fingers through his hair and whispers back, "I'm fine."

Without acknowledging me, he turns and carries her inside.

Maybe I need a little bit of Declan in me.

CHAPTER TWENTY-THREE

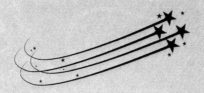

SKYLAR

I wake in the middle of the night to a noise coming from my living room. I look at my phone and see that it's just after three in the morning. I also notice that Lance hasn't called. I hate how upset he was when he left. I hope he can forgive me. The pain I saw in him has me worried that he won't.

I was so caught up in my own torment that I didn't consider his. He was right in everything he said to me. I want to make it right. I want to love him the way he loves me. He deserves nothing less. I can only hope he gives me the chance.

I listen for a moment, but don't hear anything else. Maybe I dreamt it. It's been a restless night for me.

I rub my eyes as I contemplate getting up. I'm fairly thirsty. I'll grab a bottle of water from my kitchen and look around. I'm sure it's nothing.

In my groggy state, wearing a small tank top and sleep shorts, I walk out of my bedroom.

I'm jolted to an alert state by the fact that there's a man

dressed in all black, wearing a black ski mask, charging right at me.

My heart starts to beat fast, but adrenaline courses through me.

My karate instincts take over, and as he approaches me, I surprise him and deliver a hard roundhouse kick to his stomach. He grunts and goes down with a loud thump. He's on the ground holding his stomach.

I attempt to deliver another kick to the ribs when he catches my foot, pulls it, and brings me down to the floor. Hard.

Shit. I should have run out the front door as soon as he went down.

Despite my attempt to kick my way out of it, he quickly rolls and pins me to the ground. His front to mine. He must have a hundred pounds on me. I can barely move. I'm internally freaking out, though there's something familiar about him.

He straddles my legs such that I can't move them, and grabs both of my wrists with one seemingly giant hand.

He moves his mouth to my ear. I take in the familiar scent as he whispers, "This is what you wanted, sweets."

He turns his head so our eyes meet. His eyes are the only thing I can see on his body. I immediately relax as I stare into my favorite pair of blue eyes. It's Lance. I let out a breath of relief.

"Oh my god, Lance. Are you okay? Did I hurt you?"

He covers my mouth with his hand and growls out, "Don't speak unless I give you permission. Don't fight and I'll make this as painless as possible."

Realization hits me. He's trying to give me my intruder fantasy. I can't help but smile under his hand. I guess he isn't in too much pain if he's staying in character.

I simply nod my head.

With his other hand he pulls out a switchblade. My eyes widen when it flicks it open. He's *really* getting into character.

I try to move, but he's rendered me completely immobile. He whispers, "Don't move."

He softly runs the flat side of the blade across my chest. It's cold, but I can't help but love how into the part he's getting. I moan when he moves it across the tops of my breasts.

Taking the blade to one of the straps on my tank top, he slices it in half. I gasp in shock.

He then does the same thing to the other side. He growls, "You better cooperate."

I play my part and say, "Please don't hurt me. I'll do anything. Just don't hurt me."

"Good girl." He closes the switchblade and returns it to his pocket. "Now I'm going to remove my hand. We're going to get up and you won't fight me. Understand?"

I nod again as he removes his hand.

I think I want to have a little fun with this though.

He stands. As soon as his weight is off me, I spring up and sprint for the front door.

He immediately catches me and pins my body to the door. His front is to my back. He pushes hard against me. I can feel his erection. This is turning him on. It's turning me on too.

He places his hand over my mouth. "That was a *big* mistake."

While keeping one hand on my mouth, he slowly drags the other up my bare leg, brushing against my center. He pauses and applies a little pressure. I'm sure he can feel how wet and warm this is making me.

He slides my sleep shorts and panties to the side and slips two fingers inside me. He pushes in deep and growls, "This is mine."

I've never seen this side of Lance. I'm undoubtedly

dripping onto his hand. I move my hips, encouraging him to continue, but he immediately pulls his fingers out.

He lifts the fingers that were inside me and rubs them across my lips before I hear him suck them into his own mouth.

He whispers into my ear, "Your taste is for me and only me."

I lick my lips and taste the saltiness he left behind. I'm contemplating begging him to end the scene so he can fuck me right here, when he wraps his arm around my waist, picks me up, and carries me toward my bedroom.

He roughly tosses me on my back onto the bed, immediately straddling my body with his again. His legs are over my hips. Fuck, this is hot. My entire body feels like it's on fire.

He pulls out long-chained handcuffs. I can't believe he brought handcuffs. I do my absolute best to hide my smile.

He cuffs one wrist, runs the chain around the spindle on my headboard, and then cuffs the other wrist. I must be deranged because all of this is genuinely turning me on. He's completely exceeded the fantasy.

The switchblade is open and in his hand. He again runs the flat part of the blade over my chest and whispers, "Are you going to cooperate, or will I have to hurt you?"

I breathe, "Yes, sir, I'll cooperate. I promise. Just don't hurt me. I'll do whatever you want."

He nods and whispers, "That's a good girl."

Why does him saying that do things to me?

Lifting my shirt from my body, he uses the knife to slice it open down the middle, exposing my breasts. I swear to God, I almost come on the spot.

Looking down at my chest, his breathing begins to pick up. The huge bulge in his sweatpants becoming more pronounced.

He runs the cold blade softly around each nipple. In a gravelly voice, he says, "So perfect. Cooperate so they stay that way."

The mixture of both fear and anticipation is making me overheat. My breathing becomes labored. I can feel my cheeks flushing. My entire body is flushing. I have to wiggle and rub my legs together to get a little relief.

After lifting the bottom of his ski mask to his nose, he bends forward and flicks my nipple with his tongue, teasing it.

He closes the switchblade and places it on the bed. He grabs my breasts with both hands and slowly sucks one of my nipples into his mouth. As soon as he increases the level of suction, I can't help but let out a moan.

He immediately releases my nipple from his mouth. His eyes move to meet mine. "This is for my pleasure, not yours."

We both know that's not true, but I nod in agreement.

He slides his body down mine. He roughly rubs his hand back and forth over my pussy. I have to bite my lip to stifle my moan.

While maintaining eye contact with me and practically snarling, he grabs my sleep shorts and rips them off my body. I'm not sure I've ever seen a sexier image than what I'm looking at in my bed right now. I can feel a shot of wetness spill from my core.

Removing his mask completely, he bends back over, runs his nose through my drenched center, and inhales deeply.

He whispers, "Fuck. You smell good and you're so wet." His tongue slides out of his mouth and he licks my pussy through my panties.

I manage to control myself from jerking toward him begging for more pressure. I feel like I could explode at any moment. A few real licks would definitely do the trick.

He pulls away and runs his hand through his hair. It's messy from the mask. He's so fucking hot. I want him on me and in me. I don't think I've ever wanted anything more than I do him in this moment.

I lose my battle of self-control and thrust onto him, desperate for more contact.

"Please, Lance. I need you. Touch me. I'll do anything."

"Anything?"

I nod. "Yes, just touch me. Make me come. I need it. I need you. I'm begging you."

"I'm going to hold you to that."

"Fine. I'll do whatever you want. Just get your hands on my body." I'm panting like a dog.

Smiling, he grabs the switchblade again. He opens it and slices my panties right off my body. He balls them in his hand and brings them to his nose, taking another deep inhale, and then places them in his pocket. Saliva physically pools in my mouth at that sight.

His eyes are wild with a mix of anger and want. Like the freak I am, that vision drives me crazy with need.

Sliding his black sweatpants down just enough to free his enormous cock, it springs forward, looking willing and ready.

He gives it a few pumps. My tongue is practically hanging out of my mouth as I watch him do so.

He demands, "Open your mouth and stick out your tongue."

I happily do as instructed while he climbs up my body.

"Lick your lips. Get them nice and wet."

Again, I do as instructed.

He traces his tip around my lips and then to my tongue. I can taste the precum leaking out of him. I move my tongue around and lap it up.

"Good girl."

I assume he's about to slide it into my mouth, but in a quick and unexpected move, he moves down my body and slams, I mean *slams*, his cock into me. There's no gentle entry.

He's immediately balls deep. It's so unlike my normal, slow-moving, gentle boyfriend.

There's also no pausing to let me acclimate. He immediately rests on his forearms and drills into me over and over like a man possessed.

He grunts out, "No one will ever touch you again. You." Slam. "Are." Slam. "Mine." Slam.

He's never fucked me this hard. He's never fucked me in anger. He's in a different world right now and is taking me with him.

The deepest depths of my body are being reached for the first time in my life. I would give anything to be able to touch him right now. I've missed touching him. I need to touch him.

My body has never felt more alive or stimulated than it does right in this moment. I can't help but wrap my legs around him pulling him as close as possible. "Oh god, Lance. Harder." He's going to make me come in under a minute.

He continues the punishing pace. My body starts shaking as my orgasm starts to crest, but as soon as it does, he pulls out.

I yell out, "No!" I thrust my hips begging for any contact. I writhe in desperation.

He quickly moves down my body. "I want it on my tongue. I want to taste your come. I get off on controlling your pussy. That's how I know it belongs to me."

Oh. Fuck.

He immediately wraps his lips around my clit. I'm pulling on the cuffs, desperate to get free. I want to break my bed to get to him.

I squeeze his head with my legs, but he slams them back open.

He shoves his fingers inside me and pushes deep. As soon as he hits the spot he's learned so damn well, my body erupts like Mount Vesuvius. I scream out. My vision turns into a black, starry night. For a moment, I have no clue if I'm floating into space or not.

It doesn't seem to end. I'm screaming at the top of my lungs. My entire body convulses over and over. I can physically feel my come seeping out of me. It's like a water balloon popping.

He doesn't let up for a second. His fingers pound into me. He's slurping me up like a dehydrated man. I can hear it.

I have no idea how long it goes on, because I've lost all sense of time and space. I just know it lasts longer than any orgasm I've ever had. Every ounce of energy has been zapped out of my body. He's sucked it out of me.

When it eventually ends, he lifts his head with wide eyes. His face is completely covered in my come. "Holy fuck, Skylar. That was the most intense thing I've ever witnessed. You went off like a fire hydrant."

I don't answer. I can't manage to form words right now. My breaths are long and labored. I don't feel like I have the ability to move any part of my body at this moment.

We stare at each other in shock for several long seconds. Eventually I manage to breathe, "Kiss me."

He shakes his head and narrows his eyes at me. "No. Time to pay the piper. You got yours, now I'm taking mine." He runs his tongue along his lower lip. "I'm about to own your body in a way you'll never forget."

He grabs my hips and easily flips me over. He lifts me so I'm on my knees with my ass in the air and my elbows and head on the bed. "Keep your eyes forward."

I turn my head back in time to watch him reach his hand into his pocket and pull out a bottle. He catches me looking at him and spanks me hard. *Really* hard.

I yell out at the surprise force of that spank. He rubs it with his hand, soothing the stinging sensation.

I hear him open the bottle, and then a squirting sound. I

feel a rush of warm fluid all over my ass and my back entrance. He rubs it up and down my backside several times.

He slides a finger down my spine, down the crack in my ass, and then eventually into my back entrance. I push back, encouraging him to go deeper, which he does. A second finger enters me, and both now go deep. Very deep. My body begins to shake. As soon as it does, he slowly pulls his fingers out.

Once his fingers exit my body, I feel his tip at my back entrance. He leans over my back. "Time to me give me something you never have and never will give another man."

At that, he pushes himself all. The. Way. In. Or at least that's what it feels like.

I yell out, "I can't take all of you. Slow down."

"I'm only halfway in."

Shit.

He waits only a few seconds before pushing the rest of the way inside me.

I scream out at the intrusion. I thought he'd go slow. He didn't.

"Lance, stay still. Give me a minute."

He spanks me again, though not nearly as hard. "I'll decide what you're getting. I'm in charge here. Not you."

Though he doesn't move. I know he'd never in a million years want to legitimately hurt me.

He's still, buried in my body, running his fingers up and down my spine and the crack in my ass. "So fucking beautiful. Do you know how hot you look with my cock buried in your tight ass?"

I have no idea what happened to my sweet, polite farm boy, but he's nowhere to be seen tonight, and I'm finding that I'm into this side of him as much as I am the other.

He moves his fingers around to my front and begins circles on my clit, which is still sensitive and severely swollen from my earth-shattering orgasm moments ago.

The pain eventually begins to leave me. I feel full, but in a good way.

He grabs both hips with his hands. "Sweets, grab onto the bars." I turn my head back as he motions his head toward the spindles of my headboard.

I grab them with my hands and prepare for the onslaught I know I'm about to experience.

He pulls his hips away from my body and then slams them back into me. I scream out again.

He starts yelling about how my ass belongs to him, but I'm barely listening. I'm managing this new, different, amazing feeling.

He rides me long and hard. I feel a buzz and tingling down the backs of my legs that I've never felt through vaginal sex.

I'm gripping the spindles for dear life. I use them as leverage to hold me in place so he can move deep into my body.

I'm close to coming. I can feel it in my legs. He reaches his hand around to my front entrance. He slides his fingers in. If I thought I felt full before, I had no idea. The feeling now is new and among the most pleasurable things I've ever experienced.

I yell out into a completely different kind of orgasm. My body almost seizes as it reverberates down my legs.

He grunts out, "Oh fuck, Skylar." He growls my name over and over as I feel him empty himself inside of me until he eventually stills.

We're both breathing heavily, covered in sweat and oily lube. With him leaning so much of his weight on me, I can no longer stay up on my knees, and I collapse onto the bed with him on top of me.

I breathe out, "Lance, unlock me."

"I'm in charge, not you."

"Lance, the scene is over. I want to see you. I want to touch you. Unlock me. Now."

He takes a few more deep breaths before I feel his weight move off me. He rises to his knees, leans over, and unlocks both wrists.

As soon as he does, I get on my knees and grab his face. I bring my lips to his and begin to kiss him, but he doesn't kiss me back.

I push harder, but he turns his head away. I lick his lips, which usually does the trick. Nothing. I see tears stinging his eyes and my heart breaks. He's still hurting. I'm the one that caused it.

He starts to pull away, but I grab his sweatshirt to keep him close. "Lance, talk to me."

He shakes his head. "Let me run a bath for you first. Your body needs it. You must be hurting."

Tears now sting my eyes. "My heart hurts worse than my body."

He turns his head back to me, his eyes meeting mine. I see an anger in him I've never seen before. With no emotion, he says, "Welcome to the club. It sucks, doesn't it?"

He pulls away, stands, and walks into my bathroom. I hear the bath water turn on.

When he returns a few minutes later, he's holding a hand towel. He carefully rubs it between my legs. It's wet and warm. He then does the same to my backside.

He's upset with me, yet still wants to take care of me. I hope that means we're going to be okay.

Grabbing my hand, he says, "Come on. Let's get you in the bath."

I don't let him pull me though. "Will you come in with me?"

He hesitates for a moment.

I don't budge. "I'm not going anywhere without you. Ever."

He remains silent.

I pull his face so our eyes meet. "I want you. Only you. I'll fight for us even if you're the one I'm fighting. I'll do whatever it takes. Get in the bath with me. Hear me out."

After a brief moment of hesitation, he gives me a small nod.

We walk into the bathroom hand-in-hand. When we're next to the bath, I turn and lift his sweatshirt over his head. I then remove his sweatpants and boxer briefs.

He stands there in all his naked glory. I can't help but move my eyes up and down his body. He's such a beautiful man, inside and out.

I turn and dip my toes in the tub. It takes me a moment to get used to the hot water, but I eventually do. I sink into the tub and motion for him to come sit between my legs.

He's a big man. It's a good thing I have an oversized tub. We'd never fit in a regular bathtub.

He steps in and sits, his back to my front. I wrap my arms around him, pull him close, and kiss up his neck. I love having him back in my arms. It's a sense of contentment I'm not sure I've ever felt before.

I grab for the soap and wash the front of his body. We're completely silent. I simply rub the soap and my hands all over him.

As soon as I wash his dick, he immediately hardens again. I inwardly smile at the way I still affect him, even when he's upset with me.

I eventually break the silence. "Lance, talk to me. Are we going to be okay?"

I can feel him swallow hard. "I won't lie. Your uncertainty hurt me, Skylar. I'm not uncertain about my love for you. I don't need to think about my love for you. I love you and that's it. No one else remotely factors into my headspace."

"If you're unclear whether you want to forgive me, why did you come here tonight? Why did you give me my ultimate fantasy?"

He lets out a breath and squeezes my legs tight to his body. "Because I can't stay away. You're in my blood. You're in my soul. My desire to please you trumps my desire for anything else."

I pull him so his head is leaning back on my chest. I run my fingertips across his chest over and over.

"I was never uncertain of my feelings for you, and I'm truly sorry for what I put you through. I just needed a minute to process what Jason told me. The entire end of our relationship was based on something totally different from what I thought. It took me nearly a year to get over him. Until you came into my life, I didn't have interest in other men. He made a huge sacrifice for my well-being. I owed him the courtesy of a little time to think about things. In the end, Lance, there wasn't much to think about."

I maneuver our bodies so I can look at him in the eyes. I grab his face. "The decision wasn't hard. I didn't consider going a different way. I know where my heart lies. It was you. It was always you. I *love* you."

I bring my lips to his. He hesitates for a moment, but then he gives in and finally kisses me back. I know we're going to be okay. My whole body relaxes.

He easily shifts me around so I'm straddling him. Our eyes now meeting.

"Did you tell him? Did you choose me to his face?"

I nod. "I did. I told him that he's my past. You're my future."

"Do you feel sadness over it?"

"I don't regret it if that's what you're asking. Even when

you left here yesterday, I didn't have regrets or think about changing my mind. It's not easy to hurt someone, especially when it's someone you once cared deeply for. I imagine you can understand that."

He nods.

"He was devastated. That *does* make me sad. I don't enjoy hurting people. But I can't let guilt dictate things for me. I have to go with my heart, and that's with you. I'm in love with you. That's what I told him."

He brings his lips back to mine and whispers into mouth, "You really love me?"

I hold his perfect face so our eyes meet. "I do. Harley told me to close my eyes and imagine my future. She asked who was by my side as my partner in my dream. I had no doubts. It was your handsome face I saw. The only one I saw."

He nods. "I saw Roseanne today...or I guess now it was yesterday."

"You did?"

"Yes. I started to wonder if maybe since she loves me like I love you, maybe you care for me in the half-ass way I cared for her?"

"No, Lance, I..."

"I know. I don't believe that. I immediately told her that it's time for her to try to move on. No matter what, she and I aren't happening. Even if you and I don't work out, I know what real love feels like now. I never had it with her."

"We're going to work out, Lance. You and me."

He nods, but I can tell something is holding him back. Maybe he doesn't trust me with his heart.

"She's pregnant."

"Roseanne?"

"Yes."

"You just found out?"

"Yes."

I guess we're going to be tested off the bat. "How are you managing the news?"

He's silent.

"If you want to go back to her, I'll have to understand. But know that this doesn't change my feelings for you. I love you and want you. We can figure out..."

"It's not mine."

"What?"

"It's not mine. In a drunken stupor a month or so after I left, she slept with a guy who's been pining after her for years. Before she went to the doctor, she admitted that she prayed hard for the timing to work for it to be mine, but it didn't."

"She's absolutely sure of that?"

"We weren't together the last six weeks I was home. I didn't think she could handle it and, frankly, I had lost interest. There was a wide nearly three-month difference between the last time we were together and her one-night stand. Her ultrasound showed that it's impossible for it to be mine."

I rub his arm. "How do you feel about it?"

He shrugs. "Honestly, I just feel bad for her. As I'm sure you can guess, getting pregnant out of wedlock doesn't go over well in our town. She'll either have to marry him or move away."

"It's terrible that she should feel compelled to do either."

"I know. I'm guessing she'll marry him. He does love her. He always has. I knew it. She knew it too. Maybe her feelings for him will grow over time."

"I hope so." I pause for a moment realizing that I'm unclear how he knows about Roseanne.

"Did you go home?"

"Yes. I needed to get out of here. I needed to see something good. I took Aunt Melissa home with me."

I smile. "You did? How did it go?"

His eyes light up. "Really well. She and my dad reconciled."

I hug him. "Lance, that's wonderful. I wish I was there for it."

"Me too, sweets."

"My dad practically sprinted to hug her. My mom was even welcoming. She asked about you."

"Me?"

"Yes. She said to give you her love."

"You're messing with me."

He laughs. "I swear. I left Aunt Melissa with them for an hour and hung with my brothers, my sister, and their families. When I came back, my mom was begging for you and me to come back for a visit soon."

"Maybe that's because of Roseanne's current situation. I can't imagine your mom is supportive of it."

"Probably a little of that, but I'm guessing that Aunt Melissa had something to do with it."

I'll have to thank Melissa the next time I see her.

I rub his face. "Are we good?"

"You can't toss my feelings aside. My feelings matter. I would never disregard yours. I expect the same in return."

I take his hand and place it on my chest over my heart. I look him in the eyes and echo the words he said to me the other day. "It's yours, Lance. I'll never hurt you again. I promise. I love you."

He pulls me tight to his body, so my head rests comfortably between the crook of his neck and shoulder. We sit in silence for a few minutes as we both enjoy being back in each other's arms. He rubs my back and peppers my head with kisses. I do the same to his neck and chest.

Out of absolutely nowhere, he says, "You know, if we have a house one day, wouldn't it be cool to have a skylight over our bathtub? We could lay in the bath together and watch the stars."

I freeze in shocked silence. I can't believe he just said that.

I can't help but begin to tremble. He pulls my head up so we're looking at each other. "What's wrong, sweets?"

If ever I was getting a sign from my dad, this is it.

I look up at him. "Marry me."

"What?"

"Lance Remington, will you marry me?"

The dimples come out and I melt. "I'm supposed to ask that question, not you."

"Then ask it."

"Not like this." He rubs my face. "I want to make it special. You deserve something special."

"That's not a *no*. Are we engaged to be engaged?"

He thinks for a moment. "Fine. Engaged to be engaged. Don't you ever tell our kids that you proposed though."

I giggle.

"What happened that made you all of a sudden ask me to marry you?"

"Lance, the last time my father took me to star-gaze was a few weeks before he died. He gave me very specific advice on the type of man he wanted me to marry."

"What was the advice?"

"To marry a man that wanted to give me the stars."

He pinches his eyebrows in confusion.

"He said to marry a man that would want to put a skylight above my tub so I could watch the stars while I bathed. He said those exact words to me."

Lance's eyes widen in shock. "It...it just occurred to me as we were sitting here. I looked up at the ceiling and thought it would be cool to be able to see the stars from here. I've never thought of the idea before."

I rub my nose along his cheek. "It was him giving me the

sign I asked for. Confirming what I already knew. You're the one. I love you."

I kiss up his neck to his ear as I lift and position myself at his ever-hard cock. I whisper in his ear, "Make love to me, fiancé-to-be," as I sink down onto him.

He then spends an hour doing just that. It begins in the tub and then continues in our bed. It's beautiful and emotional. At no point in my life have I ever felt so deeply cherished and revered.

I WAKE in the morning as I always do with Lance, on the cusp of an orgasm. I hear noises coming from my kitchen, but I just don't care. I want to remain in the moment with him, and I do.

When I'm done, he looks up at me with his blue eyes and sexy messy morning hair. In an equally sexy morning voice he says, "I think we have company."

I run my fingers through his hair as I nod. "I know we do. At least they didn't come in here this time."

He smiles. "I locked the door."

"Smart."

"We should get dressed and go out there."

I shake my head as I pull him up to me, kiss his lips, and then continue kissing my way down his body. "They'll just have to wait."

After I take care of my man, we get dressed and walk into my kitchen to see Mom, Harley, Reagan, and Aunt Cass making breakfast.

I had updated them that Lance left yesterday in a distressed state, but obviously I never told them he came back in the middle of the night. I'm sure they're here thinking they need to cheer me up.

They all turn when they hear us walk in. Mom smiles. "Lance is here, how wonderful. We're so happy to see you."

"Good morning, Mrs. Knight."

"Ah, Lance. For the thousandth time, call me Darian."

Harley and Reagan smirk at each other. Reagan turns back toward us. "Lance, have you been tasting the rainbow this morning?"

I roll my eyes. "Here we go again."

Harley shrugs. "Maybe he had some peaches and cream for breakfast already."

Aunt Cass catches on to what they're doing. "Or maybe he had some pink lemonade."

Mom just shakes her head. "Will you three stop embarrassing them." She smiles. "If he wants to dine at the Y or eat on the Ritz, he's more than welcome."

All of us except Lance start laughing hysterically. His face is down, but I can see a smile threatening to break though.

He lifts his head and licks his lips. "What can I say? Sometimes I just like to savor the mango."

He smiles and the laughter from all of us increases in volume.

He pulls me into his arms and kisses me. "I'll leave you crazy ladies to your breakfast. I'll see you later, sweets."

"Okay." I pull him to me and kiss him one more time.

Reagan looks at him and smiles. "I'd kiss you too, Lance, but I think I'm gonna pass on ever kissing you in the morning."

He turns to her and deadpans, "Then if I were you, I wouldn't kiss Skylar either."

I widen my eyes and put my hand over his mouth while my sisters laugh.

His dimples peek out from underneath my fingers. I shake my head. "Thanks for that. They're going to be relentless. But I'm glad you're more comfortable around them."

I whisper in his ear, "I love you."

The dimples stay out, and all is right in our world.

He leaves, and I unashamedly watch him go.

When the door closes, I hear Reagan say, "You're so damn smitten, I can't believe there was a remote question about this."

I turn. "There wasn't. I just needed time to let Jason go after the sacrifice he made for me."

Mom rubs my back. "How did it go with Jason?"

"He took it hard. My heart breaks for him, but he's a wonderful man and he'll find someone. I know he will."

Reagan passes me a plate full of breakfast foods. "Are you hungry or are you full from slurpin' the gherkin?"

Yep, I knew that was coming.

CHAPTER TWENTY-FOUR

LANCE

I knock on the door at Darian and Jackson's house. Jackson answers. "Hey, Lance. I wasn't expecting you. Is Skylar with you?"

"No, sir. I was hoping to speak with you and Mrs. Knight."

I hear Darian's voice as she approaches the door. "Only if you call me Darian."

I smile. "I'll try, ma'am."

She arrives at the door and gives me a disapproving look.

"I'll try, Darian."

"That's better. Come in."

We all walk through the house and sit down. I turn to Darian. "I don't know if she mentioned it, but Skylar proposed to me."

Darian smiles. "She didn't mention it, but that sounds like Skylar. She must have received a sign and immediately acted on it."

I can't help but smile at that. Her dad wasn't the only parent who understood Skylar.

"I told her I'd like to do the asking. Maybe I'm a little old-fashioned that way. I'm here to ask for your permission."

Jackson stands. "This is between you and Darian. I'll leave you to it."

"I'd like you to stay. This involves you too."

He nods and sits back down.

Darian says, "You don't need my permission, Lance. You need hers. If you'd like my blessing to ask her, that's different, but the permission comes from her."

I nod. "You're right. I'd like your blessing."

"It's yours."

"Thank you. I can't yet afford a fancy ring like those Harley and Reagan have..."

Jackson puts his hand on my shoulder. "I'll give you the money, Lance."

I shake my head. "No, sir. I'll be the one buying the ring for my future wife."

"Okay, so what can we do to help?"

I turn back to Darian. "When I was walking around downtown one day, I came across a small shop that sells rings made from meteorites, moon rock, and other space matter. Do you think Skylar might like something along those lines? They were much closer to my budget. One day in the future, I'll buy her a ring like those her sisters have, if that's what she wants."

Darian grabs my hand. "Lance, you know Skylar. You know she'd prefer something like the rings you mentioned more than any big diamond."

I nod. "I think so too, but I wanted to check with you. Will you come with me to help me pick one out?"

She smiles. "I'd love nothing more."

"Thank you." I turn to Jackson. "Adam Bancroft sits on the Board of the space museum, right?"

"I believe so."

"Do you think we can call in a favor?"

"Tell me what you have in mind."

SKYLAR

I look up and breathe loudly. "That was amazing."

He kisses my neck as he sets my feet on the ground. "Always is."

The hot water sprays on us as our breathing evens out. "Sweets, we need to finish in here. We're on a schedule. You distracted me."

I smile. "I think you enjoyed the distraction."

"I did." He smacks my ass. "Now hurry up."

"Will you tell me where we're going?"

"No."

"What should I wear?"

"I prefer you naked, but jeans are fine too."

We dress, head out, and arrive at the Franklin Institute Space Museum.

I smile at him as I grab onto his arm. "I've never been here at night. What a great idea. This will be fun."

It doesn't look open, but Lance seems to know what he's doing. When we walk in, a man greets us.

"Mr. Remington?"

"That's me."

"Right this way."

I glare at him. He's up to something.

The man leads us into the planetarium, which is a huge, round theater with a round ceiling covered in screens. It's dark and the stars are on full display on the screen. They do an amazing job at making it as realistic as possible.

I look up and smile. "Thank you. I love it here. I used to come here all the time as a kid."

The man leaves and Lance walks us to the center of the room. There's a big, fluffy blanket spread out with chocolate cake, two forks, and a bottle of wine with two glasses.

We sit down. I smile at him. "Are we having cake for dinner?"

He grins. "We are."

"Perfect."

We eat, drink, talk, and point to all the constellations we know. It's the sweetest, most romantic thing anyone has ever done for me.

When we're done eating, we lay down. I snuggle into him.

"Sweets, tell me a fun fact about the stars."

"You know everything."

"Give me something."

"Hmm. The bigger the star, the shorter the life."

He squeezes me. "I didn't know that one. See, I don't know everything."

"I didn't know that fact until after my dad died. I was trying to make sense of him dying so young, when I came across that fact. He was the biggest star. That's why his life was shorter than most. At least, that's what I told myself."

"I have no doubt it's true."

I run my hand over his chest. "Now you tell me a fun fact."

"Let me try to think of something you might not know."

He pauses for a few moments.

"There are about a million different theories on shooting stars and why we wish on them. There's an obscure one that I choose to believe. It's based on the Greek gods. Occasionally, they look down on us to see what we're doing.

To make sure we're behaving. When they lean over, rocks fall into our atmosphere. They burn on entry, causing the appearance of shooting stars. When we see the shooting stars, we know we have a direct line to the gods. We know they're listening. We tell them our wishes so they can make them come true."

I love that in this moment, when I know he's about to propose to me, he's unknowingly telling me the same story my father told me the first night we spent looking at the stars together. I think I'll keep this one to myself. I know this is my dad's way of giving me his blessing.

Lance turns to me. We're nose to nose, though my head is still on his arm. With his other hand he reaches into his pocket and pulls out what I assume is going to be a ring, but it's three pieces of paper. He hands them to me.

I read the first. *The stars are the streetlights of eternity.*

I move on to the second. *You are my sun, my moon, and all of my stars.*

And finally, the third. *I love you more than all the stars in the sky.*

When I look back up at him, I notice he's holding a different-looking ring.

I lean into his lips and kiss him. I can't help myself.

"Sweets, let me get this out."

I giggle and nod.

"When I wished for someone special in my life, the gods must have been listening because they sent me you. Skylar, I love you. I want you to have these notes. You and I together can create a new book about love and the stars, full of our own notes."

He holds up the ring. "This ring is made from a meteoroid that must have once been a shooting star."

He turns my chin so we're both looking up at the screened ceiling. The stars spell out *Marry Me?* above us.

I turn back to him with tear-filled eyes but a big smile. "I thought I already asked you to marry me."

The dimples come out. "I told you I wanted to ask."

"Maybe I should make you wait like you did to me."

He rolls on top of me. "I'm holding you hostage until you say yes."

"Ooh. I'm up for a little hostage role-play."

He narrows his eyes at me, but I hold out my finger and he slides the ring onto it.

"I love it. It's perfect."

He kisses me. "You're perfect."

EPILOGUE

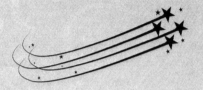

THREE MONTHS LATER

LANCE

I'm in the front row, Darian on one side of me, my mother on the other. We're all standing, applauding vigorously.

Darian is covered in tears. She turns and leans into me. "Thank you for pushing her to do this. She was amazing."

I smile with pride. "She sure was."

I turn to my mom who's also clapping and smiling. "Wow, she's genuinely talented. She really knows how to get into a role."

I can't help but inwardly laugh. She's got no idea how true that statement is.

After some more than gentle pushing, Skylar tried out for a local community theater production of Grease. She won the role of Sandy, apparently the same role she had in the last play she was in as a teenager. I can't blame the casting director. Not only is she incredibly talented, but she's got the looks of both an all-American girl and a vixen all in one. I haven't been able to take my eyes off her all night. If I'm being honest, I haven't been able to take my eyes off her since I spilled my beer on her all those months ago.

Her being in the play has been a large time sacrifice for us, but seeing the smile on her face as she bows and stares at me makes it completely worth it. I've missed spending every evening with her, as the rehearsal schedule was brutal, but I know she needed this as her final step in healing from the loss of her father. She loves her job, but she abandoned this part of her when he passed, and I know she missed it.

The whole family is with us, mine included. We've managed to take up the first three rows in the theater. All of mine and Skylar's nieces and nephews are looking at her like she's a star. She *is* a star. *My* star.

When she walks out of the dressing room, it sounds like a stadium clapping for her. Everyone hugs and kisses her. She's being showered with flowers and praise. She looks so happy. I'm proud of my girl.

She maintains eye contact with me, trying to work her way down the line toward me while still graciously thanking everyone. I'm waiting with peach roses, her favorite.

When she eventually gets to me, she leaps into my arms, wraps her legs around me, and kisses me. She hugs me and whispers into my ear, "Thank you for making me do this. I needed it. I love you."

I pull back so I can look her in the eyes. "You were incredible, sweets."

She gives me such a genuine smile.

I whisper. "Can you bring home the tight leather outfit you wore in the last scene?"

Her face flushes and she whispers back, "It's already in my bag."

A MONTH LATER ~ SKYLAR'S BACHELORETTE PARTY

SKYLAR

"Reagan, I can't believe I let you talk me into a strip club. You know it's not my thing."

She rolls her eyes at me. "I got married quickly and didn't have a bachelorette party. Harley was knocked up when she got married, so she didn't have one. This is for all of us. Suck it up. It wouldn't kill you to let loose and have a little fun."

"I'm sorry that looking at strange naked men isn't my definition of fun. I'd rather look at the hot naked man at home waiting for me. He's way hotter than these guys will be. For what it's worth, you have a hot man waiting at home for you too."

"True." She throws her arm around me. "Let's have a few drinks and enjoy the show."

She slides two lemon drop shots in front of me. "Take both of these to chill the fuck out."

I take them because I might need them to get through this.

When I'm done, I look around at our group. "Why did you let Jade come? She's only eighteen."

"She has a good fake ID. So did you at that age. She's been begging to come for weeks. Melissa said she'd keep an eye on her."

We're in a huge booth with my sisters, Jade, my mom,

Aunt Cass, Kylie, Melissa, Lucy, Reagan's friend Jasmine, Harley's friend Angelina, and five of my friends, including Randy. Jess gave birth to a baby boy a few weeks ago, so she wasn't quite up for coming.

I'm happy that Lance's sister, Lucy, decided to come. His mother declined. I certainly understand why. I've gotten a little closer with Lucy. She's not quite as uptight as I initially thought. She fits in well with my family and she's made a huge effort to build a relationship with me.

Melissa is doing her best to rein in Jade, but it's no easy task. She's a wild child and is sneaking shots every time Melissa turns her head.

Randy leans over. "I'm so excited for this. Thanks for inviting me."

"I hope Gary wasn't too jealous."

"He knows you and I are besties, and I'll be coming home turned on. He'll be fine."

I smile.

The lights dim and the music starts. I let out a breath. Here we go. In a few hours this will thankfully be over. All I want is to go home to Lance. In just a few weeks I'll get to call him my husband. I have to pinch myself at how lucky I am to have him. A man that loves me so completely. A man that I know would do anything for me. A man that looks at me like there's no one else in the universe.

Three men dressed as firemen saunter onto stage to a sea of screams. Reagan turns to me, "Have you ever done a fireman role-play?"

I give her the finger and she laughs.

The men are wearing fireman jackets, pants, helmets, and have masks covering their faces. They're all extremely big men. I imagine there must a lot of muscles underneath those uniforms. I also imagine we'll be seeing it soon enough.

They're dancing around, though the one in the middle is by far the best dancer. He must be the main guy.

They shake their asses, swivel their hips, and do what strippers do. The women go crazy and throw money at them.

The guy on the right slowly peels open his jacket, just enough for a bit of his broad chest and chiseled abs to show. His abs are amazing. He must have an eight-pack. The women all yell as his baby oil lathered chest and abs come into full view.

Reagan whispers, "What the fuck?" To no one in particular.

I look at her in question. She points to the guy with the open jacket. "That's my husband."

"What? That's Carter?"

Mom shakes her head. "There's no way. You can barely see any of him, and why would Carter be dancing here?"

Reagan shakes her head. "Mom, I've touched, kissed, and licked every inch of his body. I know my husband's chest and abs. That's him." She looks around the table. "Fair warning, if he's wearing a G-string, every one of you will be ruined for all other men." She mumbles, "He's definitely ruined me for anyone else."

She stands and waves cash for the dancer to come over. He dances our way, swaying his hips and rolling his abs to the beat of the music.

He approaches Reagan with his hands behind his head, which opens his jacket a bit more. She slowly runs her hands down his exposed chest and abs until she reaches his waistband.

A normal person would place the money in that waistband. Reagan isn't normal. She pulls on the waistband of his pants and shoves her hand all the way down. Turning around with a big smile, she says, "Yep, this is my husband."

He rips off his mask with a big smile. "What if it wasn't me?"

She runs her fingertips back up his abs and then chest until she reaches his face. She rubs her hand over his cheek. "I know what's mine, baby. I never had a doubt."

He bends and kisses her. Per normal for the two of them, they kiss in a manner uncaring that anyone is around. He eventually lifts her, and her legs immediately wrap around him.

Those two nut jobs dance all around the stage, much to the jealous chagrin of every woman in here. I hear a couple of them booing the fact that Reagan's monopolizing one of the dancers.

One of the other firemen dances over to our table. He starts moving his hips in a circular motion, clearly looking for both attention and money. A woman from a different table runs over and rips open his jacket. We see yet another broad chest and chiseled abs.

Harley gasps. "Oh my god. That's Brody."

What the hell is going on here?

She motions for him to come to her. He half sits on Harley's lap and rubs his ass all over her. She wraps her arms around him and runs her hands up and down his chest and abs with a huge grin.

She says, "Don't tell my husband, but you have a much better body than he does. I might have to go home with you tonight."

He stands, rips off his mask, and turns around with narrow eyes. Harley giggles.

"Did you know it was me?"

She stands on her tippy-toes and nibbles on his lower lip. She rubs her fingertips across the top of her chest, drawing his attention. "If someone ripped open my top and you saw my chest and stomach, would you know it belonged to me?"

He moves his eyes up and down her body while licking his lips. After landing back on her massive chest, he nods. "I'd know your body anytime, anywhere. I know it better than my own."

She smiles in triumph as he scoops her up and carries her to the stage with him.

That leaves the last fireman on the stage. Judging by his moves and the company he's keeping, it's Lance. My Lance. All of a sudden, my bachelorette party is looking much better.

He manages a full-blown professional dance routine. Every strip club cliché song is played while he dances like he's been doing it his entire life. When *"It's Raining Men"* plays, he may get more money thrown at him by the crowd than I make in a year.

When his jacket is eventually opened, my suspicions are confirmed. That's my fiancé dancing at a strip club.

The ladies all scream when they see his NFL tight end-looking chest and abs. Hands off, he's all mine.

He motions for me to join him on stage. I'm pushed there by everyone at my table.

He places me in a chair in the middle of the stage. The lights all go out, except a spotlight on us.

"Holding Out for a Hero," from *Footloose*, starts playing on the speakers. The very song I was imagining when I saw Lance on his tractor.

He then dances and achingly slowly strips for me. I'm enjoying it, but I'd *really* enjoy it if we were alone.

As if hearing my thoughts, he whispers, "Pretend we're alone, sweets."

He never stops dancing. He's in my lap, he's rubbing on my back, he's rubbing on my front, he's upside down. He spreads my legs and dances between them, gyrating all over the floor.

Every few minutes he removes something. He's down to

just his pants. The ladies here are going nuts for him. I don't blame them. They're throwing twenty-dollar bills at him like they're on fire.

He bends and runs his tongue through my mouth. He's so fucking hot. All the women scream again, most of whom don't realize he's mine.

He turns toward the crowd, with his back to me. He bends over and slightly tugs down the waistband of his pants, baring his perfect ass to just me.

He slowly shimmies down to his knees, turns around, and buries his face between my legs. Throwing my legs over his shoulders, he picks me up and stands with his face still buried.

I'm wearing a short dress. He manages to pull my panties aside and take a swipe. My face must show it because I hear my sisters laughing hysterically.

He manages to dance around like this for an entire song.

When the song ends, he mercifully places me back in the chair. He mouths, "Just you and me."

I mouth back, "I love you."

He smiles and I can't help but smile back at those mouthwatering dimples.

Facing me, with his back to the crowd, he takes a big breath. He winks at me and then rips off his pants. The crowd goes insane. My sisters and friends are now on the floor laughing.

Lance is in a G-string. And not just any G-string. It's decorated with stars, with the Big Dipper on the front.

THE END

FOR A SNEAK PEEK at Indecent Ventures, the second book in the series, please flip ahead!

ACKNOWLEDGMENTS

To the Queen, TL Swan: This amazing journey would never have begun if not for you and your selfless decision to help hundreds of women. You are a shining example of the girl power quotes I place in each dedication. Those are for you, girlfriend. This crazy and unexpected new path in my life has brought me so much happiness. I owe it all to you. Please know that I try every single day to pay it forward.

To Lakshmi and Thorunn: This book would not be what it is if not for the input from both of you. You battled with me in those first few drafts to make this book so damn special. **Lakshmi**: You are my favorite perv. Thank you for the daily reminders of your perv status. Your audio messages brighten my days. Thank you for always being there to give me advice or to give me a thirst trap. **Thorunn**: You are my self-proclaimed 'theoretical bitch'. You have become my sounding board and trusted advisor. I can't begin to tell you how much a value our friendship. I can't wait for you to join me as an author (hint hint). You'll undoubtedly shine bright and I will be your biggest cheerleader.

To Jade Dollston and Carolina Jax: You are my bookish besties. Our daily texts are my lifeline. I love the support we have for each other. I adore and trust both of you wholeheartedly.

L.A. Ferro: Despite me being older, I look up to you. You're innovative, forward thinking, and are selfless. You're always willing to help your author friends, and at times, you're even my therapist.

To Katy Brown: Your support is unwavering. Thank you for all of your help.

To My OG Beta Readers Stacey and Fun Sherry: Thank you for being there for me since day one. You've been my sounding boards and biggest, and hottest, cheerleaders every single step of the way.

To My Badass ARC and Street Teams: You bitches are the best. I appreciate every single ounce of support you throw my way. Your constant words of encouragement keep me writing. Our daily street team group messages always make me laugh. I love that you not only support me, but you support each other.

To Chrisandra and K.B. Designs: **Chrisandra**, thank you for making me feel illiterate. That's what makes you such a great editor. **Kristin**, thank you for helping this artistically challenged woman. You have breathed life into all of my books. I'm so proud of them thanks to you.

To My Family: I truly feel bad for you. An immature mother and wife can't be easy. To my daughters, thank you for tolerating me (ish). Thank you for telling everyone you know that your mom writes sex books. I appreciate that by the time you were each six, you were more mature than me. To my handsome husband, thank you for your blind support. You never question my sanity, which can't be easy. But let's face it, you do reap the benefits of the fact that I write sex scenes all day long.

ABOUT THE AUTHOR

AK Landow lives in the USA with her husband, three daughters, one dog, and one cat (who was chosen because his name is Trevor). She enjoys reading, now writing, drinking copious amounts of vodka, and laughing. She's thrilled to have this new avenue to channel her perverted sense of humor. She is also of the belief that Beth Dutton is the greatest fictional character ever created.

AKLandowAuthor.com

ALSO BY AK LANDOW

City of Sisterly Love Series

Knight: Book 1 - Darian and Jackson

Dr. Harley: Book 2 - Harley and Brody

Cass: Book 3 - Cassandra and Trevor

Daulton: Book 4 - Reagan and Carter

About Last Knight: Book 5 - Melissa and Declan

Love Always, Scott: Prequel Novella - Darian and Scott

Belles of Broad Street Series

Conflicting Ventures: Book 1 - Skylar and Lance

Indecent Ventures: Book 2 - Jade and Collin

Unexpected Ventures: Book 3 - Beth and Dominic

Enchanted Ventures: Book 4 - Amanda and Beckett

Signed Paperbacks: aklandowauthor.com/books

PROLOGUE ~ INDECENT VENTURES

BELLES OF BROAD STREET BOOK 2

FOUR YEARS AGO

REAGAN'S TWENTY-EIGHTH BIRTHDAY PARTY

COLLIN

"You better be on your way."

"Carter, I told you I'd come. I'll make a brief appearance."

"What do you mean by brief? It's my wife's birthday party. You're my closest friend. It better be more than brief. Since when do you pass up the chance to party?"

I blow out a breath. "I just left a construction site outside of town. I need to run home to shower, and then I'll be there. I promise."

I hear him whisper, "Holy shit."

"What's wrong?"

"Reagan just walked out of our bedroom dressed for tonight. Fuck, my wife is hot."

I can't disagree with him on that. Reagan Lawrence is the hottest, most perfect woman ever created. I guess she's Reagan Daulton now. They recently got married.

I hear a slightly muffled, "Sorry, babe, we're going to be late. Lift up your dress."

I swallow at what that must look like. My cock starts to harden.

"Carter, I think Reagan told me she wants a threesome for her birthday."

"No, she didn't, asshole. Nice try."

I can't help but let out a laugh.

"We used to share women all the time. You're going soft."

"Not my wife. I'm not sharing her. Ever. She's all mine. No other man's hands will ever touch her body again. You'll understand that feeling one day."

Unlikely.

"Can't blame a guy for trying."

I hear her in the background. "We don't have time for sex, but how about I suck your..." The line goes dead.

Of course she would offer to suck his dick. On her birthday. She's perfect.

My cell phone rings again. There's no way it's Carter calling back. We're best friends, but a blow job is a blow job. I get that. I look at my screen and see that it's my brother, Cormac. I accept the call. "What's up, Mac?"

"How did the Paulson job go today?"

"It was fine. Another boring, cookie-cutter home is well under way. We're ahead of schedule. Stop babysitting me. I know what I'm doing. It's not that hard to build the same house over and over again."

I work with my brothers at Fitz and Sons Construction. My father, Nolan, started the company, and Mac, Shane, Braden, and I all work there. Mac is the oldest and has taken a quarterback-type role in our operations. Self-appointed. Being the family goofball means that none of them think I can do my job properly, and none of them take my ideas seriously.

"Sometimes you need it. I'm glad it's going well though. How are the plans coming for Carter's house?"

Carter and Reagan are building a giant mansion in a Philadelphia suburb. No expense spared. They hired us to build it. I'm thankful to my best friend for this job. It's one of the biggest in our company's history. Every contractor wanted the job and submitted bids. Carter and Reagan didn't even consider them. They hired us immediately and Carter insisted on incorporating all my crazy, unusual ideas. He's the best friend you can imagine. I'm the dickhead that has a thing for his wife.

"I'm just waiting on the final permits and a few materials bids. We should be good to break ground in the next few weeks."

"Look at you being a grown-up, Collin. Following through on something for once."

"Screw you. I'm thirty-four. I *am* a grown-up."

"In age, not maturity."

"I'm giving you the finger." I'm literally giving the finger to my phone right now.

"Exactly. Back at you. What are you up to tonight? Ash and I are hanging at home with the kids. You're welcome to come over."

"As enticing as a Saturday night with you, your wife, and kids sounds, I have other plans."

"What's her name? Or is it names?"

"It's not a date. It's Reagan's birthday party."

"Have you told Carter that you're in love with his wife?"

"Fuck you. I'm not in love with her."

"Sure."

"I'm not." God, I hope I'm not. I'd be an asshole friend if I was. "I just want a woman exactly like her."

"Hot?"

"It's not just that she's hot," which she is.

"Great body?"

"Yeah, yeah. That too. But it's everything. Her personality, her brashness, her lack of filter, her intelligence, her confidence. I dig all of that. It's so unique to find those things in a singular woman."

"Well, keep the stallion in the corral. Carter's project is huge money for us. Don't fuck it up."

"It has nothing to do with the money. Carter is my best friend. He's like a brother to me. I like him better than I like all of you. I would never want to jeopardize that. I hate myself for being attracted to his wife. I'll get over my crush. It's not like I would ever act on it."

"Good. Behave tonight."

I can't help but smile. "Never. There's no fun in being well-behaved."

We hang up and I head home to shower and get dressed. I'm in a black suit and a blue button-down shirt that matches my eyes. No tie. I'm sure every other man will be in a tie. It's just not my style.

I brush the top of my hair back. The sides are short and don't need to be brushed. The top is a little longer. My face is clean shaven. I look damn good. Eat your heart out, ladies.

I arrive at the hotel. It's in an older, famous Philadelphia hotel. I look up at the giant chandelier in the lobby. I wonder what kind of crane they needed to get that sucker in here. I don't envy that crew.

I make my way to the ballroom. The party is in full swing. Carter must have dropped a bundle on this.

Several bars, crazy décor, a band, lighting, and an endless supply of upscale food. There must be over three-hundred people here. Everyone loves Reagan. What's not to love? Ugh. Stop, Collin.

Carter and Reagan see me and immediately make their way over. Reagan looks gorgeous. She's tall, probably about five feet, eight inches. Closer to six feet when in heels. She's got wavy, natural blonde hair, the most expressive blue eyes, huge breasts, and a flawless curvy figure. She's all woman. A perfect woman. She's wearing a blue, strapless dress that hugs her figure and makes my heart race.

I'm six feet, three inches, but Carter probably has an inch or so on me, and a good amount of muscle. I'm muscular, but he's a giant. Admittedly, they're a good-looking couple.

He smiles and gives me a big hug. "Finally. I was afraid you weren't coming."

I lean over and kiss Reagan's cheek. "I wouldn't miss a party for the future Mrs. Fitz."

Carter narrows his eyes at me, but I simply grin. I turn to Reagan. "You look beautiful. Happy birthday."

"You're making my husband jealous." She licks her lips. "Keep doing it. I like when he goes all alpha possessive on me."

Carter grabs her hip and pulls her close. He lifts an eyebrow. "Is that so?"

She leans her entire body into him, runs her hand up his chest, and gives him a nod. The sexual tension between them is making it hard to breathe. It's always high. I would kill to watch them go at it. Actually, I would kill to be a part of it.

I let out a quick whistle to break their trance. They

both turn to me. Reagan asks, "Have you seen my sister? I haven't seen her in a while."

"Which one?" Reagan has two sisters. Harley is older and Skylar is younger. They both look like models too. The whole damn family does.

"Skylar. I might need to call her. I want her with us when I speak in a little while. I hope she's off getting some ass. She could use it."

I can't help but laugh. I love the way Reagan speaks. She's like one of the guys.

Carter grabs her hand. "I'll help you find her." He turns to me. "We'll have a drink later?"

"You bet."

"Are you okay alone?"

"I'm not a child. I can manage myself. There are tons of hotties here to occupy my time." I give him a wink. "I'm going to grab a drink at the bar, maybe a woman too. I'll see you guys later."

They walk off and I can't help but watch her ass as they go. Such a perfect...damn it, Collin. Stop. She's off limits.

I turn and head toward one of the bars. I'm stopped by one or two people that I know, but I keep the conversations short.

I approach the bartender and order a double whiskey. I lean on the bar with one elbow as I take in the party. People are having a good time. They're dancing, drinking, eating, and laughing. I guess I should expect that from anyone that knows Reagan.

I can't help but smile for my friend Carter. He deserves this life. He got a shitty draw growing up. He may have grown up with money, excessive money, but I wouldn't have traded places with him for all the money in the world. His dad is a pretentious, abusive asshole, his mom is zoned out most of the time, and he lost his only sibling when he was a little kid. His house was stuffy, cold, and miserable. The only family member he was close to was his grandfather, and he died in a plane crash when we were in junior high.

Carter loved hanging at my house. The whole house could have fit in his foyer, but he loved my happy, hectic home, full of my crazy, loud family.

Now he has Reagan's crazy ass, big, close family. They spend a ton of time with them. He's never been happier, and I'm thrilled for him. Yes, I have a crush on Reagan, but it's because she's so great and Carter is a lucky man. I know I'm a bit of a playboy, but I think I want the same thing one day. If only Reagan had a twin sister. Her older sister is married, and her younger sister, though just as hot, doesn't have Reagan's dynamic, filterless demeanor. Oh, and she also can't stand me. She makes that abundantly clear every time we're together.

I hear a woman's voice next to me. "I'll have a vodka tonic." She pinches my ass. "And one of him."

I turn around. She looks me up and down. "Ooh, this evening just got a lot more interesting."

I give her an obvious once-over. She's very tall. Well over six feet in heels. She's a leggy blonde, with familiar blue eyes. A little skinny for my tastes, but she's gorgeous. She looks like she's in her mid-twenties, putting her about ten years younger than me.

She smiles when my eyes eventually meet hers. It's full of mischief. "Do you like what you see?"

I nod. "I imagine most men do."

She crosses her arms. "I'm not interested in their opinions. I'm interested in yours."

I shake my head. "Sweetheart, I'm the Big Bad Wolf. You want no part of me."

She runs her hand down her red, form-fitting long dress. "As the story goes, Little Red Riding Hood couldn't manage to stay away from the Big Bad Wolf."

Ooh. I like her playfulness.

I run my finger up her arm. "What does Little Red Riding Hood have in mind for this evening?"

She runs her tongue over her plump, red-painted bottom lip. "To see just how big and bad your wolf is."

I can't help but let out a laugh. "Why don't we start with your name, beautiful."

"I'm Jade. What's your name?"

"Collin. How do you know Reagan?"

She hesitates for a brief moment, but then answers, "I work for her."

"Oh, then you work for Carter too. I'm his best friend."

Her eyes light up. "Interesting." She takes a few sips of the drink I hadn't noticed the bartender leave in front of her. I guess I've been staring at her. She's an undeniably stunning woman. She could model. Maybe she does.

Carter and Reagan run Daulton and Lawrence Holdings, one of the biggest companies in the world. Reagan is the CEO and Carter is the president. They're Philadelphia's biggest power couple.

"What is it that you do, Collin?"

"I run a construction business with my family."

She tilts her head to the side. "So, if you were to take your shirt off, would I see muscles from all your *hard* work?"

"I'm in management, but I do like to get my hands dirty now and then."

She grabs my big hand and runs hers over all the callouses. "Maybe they should get dirty tonight."

"Is that what you want?"

She nods.

I intertwine my fingers through hers. She curls her delicate, soft fingers through mine.

"I like how rough your hands are, Collin."

I pull her to follow me. "Do you like it rough?"

"I do."

We enter the hallway. I open one door and quietly peek my head inside before quickly pulling it out and closing the door before Jade sees anything.

"Umm, that was occupied." That was Reagan's stepfather, Jackson, drilling her mother. Damn, her mom's body is as hot as hers. That fucking family. They got all the hot genes on the planet.

I try the next door, but it's locked, and I hear moaning. Jade giggles. "It sounds like we're not the only ones with this idea."

I nod in agreement. "Seems like it."

I get to the next door, and it opens. Unfortunately, it's a supply closet. There are several high shelving units with supplies lining them. I turn to leave. She pinches her eyebrows together. "What's wrong?"

"I'm not taking you in there. It's a fucking supply closet."

"Collin, we don't have much time. This is fine."

She turns the light on and pulls me into the closet, closing and locking the door behind us. She pulls my shirt to her and immediately brings her lips to mine. She bites my lip. Hard. Damn, she's really aggressive. I love it.

I pull her dress up so I can lift her, and she wraps her mile-long legs around me. Turning, I push her against the door. I grab her exposed ass with both hands and slide my tongue into her mouth. She tastes like vodka and mint.

I move my tongue around until it meets hers. As soon as it does, she pushes it into my mouth. Our kiss turns hard and deep, lips pressing and tongues battling for supremacy. I grind my hardened cock into her center, and she lets out a moan. She digs her nails into my neck. She whispers into my mouth. "Fuck me, Collin. Now."

"How do you want it?"

"I told you. Rough."

"Of course it's going to be rough. I meant which hole."

Her eyes widen, which tells me all I need to know. The front.

She attempts to play it cool. "Whichever one you want."

I run my thumb and pointer finger up her neck, applying a little pressure. I need to test my boundaries. The more pressure I apply, the more her eyes flutter.

I whisper in her ear, "Do you like my hand around your neck?"

She tightens her legs around me and manages a, "Umm hmm."

"Use words. I like words."

She breathes, "Yes, I like it."

I reach my other hand down and slip her panties to the side so I can run my fingers through her drenched core. "Seems as if you *do* like it."

I sink two fingers deep into her and she lets out a loud moan. "You're very needy, Jade. You seem to want it very badly."

She whimpers, "Yes."

"Yes? Use more words."

"I want it. I want you."

I pull my fingers out of her. I use them to rub around her kiss-swollen lips. I can tell a lot about a woman from her reaction to tasting herself.

She traces her lips with her tongue. "Hmm. Good."

I smile as I place her on her feet. I look around and grab an extension cord that's on the shelf. "Give me your wrists."

She visibly swallows, telling me she has a small amount of fear, but then does as I asked. I wrap the cord around her wrists, leaving some room at the end. I move her so her front is facing one of the shelves, using the remaining part of the cord to tether her to the shelf stand with her hands above her head.

I pull her dress over her ass to her waist. She's wearing a red thong. I rub her. "You have a perfect ass, Jade."

"Is...is that where you're going to take me?"

I can tell she's new to it. "Not with my cock. No lube."

I see her shoulders relax. I turn her face, so our eyes meet. "If there's anything you're not into, speak up."

She leans her head toward mine and licks along the seam of my lips. She pulls her head back up. "I'm up for anything. We just can't be gone for long."

"Did grandma give Little Red Riding Hood a curfew?"

She smiles. "Something like that. Get moving, Collin."

I pull her thong down her legs. I bunch them in my fist and shove them in her mouth. "As much as I want your words, trust me, you're going to need that for what I'm about to do to your body."

She nods as she turns her head and faces forward.

I unbuckle my belt, unzip my pants, and pull out my cock. I grab a condom from my wallet and sheath myself.

I spread her legs wider and run my fingers through her pussy again. "Are you ready? It feels like it to me."

She mumbles, "Umm hmm."

I bring my tip to her entrance and slowly slide into her. She's so tight. I have to wiggle my way in.

She gasps as she tilts her head back. She mumbles some version of, "Oh, fuck."

I grab her hair and turn her head so our eyes meet again. "Am I the biggest you've ever had?"

She nods.

"Fuck yeah, I am."

I let go of her hair and begin my movements inside her. I wrap my arm around her front and pound into her with forceful thrusts as deep as I can go. Over and over. Harder and harder.

She's moaning and writhing. I'm glad I stuffed her panties in her mouth, otherwise it would be too loud in here.

She sticks her ass out allowing me to push deeper into her. "That's right, Jade. You like it deep, don't you? You feel incredible."

She manages to pant out, "Yes, yes." I see her arms pulling on her restraints, desperate for more.

I wrap one of my big hands around her neck and squeeze. Her moans get louder. This girl likes all the things I like.

I look down at her perfect ass. I wish I could take that, but I know she's not up for it. Maybe a little finger play, though.

I spit into the crack of her ass and use my thumb to rub my saliva around her puckered hole. I feel her stiffen a bit.

I lean over to her ear. "Just my finger, not my cock."

She nods.

I haven't let up my pace, but I slide my thumb in her back entrance. She's tight. As suspected, no one has been here before. The thought of being the first nearly sends me over the edge, but I hold off. She needs to come first.

As I slide my thumb in, I can feel a shot of moisture in her pussy and then she squeezes my cock. She's about to come.

She yells out, albeit garbled because of the panties in her mouth. "Ah, Collin."

Her pussy trembles as she comes on a loud scream. As soon as she does, I let go too with an unusually loud grunt for me.

Fuck, that was good. After taking a few moments to catch my breath, I pull out and make quick work of the condom. I tuck myself back in and refasten my pants and belt.

Her hands are still bound, but I'm able to turn her around. We're both still breathing loudly. Her arms are above her head and her red dress is around her waist. She's bare and exposed to me. Those long legs on full display in her red *fuck me* heels. Her face is flushed with a post-orgasmic glow. I don't think I've ever seen anything hotter.

I hold my hand in front of her mouth and she spits out her panties. I bring them to my nose and inhale deeply.

"Hmm. You smell good. I wish I got to taste you. Maybe another time."

She stares at me with all the confidence and bravado in the world. "It's still on my lips, if you need a little taste."

I grab her face and give her a hard, wet kiss, licking

all around her lips. I pull my head away and lick my own lips. "You're right. It's delicious."

"Can you untie me now?"

I shake my head. "In a minute."

I bend down and hold out her panties. She lifts her feet, one at a time, so I can slip them back on. I pull them up and then pull down her dress, smoothing it out for her.

She looks at me in bewilderment. She's not used to any aftercare. She must have only been with assholes.

I stand and untie her. As soon as I do, she rubs her wrists.

"Was it too tight?"

She shakes her head. "No, I liked it."

I bend again and grab her purse, which she must have dropped when we walked in. She opens it, pulls out her lipstick, and reapplies it.

She removes a tissue from her purse and cleans my face. She winks. "I don't want the other ladies to think you're taken."

"Maybe I want to be taken for the night. Why don't we head back to my place for another round? No one will miss us."

She smiles. It's not the mischievous smile I saw earlier. It's sweet. She's happy that I want another round.

As quickly as it came, it leaves. "I'm not sure I can. Let's get back out there. I know Reagan is giving a speech. I shouldn't miss it."

"Okay."

I take her hand in mine and we make our way back to the ballroom. As soon as we enter, she drops my hand like a hot potato.

I'm about to ask her about it when I hear Reagan on

the microphone. "I don't want to stop the fun for long, but I want to say a quick hello. Thank you to everyone for coming tonight to help us celebrate. This was supposed to be a wedding reception, but Carter insisted on it being a birthday party for me instead." She looks at him with more love and need than I've ever seen in my life. "Let's just call it both and skip to the part where you kiss the bride."

She pulls him to her and kisses the living hell out of him. It's over-the-top and totally inappropriate. Perfect for the two of them. I can't help but smile and then let out a big whistle.

People join in and yell out. People even clap for the live porn show we're watching.

When it eventually ends, Reagan just gives a big, *I don't give a fuck what you all think*, smile. "Wow. I can't wait for the honeymoon."

We all laugh.

"While we're celebrating, I want to mention that it was my cousin Jade's birthday last week. Where are you, gorgeous?"

Jade, still next to me, raises her hand. Cousin? I thought Jade said she works for Reagan.

Reagan then waves Jade up to the front of the room and Jade walks up to her.

She pulls Jade close to her. "Happy birthday, beautiful. She's eighteen now, gentleman, so take a number. The line is going to be long."

I turn to the stranger next to me. "Did she just say *eighteen*?"

He nods. "It's hard to believe. Kids look older and older these days."

Kids. My throat starts to close. I'm covered in sweat. She's eighteen. Holy fuck. I just had sex with an eighteen-year-old. An eighteen-year-old who was seventeen last week.

I can't breathe. I start coughing uncontrollably. I feel like there's cotton lodged in my throat.

I run toward the bar. I croak out, "Water. Hurry." Maybe a fucking defibrillator.

I wipe my sweat-filled face with a napkin while I wait. He brings the water quickly and I down the whole glass in one go.

The band starts playing again. Some people go toward the dance floor, but others begin making their way back to the bar.

I look around for cops. No, she's an adult. Barely, but she's an adult.

I rub my face. Oh god. No one can know about this. Ever. It's Reagan's cousin. Carter will kill me. He'll hate me. Reagan will hate me too.

I need to get the fuck out of here before anyone finds out. I practically leave a trail of smoke behind me as I hightail it out of there.